Wicked After Midnight

Wicked After Midnight

Midnight Blue Beach
Book One

BY

OLIVIA JAYMES

www.OliviaJaymes.com

WICKED AFTER MIDNIGHT

Wicked After Midnight

Shocking revelations...

After a night of tequila shots with her two new friends, Bailey Scott discovers that their husbands all died on the exact same day five years ago. Shocked, hung over, and in deep denial, she vows to put the entire evening behind her and never give it another thought. Clearly the universe is messing with all three of them but she won't let it drag her back to that dark place. She's worked too hard to move on.

But the past refuses to rest in peace...

Chase Jennings has his work and his friends and although it sometimes gets lonely he's happy. Sure he'd love to share it with a woman but he simply hasn't found the right one yet. However there is one shadow in his otherwise sunny life that he can't seem to shake. He has never forgotten that summer so long ago when a young girl was brutally murdered at his parents' summer camp. Although there were plenty of suspects there was little evidence. Everyone has forgotten it but Chase can't seem to put it behind him.

Everything she thought she knew is false...

When their two worlds collide, Bailey and Chase reluctantly team up to investigate the tenuous connection between that murder twenty years ago and her husband Frank's death. As the pair fights their growing attraction, they uncover deadly secrets that will change their lives and that of others. All they have believed will be called into question and the only thing they can count on is the blossoming love that brings them ever closer together.

But the universe isn't nearly done with them yet...

Series description:

Three successful women. One devastating discovery. The truth must be found, but the search uncovers a destructive power struggle that goes far beyond their wildest dreams. The stakes have never been higher and it could cost them everything. Even their own lives. Welcome to Midnight Blue Beach.

Chapter One

Twenty years ago…

SHE'D DISAPPEARED FROM the campfire with some boy. It was always that way. Young and pretty, she had all the males at the camp under her spell. Gwen drank up the attention too. She'd flirted, danced, and giggled her way through every guy their age this summer. She thrived on the attention.

Making his way down to the lake, he could hear the giggles and sighs plus the whispered words from a lower register. A male voice.

She wasn't alone but then she'd never liked being on her own. She always wanted someone there.

The tinkle of laughter drifted around him, although most of the couples had turned in for the night. There were still a few by the lake but he knew that spot at the river bank would be deserted. No one went down there when it was dark. The lights from the camp didn't go that far.

A rustle of grass and he watched the boy and Gwen head back to the camp, their fingers entwined. He followed them, staying back so they couldn't see him but he could see them. The boys' cabins were closest and the couple kissed briefly before separating, the boy disappearing into the dark structure. Gwen turned to go to her own cabin but he rushed forward, determined to talk to her.

"Gwen."

She stopped and twirled around, her lips in a thin line and her hands furled into fists.

"What now? It's late."

She was mad about earlier but she wouldn't stay that way. A little moonlight and some compliments and she'd be all smiles.

"We need to talk."

Gwen sighed and shook her head. "We've already talked."

Just play along. Make her think you agree.

"I know. I just wanted to apologize about this morning. I was out of line."

Her expression softened and even her shoulders relaxed. She reached out and pulled him into a hug, the scent of her strawberry shampoo filling his nostrils. She felt small and fragile in his arms as if she might snap in two with a strong gust of wind.

"I hate it when we argue."

"Me too." He tugged at her long ponytail, the hair silky between his fingers, his fingertips brushing the soft skin of her neck. "Let's go for a walk. You can tell me about Cindy and Matt. It looked like they were fighting tonight."

She giggled and smiled, their earlier animosity forgotten. "Matt was flirting with Emily, and Cindy got mad. You should have heard what they said to each other."

He tugged at her hand, wanting to lead her away from the others. "Come tell me about it then while we're walking."

Biting her lip, she glanced over her shoulder to the girls' cabins. "I don't know. It's late."

"C'mon," he cajoled. "I know you're not any more tired than I am. Just a little walk."

She gave in, as he'd known she would. "Just a short one."

She linked her arm with his and he guided them in the direction of the river. Following him like a docile lamb, she chattered on about Matt and Cindy and Taylor and Emily plus some others that didn't matter. He didn't care about those people. No one understood what was important.

What he needed.

The moon cast a glow over the rippling water of the James River. The branches of the trees cast shadows on the banks and the leaves rustled softly in the light breeze. The scent of damp earth and grass seemed to suffocate him and he took a deep breath to clear his hazy thoughts. She was standing at the water's edge with her back to him but humming her favorite song, some dance number that annoyed him every time he heard it.

"Isn't it beautiful?" She looked back at him, a smile on her full, pink lips. "The cool night air is such a relief."

Gwen had sunburn on her shoulders from swimming. He'd rubbed soothing cream into her parched skin but she'd gone back into the pool again today, complaining about the hot weather.

"So what should we do tomorrow?" he asked, slowly reaching down for a large rock stuck in the sand. His fingers flexed around the rough surface. He'd placed it here a few days ago in preparation for just this moment.

He was relieved she was looking away from him. He didn't

want to look into her eyes.

"I want to go horseback riding. We should all go."

His chest squeezed so tightly he could barely breathe. The urge to hurt more powerful than the urge to soothe. He needed to set things right again.

"You can have anything you want," he said softly, pulling his arm back as he stepped closer. Another whiff of shampoo hit his nostrils and for a moment he almost dropped the rock, almost stopped but then she started talking about going home. Her family. The parties. He couldn't let that happen.

Acid churned in his stomach, eating away at his insides like tiny, buzzing insects swarming his abdomen. Rage burned in every vein and pore of his body, white-hot, sweeping through him like an out of control wildfire. His vision grew blurry, whether from sweat or tears, he didn't know. It was too much and not enough all at the same time. How much was he supposed to endure? It wasn't fair.

Mustering all the strength he could he threw his arm forward, anger and hate amplifying the force until he felt the impact of the rock and her skull ricochet through the tendons of his hand all the way to his shoulder. It made a dull thud sound that belied the power behind the hit.

She'd cried out but they were too far away for anyone to hear. He'd made sure of that. His fingers were covered with warm, sticky blood and he threw the rock into the river where it sunk to the bottom immediately. Turning his hand over and back, he examined it, studying it as if it belonged to someone else. Detached from his torso and floating independently in the air.

A soft moan from Gwen brought him back to that moment. He knelt down next to her and ran his hand over her golden hair that was quickly becoming saturated with blood.

"Easy there, baby. I'm going to take good care of you."

Chapter Two

Present Day...

B AILEY SCOTT DUCKED behind a large column and with one hand holding her wine glass adjusted the neckline of her slinky black strapless cocktail dress that had slipped down an inch too far. Flashing the high society of Midnight Blue Beach might increase traffic to her bakery but it wouldn't endear her to the stuffy old farts that populated events like these.

Of course, it might say something about herself that she was here too.

Keeping a low profile, Bailey relaxed and enjoyed watching the guests mingle and impress. It was only a cocktail party but the men and women of the town hadn't skimped on attire.

A redhead, the wife of a local attorney, stood a few feet away with her friend, a gorgeous divorcee and business owner. They were chatting animatedly about the summer holidays and kids out of school. The redhead's expression turned from happy to stormy in an instant.

"Can't we have one party where she doesn't show up?" the woman hissed, leaning forward so no one would overhear. "She has some nerve."

Her friend looked over her shoulder and snorted. "That girl has some king-sized balls. She works with practically every charity in town and attends every single party."

Bailey's gaze followed theirs to where Willow Vaughn stood, chatting with two older gentlemen. Willow was around Bailey's age and was rather notorious in Midnight Blue Beach for her past as a high-dollar stripper before she married her husband. With her perfect figure and face, it was easy to see why Willow had been successful in her past profession.

The redhead wrinkled her nose in disgust. "Look at that dress. Showing off what God gave her, that's for sure. Just goes to prove that money won't give you class."

Bailey didn't think the dress was that bad. It was a dark purple with a plunging back that went perfectly with Willow's unusual coloring – golden skin paired with light brown hair. So different from Bailey's chestnut hair and fair skin.

The friend nodded in agreement. "You'd think a widow would have more decorum. Her husband is six feet under and she's out chatting up rich men, looking for husband number two."

Muffling her chuckle, Bailey wondered what the two women thought about her own widow status. Since Frank had died, she'd found that other women either pitied her or feared her – as if she was out trolling for a new husband and anyone's man would do. Personality not important, only a penis required. Ability to kill bugs a bonus.

A scuffle on the other side of the large ballroom caught her attention. A wave of gray smoke billowed from the left side of the room where servers were streaming out of a doorway, coughing and covering their faces with napkins. More people were running out of the entrance including several cooks, which gave Bailey the impression that a fire extinguisher hadn't been sufficient.

Time to exit the building.

Despite the soaring ceilings, the room was beginning to get smoky, making her eyes water, and the other guests were beginning to notice that something was amiss. The crowd was moving toward the large double doors at the front of the estate and Bailey went too, breathing in a lungful of fresh air once outside.

She certainly hoped everyone in the kitchen was safe and unharmed but this was a terrific excuse to leave the party early, go home and watch a movie marathon. This night might not be a total loss after all.

BAILEY HAD PARKED her car at the far end of the lot and was almost there when she heard a woman curse a blue streak, four letter words thrown out in a pain-filled voice. She craned her neck to find the female and finally did – one row and three cars over.

A blonde was bent over, rubbing her ankle and being helped by none other than the notorious Willow Vaughn. The blonde held up her shoe in one hand and the broken heel in the other.

Slipping through the parked cars, Bailey approached the other two ladies. "Are you alright?"

The blonde straightened and rolled her eyes, a wry smile on

her lips. She was pretty in a delicate sort of way with a small nose and chin. Dressed in a red, floaty creation she had an ethereal quality that Bailey would have described as cute.

"The heel on these brand new shoes snapped off in that hole right there and I twisted my damn ankle. I swear I can't walk and chew gum at the same time."

Bailey wasn't a doctor but she was always prepared for a wardrobe malfunction. Or at least a trip to the gym when she had time. "I have a pair of tennis shoes in my car. It might be easier to walk in them rather than those heels."

"Are you kidding? That would be great." The blonde peered at Bailey's feet. "I think we might not be the same size though."

Considering there was at least three inches difference in their heights, she was surely correct. "They're lace ups so it won't matter too much. I'll get them out of my car. My name's Bailey, by the way. I own the bakery on Beach Boulevard. Sinful Delights."

The other woman shook her hand and sighed dramatically. "I'm Willow Vaughn and I've had your Sinful Delight Dark Chocolate Cake. It's heavenly, just perfect."

The blonde also held out her hand. "I'm Peyton Nelson and I'm glad to meet both of you. It sounds like I'm going to have to give that chocolate cake a try."

"You'll love it," Willow assured her, looking around the parking lot. The crowd was milling about, waiting to get back in. A mischievous grin broke out over her face. "Listen, I could really use a drink. A real one with vodka, gin, or whiskey. Not that watered down crap they serve at these shindigs. Are you interested?"

Bailey and Peyton exchanged a glance and a smile. The last place Bailey wanted to be was back inside.

"I'm in," she said with a nod.

"Me too. Lead the way to the booze and the comfortable shoes," Peyton laughed, allowing Bailey and Willow to help her limp to the car.

"I know just where to take you," Willow said.

BAILEY WAS SITTING with her two new friends and drinking a martini in a cheesy beach-themed dive bar that was so small it only held six tables, all open to the elements. Luckily, it was a lovely night, not too hot or humid.

The bar itself looked suspiciously like an old, tiny RV with the wheels rusted so they couldn't drive on them any longer. The bartender, on the other hand was sexy as hell although way too young, and the drinks were strong. Bailey's daddy would have said they were strong enough to put hair on your chest.

Bailey studied the cramped space and rickety tables. They looked a little out of place with their expensive cocktail dresses while the other patrons were wearing shorts or jeans. "What's this place called again? It's legal, right? We're not going to get raided and end up in jail? I have inventory in the morning."

Willow laughed and sipped at her Jameson's whiskey, neat. "It's called Ted's, and yes, it's completely legal. He's a good friend I met when doing some volunteer work at the hospital and he follows all the laws. I promise you'll be at work tomorrow morning."

Peyton swirled the shot glass of tequila before knocking it back. "I like it. It has…character."

"That's a nice, polite way of putting it." Grinning, Willow signaled for another round. "So tell me something about yourselves, ladies. Who wants to start?"

A second martini was placed in front of Bailey and she downed the last of her first, the heat expanding in her belly. This was way better than that uptight party with fancy, shmancy wine. She couldn't remember the last time she'd had some plain, old-fashioned fun.

"Start?" Bailey asked, her brows pulled together. "I'm not sure what you mean."

"Your life story," Willow prompted. "There's still four and a half hours before last call. I figured our life stories would be a good way to fill the time but I'm willing to discuss something else. Who are you planning to vote for this election? Or we could talk about sex. Your call."

It had been drilled into Bailey from the time she was in diapers to never discuss politics, religion, or sex. Especially with people you had just met.

Plus she didn't have a sex life to speak of and wasn't all that eager to admit it.

"I'll do it," she volunteered. How bad could it be? She'd leave out the upsetting parts. These women would never know the difference. "Where should I start?"

"At the beginning. Where were you born?"

That was an easy question.

"In the Midwest. With the corn and the cows."

Chapter Three

THE BAR WAS spinning and Bailey's cheeks were flushed with heat. Several martinis over the last few hours had left her with a distinctly disturbing problem.

She couldn't seem to shut the hell up.

So far she'd told Peyton and Willow about the night she'd lost her virginity, and also about the time she and some college classmates had garbed the alma mater statue in a dark black cloak and put a scythe in its hand as if it were the Grim Reaper. Thank goodness there weren't remote cameras and cell phones to record a person's every move back then.

Peyton was also affected by the alcohol, her body swaying in her chair in time with the sound of the waves breaking on the beach. Willow, on the other hand, appeared no worse for the wear. The woman could hold her liquor, which made Bailey admire her all the more.

They had yet to hear Willow's life story but already she could tell that her new friend had a spine of solid steel and the smarts to go with her bravado.

"So was it hot?" Peyton teased. "My first time sucked. I'm

always hoping to hear someone say that their first time was amazing. Heck, I'd accept fair to good."

Remembering that night long ago, Bailey smiled. "The beginning was very good. But the end not so much. It hurt and I'm a wuss about stuff like that." She elbowed Willow, almost spilling her drink in the process. "What about you? Anything to write home about?"

The smile on Willow's face vanished and she shook her head. "No, it wasn't good at all. Just some guy who talked a good game and I fell for it hook, line, and sinker. After he got what he wanted, he moved on. I knew then that I had to get a hell of a lot smarter about men or I was going to end up perpetually broken hearted."

It was hard to believe any man would leave Willow. Tall and slender in her dark purple cocktail dress, her golden brown hair was pulled up on top of her head in a mass of curls showing off a graceful profile. Even her eyes were a soft shade of amber, almost the color of brandy. She doubted seriously if Willow had trouble attracting men.

Bailey frowned and took a large gulp of her martini. "I don't know shit about men. I've been married and didn't learn a thing."

"I learned that all men are the same," Willow declared. "All of them. Old, young, fat, thin. It doesn't matter. So if you know one, you know them all."

Peyton looked skeptical, shaking her head. "That would certainly be convenient but I'm not sure I believe it."

Shrugging, Willow eyed two men sitting a few tables away. "That's been my experience but your mileage may vary. For example, I bet I could get those men to buy us a round just by giving them a certain look. They won't need much encouragement."

No, no, no, no.

Bailey grabbed Willow's arm to get her attention. "Let's not, okay? I believe that you can do it but let's not invite them over. It's just us girls."

Peyton lifted her glass and giggled. "Here's to just the girls."

Bailey would drink to that. This entire evening had been more fun than she'd expected when she dressed this evening to go out.

Willow sipped her whiskey and wrinkled her nose. "I heard you say you'd been married. Is he home tonight or did you split up? Or is that a rude question? Dammit, I swear I'm not this nosy when I'm sober."

Concentrating on inhaling and exhaling, Bailey took a moment before answering. It had been five years but the memories could still sneak up unexpectedly and knife her in the heart. She'd moved on with her life and most of the time she was fine and happy...then something would bring it all back again. A few years ago she'd decided to be happy and she was, but that didn't mean the past was completely erased. It still had some power.

"I don't think much is rude after talking about losing my virginity. Actually, I'm a widow. My husband passed away in a scuba diving accident in Turks and Caicos."

She didn't imagine the stunned looks on Peyton and Willow's faces nor their swiftly indrawn breaths. They were clearly shocked and Bailey wasn't sure why. She might be young to be a widow but it wasn't unheard of. Willow was a widow herself after all.

"Did I say something wrong?" she asked uncertainly, watching them over the rim of her glass. "You both look pale."

Had the booze hit them at exactly the same moment? They looked like they might be sick.

Willow placed her glass down on the table with a shaking hand. "You didn't say anything wrong. I was surprised, that's all, because I'm also a widow."

The last words came out shaky and strangled.

Peyton's hand jerked, spilling part of her mojito on the table. Cursing, she tried to mop up the liquid with a tiny bar napkin but it wasn't cutting it. Bailey dug in her purse for some tissues, dabbing at the spill.

"How did your husband pass on?" Peyton asked, her tone unsteady and her lips pressed tightly together.

Willow swallowed hard and stared into her drink. "He drove drunk and ran into a tree. Luckily it was a one-car accident."

The last thing Bailey wanted to do was upset her new friend. Patting Willow's shoulder, she wanted to change the subject, but what topic could possibly lighten the atmosphere now? This was why she rarely revealed this part of her history. It made everyone sad and that was one thing she was trying not to be anymore.

"I had heard he'd passed away," Bailey finally said, the acid in her stomach churning. "Recently?"

Something of a workaholic, she didn't keep up on current events in the area like she should. She only watched the local news for the weather and they were wrong half of the time.

"It was a while ago."

The silence stretched on, the tension at the table thick and uncomfortable. That was the thing about death. It could stop any conversation cold.

It was several minutes later when Peyton spoke up, her voice so soft it could barely be heard.

"Allergic reaction."

Bailey leaned forward, not sure she'd heard correctly. "What did you say?"

Peyton's entire body was shaking, head to toe, and her face had turned a ghostly white.

"I said allergic reaction. To peanuts." A tear streaked down Peyton's cheek. "That's how Greg died."

It was as if the bottom fell out of Bailey's world and she was falling fast toward a sudden and violent stop. She had to force her trembling lips to move.

"Who is Greg?"

The question came out strangled as if someone had her by the throat, slowly squeezing the life out from her body while she struggled and clawed for oxygen.

"My husband," Peyton whispered, her knuckles white where she gripped her glass. "Greg was my husband."

Three women who met because of a kitchen fire and a broken high heel. Three young widows. Perhaps Bailey had finally met women who could truly understand.

If nothing else, this entire evening would make a great story.

If anyone believed it. She wasn't so sure she did.

WILLOW KEPT SHAKING her head and drinking her whiskey

while Peyton appeared to be in some state of shock, her face still pale. Bailey wasn't exactly one hundred percent sure that all she had experienced tonight was even real. It felt strange in the extreme to be discussing Frank with two women who had never met him, but understood what she'd been going through for the last five years.

If anything, Bailey felt numb. Her mind was firmly in charge and not allowing her emotions to overwhelm her in any way. It was only temporary and eventually she'd have to deal with all the pain and guilt simmering inside but at the moment she allowed a chill to invade her bones, spreading to every limb. This was safer, controlled. Falling apart was best done in solitude.

Willow refilled her glass, having long ago told the bartender to simply leave the damn bottle.

"It's going to be a long night," she'd told him. "No sense wearing yourself out walking back and forth."

He'd left the bottle along with a pitcher of martinis and another of mojitos, and then come back with a large bowl of pretzels urging them to eat so that there would be something in their stomachs soaking up the alcohol. As nauseous as Bailey was she couldn't imagine a morsel of food passing through her lips ever again.

"I think the guilt is the worst," Willow said, her eyes glazed with tears or booze. "What did I not do that would have made him stop drinking and whoring? I think about that. If I could have stopped him, he would be alive now."

"You don't know that," Bailey protested, knowing that guilty feeling all too well but for a far different reason. "He could have died from something else. When it's your time to go... Besides, you can't make a grown man stop doing anything that he wants to do. It sounds like your Alex didn't treat you right."

Shoving a stray curl behind her ear, Willow shook her head. "It wasn't always like that. I know people think I married Alex for his money but the fact is I loved him. Very much. He came into that nightclub and swept me off my feet. He was my knight in shining armor, at least for awhile. Then he changed and I don't know what I did to make him do that."

"Another woman?" Peyton asked, her tone timid. "I know Greg had them. Many of them. After awhile I stopped caring so much."

Willow rolled her eyes. "There were women. Lots of them. And wild weekends, fueled by the booze and drugs. Sometimes it felt like he was pushing me away with both hands and then there would be times he would cling to me and beg me not to leave like a little boy who had displeased his mother. He was so sad and lost and I couldn't help but try and take care of him."

"You didn't do anything. He made those choices. It's not your fault."

Perhaps if Bailey could convince Willow, she could somehow convince herself.

"It's not your fault either," Willow said to Peyton. "If he was cheating on you then he wasn't a good husband."

"I was a bad wife. I didn't love him. Not really."

"Did you cheat?"

Peyton's eyes widened and she shook her head. "Of course not. I'm just saying that there's plenty of blame to go around."

Bailey drained her glass and slapped it down on the table, enjoying the pleasant buzz. She rubbed her icy fingertips together, barely feeling the friction of flesh on flesh. She did the same with her toes and enjoyed a moment of satisfaction. She couldn't feel a thing and was glad. The numbness was preferable at a moment like this.

"The sad fact is that if we had grown old with our husbands we wouldn't have this soul-crushing guilt. But because they died young, we think it was somehow our responsibility to make every day of their lives Disney World. That we should have made them deliriously happy and ignored the shitty things they did to us. I'm going to say this out loud and I've never told another living soul. I was thinking about divorcing Frank when he died. I'd even contacted an attorney. There, I said it."

She actually felt a little better. Maybe she should have said it a long time ago, but whom would she have told that would understand?

"You don't have anything to be guilty about either." Willow poured Bailey another drink. They definitely weren't going to be driving themselves anywhere when this place closed down. As it was, her stomach was doing somersaults and the room looked decidedly wavy. "If you were that miserable he probably was too."

"He was so cold to me. I sometimes wondered if he'd even notice if I up and left one day." Bailey sighed and let her mind wander back, feeling the pain of being ignored acutely. She hadn't loved Frank by then but his total indifference had been a blow. "You'd think after so many years I wouldn't give a shit but it still hurts. How do you blow off a wife and act like she doesn't exist?"

"How long has it been?" Peyton asked. "Greg died five years

ago so I know what you mean. He shouldn't have the power to hurt me anymore."

"Five years for me too. July twenty-first."

Willow almost dropped her glass but caught it just in time, the contents sloshing onto the table. "No fucking way."

Peyton's gaze darted around the table, a sheen of sweat on her forehead. "Am I asleep? This is too strange. It can't be real. Somebody pinch me."

Willow reached over and did the deed, causing Peyton to yelp in pain. "Ouch! Shit, that hurt."

"Then you're awake," Willow replied with a cynical laugh. "I think we all are although this is some Twilight Zone and Outer Limits shit. I barely passed math in high school but the odds of this have to be astronomical. My husband died five years ago. On July twenty-first."

Peyton closed her eyes and nodded. "July twenty-first."

Bailey was holding onto that numbness like a life preserver. She didn't have the luxury of allowing herself to feel anything right now. Frankly, she didn't know how she was supposed to feel or react. It was bizarre and almost supernatural except she didn't believe in any of that. There had to be a logical explanation for this but she couldn't think of one off the top of her head.

She tried to explain it anyway. "They say that everyone has a twin somewhere in the world but they rarely meet up. I guess it's possible to meet other people whose husband died on the same day. I bet there are hundreds, if not thousands of widows walking the earth that lost their spouse on that date. It's just quirky and unusual."

Willow stared at Bailey as if she'd lost her mind and maybe she had.

"I guess you're one of those optimists."

"You aren't?"

Willow shrugged. "I'm pragmatic. I don't care if the glass is half full or half empty, I just want to know how I can fill it."

Fair enough.

"You haven't said much, Peyton."

The blonde took a large breath and exhaled slowly, placing her hands flat on the table. "I think this is crazy and that I'm going to wake up and this won't have happened. It's surreal."

"I'll pinch you again," Willow offered.

Peyton moved her arm out of Willow's reach. "No, thanks. The thing is I haven't said much because I have a question. What happens now? This strange cosmic thing has brought us together in this moment in time. What do we do? Buy lottery tickets? Go on Jerry Springer? This is too bizarre. Aren't you freaked out? I sure am. My whole body is shaking and my heart is racing almost out of my chest."

They all looked around at each other and no one had an answer. Bailey was still trying to wrap her alcohol addled brain around it. It was too weird and spooky, and it had brought up a past she'd thought she'd left behind.

Bailey reached for the pitcher of martinis in the middle of the table. "I don't know what you all are going to do but I'm going to have another drink. Then later I'll figure out how to deal with it. Nothing in my life has prepared me for this."

If she couldn't deal with it, maybe she could forget it. Or ignore it.

Yes, that's what I'll do. Ignore the whole thing.

"What about us?" Willow asked, her brow lifted. "Are you going to deal with me and Peyton? Or are you going to try and forget you ever met us?"

It was a good question. As much as she'd been enjoying her new friends, they brought with them too much baggage and too much hurt. She might not have been living the most exciting life up until now but she'd been content. This accidental meet up might be a hiccup of the universe but she had free will.

Can I truly forget this ever happened? Walk away?

"I don't know," Bailey finally answered, her heart sinking at the idea of never seeing these women again. There was a big part of her that didn't want to go back but going forward was too scary to even contemplate. "I'm not sure what we should do. What do you think? All we'll do is remind each other of things we'd rather put behind us."

Peyton's lips turned down. "If we never see each other again it will be kind of sad. I was hoping we'd be friends. I don't have too many of those here in town."

Willow, however, seemed to understand Bailey's torment. "I get what you're saying. After all, we weren't supposed to meet. The party and the fire and the broken high heel. If any one of those things hadn't happened we wouldn't be here together right now. I'll respect whatever decision you come to. After all, this is a fluke."

No, it was a one in a million or billion chance and it never should have happened. Perhaps when Bailey woke up tomorrow morning she'd find out it never really had at all. It was just her imagination. A drunken fantasy.

Chapter Four

B AILEY BARELY MADE it from the taxi to her bedroom before her legs gave out and sleep overtook her. Still wearing her dress, she tossed and turned, tangled in the sheets as she dreamed of Frank. Or at least it sort of looked like Frank. Only this man's face was slightly distorted like a Dali painting and he kept pointing to her and shouting, although she couldn't make out a word he was saying. Whatever he was angry about, she wasn't going to be able to do a thing to correct it.

In her dream she stood there staring at her late husband, tears streaming down her face while he berated her for some unknown offense. She did nothing to stop him, just standing like a statue. Funny how he'd barely spoken to her when alive but now in death was pissed as hell.

When she awoke the next morning her head hurt, her tongue felt like cotton wool, and her body ached. She had to blink several times as the sun streamed in through the windows where she had forgotten to close the drapes before passing out. Forcing her feet to the floor, she padded into the bathroom to survey the damage.

Holy smokes. She looked like death warmed over.

Her long hair was a veritable rat's nest, with strands sticking out every which way. Her mascara was smeared almost to her cheekbones and her skin was pale and splotchy. The cocktail dress hadn't come out unscathed either. Wrinkled and bunched, it looked like she'd slept in it. Perhaps on a park bench and not on a comfortable bed.

Basically she looked like a vagrant.

Damn that gin.

"I'm never drinking again," she said solemnly to the horrifying reflection in the bathroom mirror. "I cannot hold my liquor."

Alcohol had been needed though. After what she had learned about her new friends, Bailey had needed cocktails. Several of them. The universe had hiccupped last night and she'd been on the receiving end of the spit. It was only by staying numb that she'd managed to hold things together. She prided herself on being in control when it mattered most.

Except that welcomed numbness wasn't doing its job this morning. Not sure if it was the booze or the revelations, Bailey ignored the pain that was beginning to seep into every bone and instead stripped off her party dress and stepped into the shower, determined to wash away the remains of the night.

After scrubbing her body from head to toe, she made a pot of coffee and took the mug outside to sit on her back patio. There was shade and a ceiling fan so it wasn't unbearably hot. Yet. It was still early in the summer though. By August she'd be sitting inside with the air conditioning all day.

Listening to the birds chirp, she couldn't stop her mind from going there. *There.* Back to Frank and their marriage. So much angst and anger. Unbearable coldness. There had been good times too and those were what had kept her there, trying to salvage something that had gone terribly wrong. She'd wanted to love someone for a lifetime but she simply might not be capable of it. It didn't seem she inspired that sort of devotion as well.

She hadn't allowed herself to think about him for a long time, although he'd sneak up on her every now and then when something was familiar. That first year she'd kept everything in the house as it was but then her family had visited, performing a quasi-intervention. They'd ignored her protests and packed up all of Frank's possessions in cardboard boxes and placed them in one of the spare bedrooms.

She'd argued that she wanted everything to stay the same but her mother and sister hadn't backed down. It was time she lived again and they weren't taking no for an answer.

"You need to move on, honey," her mother had said gently. "You can't do that with all of Frank's things as if he's still here. He's not, but you are. When you're ready to go through it all, it will be there."

That's when it hit her. Was she ready now? Today?

Maybe that was the message the universe had been trying to send her last night. It had used a baseball bat instead of a stick but she was receiving it loud and clear now that her brain was fully caffeinated.

It was time.

Standing, she headed for the spare room feeling a little less hungover. She could do this.

PRESSING FRANK'S OLD cardigan to her nose, Bailey inhaled trying to get even a trace of his scent but it had long ago faded. Now it smelled of wool and dust, and she couldn't hold back the sneeze that tickled her nostrils. She'd always liked the smell of Frank's cologne but five years stuffed in a box had obliterated it from the fabric. Nothing smelled of him anymore.

Five boxes down and about a million to go. Okay, maybe not that many but it felt like it. They were stacked all around the room and as she'd soldiered through box after box she'd been reminded of what a clothes horse her late husband was. He'd taken up more space in the closet than she had. He'd especially liked finely cut suits and Italian loafers.

She sincerely hoped whomever shopped at the local thrift store would like them as well.

So far, the belongings she'd sifted through were going straight to charity. She'd heard there was a good one that gave suits to men who were looking for a job. It would be nice to know that someone was getting good use of all of this. Her old friend Guilt set in as she realized how long she'd put off this task, walking by the door to the room day after day and not admitting what lay behind it.

She'd been in a sweet state of denial. Fun while it lasted.

"Time to wake up," she muttered to herself. "Stop being a wimp."

Wiping her dusty palms on her cotton shorts, she pulled another small box toward where she was perched on the floor, a big pillow under her bottom. This one wasn't filled with clothes and she had to lift up onto her knees to study the contents. None of it looked in the least familiar.

On top was Frank's high school diploma from that fancy private institution in New England that had given his voice an upper crust tone. There were a few spiral notebooks with class notes in them – math and history – plus a trophy from his lacrosse team. Bailey wasn't even sure what lacrosse was. Her Midwestern high school in the middle of the cornfields had a football team but no lacrosse.

"Maybe I should send this to his parents," she said to herself as she dusted off a yearbook, paging through until she found his smiling face. "All of this is from his school years. They might want this."

Except that she would have to talk to Betty and Frank Senior. They hadn't much approved of the marriage and the relationship had always been strained at best.

"Or I could toss all of this but that seems wrong. This must have meant something to him."

Frank hadn't been the most sentimental man. He'd seemed confused as to why they needed a photographer at their wedding, so realizing that he had saved all of this memorabilia was something of a surprise.

God, he looks so young.

The black and white picture was from his senior year. He looked relaxed and carefree, even naive. Life had clearly not touched him, or if it had he'd shaken it off easily. This photo showed a man who had everything in front of him.

This box was a peek into a person she hadn't known and that

made her sad. The Frank she had married right out of college wasn't someone who kept yearbooks. She would have wanted to know this man.

What happened to him? What changed? Life?

Her fingers dug into the box and landed on a stack of newspaper clippings, yellowed and brittle with age. Carefully, she lifted them out expecting to find memories of athletic glories or teenage shenanigans. When she was in high school, some kids had put crepe paper in the trees of their cross-town rival on Homecoming. Did rich kids do stuff like that too? No, they probably had servants to do it for them. Or maybe they fought pistol duels at dawn. The one thing Bailey had learned from being married to Frank was that the rich were different.

The clippings were faded and worn as if they'd been handled often. From a newspaper in Virginia, the headlines proclaimed that a teenage girl had died tragically at a local summer camp. Perpetrator unknown.

Leaning back against the wall, Bailey stretched her legs out comfortably as she read on. All the articles were about the same incident and it had to have been something important for Frank to have held onto it all these years. They might have been childhood friends.

Scanning the text, certain words jumped out such as *knife, deserted, no suspects.*

"I wonder if the crime was ever solved?" Bailey groaned and rolled her eyes. "Great, now I'm talking to myself. I need to get a dog—at least then I'll have an excuse."

Shuffling through the clippings, there were a few more details of the murder such as witnesses who saw the girl about an hour before the time of death but still no guilty party. From what Bailey could see the murderer wasn't caught. At least not in the days immediately following.

She stood, her muscles protesting the movement after sitting for so long, and headed into her small office at the front of the house. She used this area mostly for the metric-ton of paperwork that went along with owning her own business, but right now she only needed her laptop and a search engine.

She checked the article again for the correct spelling of the girl's name – Gwendolyn Baxter – before typing it in and pressing enter. A myriad of results came up and Bailey clicked on the first link, which was an op-ed piece in the *Virginia Gazette*. The writer, Leon Melrose, appeared frustrated with the efficiency of the police if the title was anything to go by – *Local Police Bungle Tragic Murder of Teenage Girl*.

Near midnight on July 21ˢᵗ, 1996, Gwendolyn Baxter, out walking on a moonless night, was stabbed repeatedly with a large knife and left for dead. Not missed until the morning, a search party was sent out to look for the girl and her body was found near the shore of the river. According to the medical examiner, she'd been dead for hours. Our local police, usually a shining example of detective work, have managed to find not one single suspect despite there being almost a hundred people less than a mile away. No one heard anything. No one saw anything. The killer didn't leave one clue behind. People are asking questions and wanting answers. The biggest question is who are they protecting?

Reading the opening paragraph a second time, Bailey stiffened as she struggled to breathe, her chest tightening painfully. At this rate, all the wonderful numbness that kept her safe would be gone and she'd have to feel every stab of guilt and sadness. Something she wasn't prepared to do.

But the universe was fucking with her again and this time she couldn't ignore it or pretend it hadn't happened.

Because Gwendolyn Baxter was killed on July twenty-first.

Just like Frank.

Just like Willow's husband.

And just like Peyton's.

This wasn't funny or quirky anymore.

If the universe wanted to make her its bitch it was going to find that she wasn't a pushover. She was going to mess with it right back.

Chapter Five

"WE NEED TO talk," Bailey announced when Willow opened her front door a few hours later. "It's important."

Willow's brows rose but she nodded and stepped back. "Sure, come on in. I didn't expect to see you again, to be honest."

"To be honest, neither did I. But I think this is something you might want to know about."

Bailey had read every article available on the Internet and even printed them off to show Willow and Peyton. She needed another opinion as to whether she was losing her mind. With any luck, she was in an alcohol-induced haze and had imagined the entire morning.

Willow led her into a large, airy room at the back of the house. The all-glass walls overlooked the elaborate pool and patio, complete with an impressive outdoor kitchen. She waved at a teal loveseat, which Bailey sank down into gratefully. Her legs had been none too steady all day.

Two excited dogs of unknown lineage circled around her

legs, tails wagging furiously. Willow sighed and lifted them, one under each arm, and placed them on the dog beds by the windows. Apparently well-trained, they settled in to munch on a few treats she sprinkled around their paws.

"So what did you want to talk about?" Willow sat down in a beige leather chair to Bailey's left. "You seemed unsure last night about seeing each other again."

Bailey had been iffy but circumstances had changed.

"The universe is messing with me again. With you too."

She didn't know how else to describe it. This was past a co-incidence but what was next on the spectrum she had no idea. She only knew she couldn't deal with it alone.

Willow's eyes had narrowed and her lips were pressed to-gether so Bailey continued on, hoping to find the right words to convey how freaky the whole thing was yet not show it.

"After what we learned last night, I decided to go through Frank's things that my sisters had boxed up for me." She didn't go into the details but since Willow was also a widow she probably understood. "I found this in a box of memorabilia."

Bailey handed over the fragile newspaper clippings to Wil-low, placing them on the end table between them. The other woman frowned but picked them up, her gaze darting left to right and then back again through the articles. When she was finished, she looked up at Bailey and shrugged.

"Am I supposed to know what this means? I don't under-stand."

Bailey pointed to the date in the article. "She was killed on July twenty-first."

Willow shook her head in denial but her skin had gone pale.

"It's a—"

"Coincidence?" Bailey finished for her. "All these coincidences are getting kind of old, don't you think? Frank kept that stack of clippings for a reason. This was a man who wasn't sentimental about anything. He barely remembered his own birthday let alone his wife's or family's. But he kept those and there has to be a reason why."

Willow dropped the clipping onto the table as if she'd been stung. "This girl, God rest her soul, was murdered. Our husbands died in accidents. It's a fluke. It has to be. One doesn't have anything to do with the other."

She sounded more desperate than sure and Bailey recognized the emotion well. She'd been swimming in it since last night but fighting against the rip tide that would most certainly pull her under. Calm and logical was what she needed to be.

The ringing of the doorbell interrupted Bailey's train of thought and Willow stood, excusing herself to answer it. When she came back, Bailey was shocked to see Peyton with her.

"So you two were going to keep spending time together." Bailey couldn't help the twinge of hurt.

"You weren't sure if you wanted to be with us but we were." Peyton sounded defensive and Bailey knew she was right but that didn't make it less painful.

"I never was in the cool crowd at school." Bailey shrugged as if she didn't care. She was an adult and things like this shouldn't bother her. Except that she'd been alone for a long time. "But I'm glad you're here. We have things to talk about."

Willow rolled her eyes and sighed. "For heaven's sake, we were not plotting anything, Bailey. After the cab came and picked you up we got to talking and decided to have tea this afternoon and talk some more. It's nice to have someone who understands. Besides, maybe that damn universe brought us together for a reason. That's what I believe, anyway."

Bailey was beginning to think that was the case although she'd never believed in fate or karma or any of that other mystical crap. Mostly she believed in hard work and effort.

Peyton settled onto the sofa. "Willow is being too nice. The fact is I begged her to see me again today. You may be able to forget about what happened last night but I can't. I didn't sleep a wink. All I could think about is Greg, Alex, and Frank. I wonder if they knew each other? That would be even more strange."

Bailey and Willow exchanged a glance.

"Strange doesn't even begin to describe this situation," Bailey said, reaching for the clippings and handing them to a frowning Peyton. "Read and then we'll talk."

Peyton shuffled the papers and then lifted her gaze. "These look old. Just what am I reading?"

Willow's laughed echoed off the vaulted ceilings. "You're reading the reason we won't be pretending we never met. I think we're stuck with each other whether we like it or not."

WILLOW HAD MIXED up a pitcher of margaritas, calling it a little hair of the dog, while Peyton read the articles. At first Bailey, still queasy from last night, didn't want anything to do with more alcohol but Willow had also brought out tray after tray of nibbles including wings and cheese sticks. Bailey's stomach had growled loudly and she'd given in, finding that junk food was exactly what she needed for her hangover. The margaritas had washed down the fat and carbs quite nicely.

"July twenty-first," Peyton whispered, her fingers playing with the stem of a glass but she had yet to take an actual drink. "What's so special about that day?"

"I think that's something we need to find out," Willow replied. "We can do a Google search on that date but I'm not sure it's going to give us what we need."

Peyton placed the clippings on the coffee table. "Have you ever heard of Chaos Theory or the Butterfly Effect?"

"I saw that movie," Bailey said, trying to remember the details but it had been years. "Supposedly one little thing can change human events forever."

Nodding, Peyton took a sip of her drink and then grimaced. "It's more than that. It's about large complex systems that appear to be orderly but really are not. Small variations can create widely different results. Supposedly, under certain conditions chaos can evolve into a pattern. Maybe that's what we're seeing here."

"Some sort of pattern that makes people die on a certain day?" Willow queried, her brows knitted together. "Wouldn't people notice after awhile?"

"Not if they don't see the pattern," Peyton countered. "Maybe the only reason we can see it is the string of events that led to the discovery last night and today. The Butterfly Effect."

Blowing out a breath, Willow took a gulp of her margarita. "So are we changing human events? Have we already changed them?"

Bailey had never liked science much and Chaos Theory was something they hadn't taught in Mr. Finch's chemistry class her junior year.

"Or it could be something else altogether," she offered. She'd been thinking about it since she found those stupid clippings and so far she hadn't been able to talk herself out of it.

Peyton reached for a cheese stick. "I'm open to any other suggestions."

Bailey took a deep breath, her gaze moving between Peyton and Willow, sizing up their reactions. She'd wanted to keep her mouth shut but it was a losing battle. Apparently she'd read too many mysteries and thrillers plus she had an overactive imagination.

"Frank, Alex, and Greg all died on the same day. Gwendolyn did too but years before. What if they were all killed by the same person? What if there's a serial killer out there who for some strange reason hates July twenty-first? There might be dozens of other victims."

Willow slowly placed her glass on the table, seeming to consider her next words. "There's only one problem with that. Our husbands died in accidents. They weren't murdered."

Slumping against the cushions, Bailey sighed in defeat. "I want to be able to explain all of this. I want it to make sense."

"It will." Peyton scooted closer to Bailey and patted her hand. "We'll find a connection. If there is one."

There had to be. It was too weird to be a coincidence. All of this was too…fucked up.

Bailey made her decision then and there. She hated the unknown and the universe could kiss her ass. She wanted to know the truth.

"I will find a connection. I'm going to pack a bag and head for Williamsburg. Visit that summer camp and maybe talk to some people who remember the murder. Maybe they know how Frank is connected to Gwendolyn. If he is at all."

Peyton's eyes were wide and she was shaking her head. "Do you think that's a good idea? More butterflies?"

Barking with laughter, Bailey was even more determined. "Afraid I'll start World War III? I just can't let this go. I'll admit this has my curiosity piqued. I want to see where Gwendolyn was murdered. I want to find out if this is one giant cluster coincidence and we should all just laugh at fate. I need to know."

Willow nodded, her expression serious. "So do I. I'm going with you."

"Alex might not have any connections at all to Gwendolyn," Bailey protested. "The clippings were in Frank's possessions."

"That's true but I want to help. I'm not going to let you do this alone. Frankly, this is the most intriguing thing to happen in years. I don't lead the most exciting life despite what the old biddies in this town might say."

Bailey wouldn't argue with that sentiment but she didn't want to lead anyone on a wild goose chase.

"Maybe it would be better if you and Peyton stayed back here and checked into your husbands' pasts. Find out all the details about their friends, schools, jobs. Put it all together and then we can compare notes. I don't want both of you to drop your lives for something that might not be worth the trip. Frankly I don't know what I'm going to do when I get there."

Peyton sighed and let her head loll back onto the couch

cushion. "I can do that. But if you find something – anything – you have to call us. I'm not going to miss out although I'm not sure I really want to know. I've already given Greg too much real estate in my brain these last five years."

Bailey smiled for the first time since yesterday. "What about the butterflies?"

Peyton was smiling too.

"Screw 'em. I've always preferred ladybugs to be honest."

Bailey was beginning to believe she couldn't move forward until she'd looked back. Way back. She didn't know just how far she'd have to go but she was willing to do it.

This was no coincidence. No chaos. No butterflies.

Frank and Gwendolyn were connected and Bailey was going to find out how.

•

Chapter Six

"RECALCULATING."

The disembodied voice of the GPS announced loud and proud that Bailey had once again managed to not follow the directions. She had checked into a hotel in Williamsburg and was now driving to the summer camp where Gwendolyn had died. The rental car was equipped with GPS but she seemed to be having issues.

The problem was that Bailey was too absorbed in her thoughts about the entire creepy situation she'd found herself in and would forget to follow the instructions from the annoying female voice even though it had warned her about the upcoming turn.

"Turn right in two hundred feet," the mechanical voice droned. "Then stay right."

Grunting, Bailey slid into the correct lane. Luckily there was no one already in it as she barely checked her mirror before turning right at the light.

"That was an adventure," she muttered under her breath. She wasn't the type that knew north from south or east from west. She navigated by landmarks, which was a problem in an unfamiliar area.

Bailey wasn't so sure that she hadn't made a terrible error in judgment coming here. Last night she had barely slept, her mind refusing to quiet down, so she'd been dragging this morning, chugging a giant coffee when at the airport. She tended to be a nervous flyer so the trip wasn't high on her fun meter nor was driving in a strange town any better. Her nerves were frayed and now she needed a Xanax to be able to handle the road trip. She couldn't get to the damn summer camp soon enough.

"Turn left in three hundred feet."

Willow leaned forward and craned her neck to see a street sign. They were out in the middle of nowhere or at least it seemed that way – somewhere between the James River and Williamsburg. "I'll happily turn left but where the hell am I supposed to do it?"

The rental car slowed to a crawl as she tried to find the turn off. She'd almost passed it when she finally spotted the sign.

"There it is. Keene Hill Camp. The branches and leaves cover almost the whole sign. It would be easy to miss this place. Maybe that's the point."

Talking to myself again.

Bailey had been aware that the campground was closed down and had been for several years. When she'd looked it up she'd found that in its heyday it had been one of the premiere summer camps for the children of the wealthy elite. They'd come from all corners of the United States to horseback ride, swim, play tennis, and make connections that would serve them well for the rest of their privileged lives.

After driving up the long, rutted road, Bailey parked the car near the first building she came to and climbed out, anxious to stretch her legs. She circled the large, dilapidated structure that had a sign hanging from a single hinge that proudly announced it was the dining hall and social center. More buildings were visible and there were directional signs mounted on posts pointing to the lake, the stables, and the basketball courts.

But there wasn't a single, solitary soul. It was kind of creepy.

Maybe if the buildings hadn't been so rundown or the greenery so completely overgrown it might not have been too bad. The place looked like it hadn't seen a human being in fifty years although Bailey knew it had been less than twenty. The camp had fallen on hard times after the murder. No one had wanted to spend their summer where someone had been brutally stabbed.

"Jesus, I'm ready for Jason to jump out any minute wearing his hockey mask and wielding a machete."

Clearly I've watched too many horror movies. Shame on me.

Bailey placed her hands on her hips and surveyed the area, not even sure where to start first. Or if she even wanted to. "This place brings new meaning to the word ramshackle."

Bailey began to head deeper into the camp. She wanted to see where Gwendolyn was murdered. She'd read all the clippings and seen the few photos but what she really wanted to see was where it actually happened. As for what she'd learn? Probably nothing except to get a better picture in her head as to what had happened that night. What it wouldn't tell her is why it was important to Frank.

She was used to being surrounded by people even in their little town so being alone was slightly unnerving. A screen door waved in the breeze, slamming against the door frame every few seconds in time with her pounding heart. The smell of dust, old wood, and grass filled her nostrils and made her sneeze a few times. In her mind's eye she could see this place filled with teenagers bustling to the lake and the dining hall. At one time this must have been a happy and lively place.

I need a better travel agent.

Bailey spotted a sign on a wooden pole pointing down a pathway to the river. Where Gwen was killed.

The hot afternoon sun beating down on her back, she trudged down the narrow path through the trees that eventually led her to a small sandy beach only about three feet wide and a hundred feet long. The river wasn't expansive and Bailey could see the opposite bank and in her younger days might have even been able to swim the distance. There wasn't much in the area but there were a few buildings on the opposite side but she couldn't see any inhabitants.

There was a rustle of grass and then the sound of someone clearing their throat. Bailey whirled around on her heel and her heart switched into a faster gear, her imagination motoring into overdrive. All she had for a weapon was her purse. She was an idiot for walking around a deserted summer camp without a way to defend herself.

"Can I help you?"

A tall, dark-haired man stood in front of her, dressed in blue jeans and a black t-shirt. Car keys dangled from his fingertips, not a machete, which immediately allowed Bailey to draw a full breath but not relax completely. He wasn't a small man and he could probably break her in two pieces with little effort.

"Can I help you?" the man repeated, taking two steps closer and sending Bailey a step back. "This is private property."

Another two steps forward but this time she stood her ground. He was only a few feet away now and she could smell the citrus of his body wash in the light breeze that ruffled his chocolate brown hair. Wide shoulders and long legs, he could be described as a handsome man although not in the conventional sense. His nose was crooked as if it had been broken once or twice but his cheekbones were high, his jaw firm, and his blue eyes stood out starkly from his tanned skin.

"I'm sorry," she said, not sure what she should tell him. Was the truth an option? He'd think she was crazy, which was surely a possibility. "I suppose you're wondering why I'm here."

"That did cross my mind. I don't get too many visitors out here. This place isn't too safe. Why don't you let me escort you back to your car?"

She'd come too far to fail this first task. Giving up was not an option.

"Gwen Baxter," she blurted, heat filling her cheeks. "I'm here about Gwen Baxter."

His friendly smile fell and was replaced with a suspicious glint in his eye. "Are you a reporter?"

"No." Bailey adamantly shook her head. "I swear I'm not. My name is Bailey Scott and I own a bakery in Florida. As for why I'm here, it's a long story."

One you probably won't believe anyway so why bother.

"I'm Chase Jennings and I own this piece of property. Now why don't you tell me why you want to see where Gwen died? What business is it of yours?"

Now he had her complete and total attention. He knew something about the events of that night from the way he said the girl's name. Bailey summoned up her courage and spoke. "You knew Gwen?"

"Yes, and now I get to ask a question again. What does this have to do with you?"

Bailey didn't like where this was going. She didn't have any answers. "Isn't it my turn to ask a question?"

Chase smiled and chuckled at her bravado. Or perhaps he thought she was funny. "I wasn't aware we were playing a game but fine. You can ask me a question."

"How did you know I was here?"

"A few of the townsfolk saw you drive in and alerted me that I had a trespasser. There are no secrets around here."

That might work to her advantage although it hadn't this time.

"I'm not trying to trespass," Bailey began, wanting to explain but frankly not knowing where to start. "It's a long story but I wanted to see where she was killed."

He cocked his head to the side and looked her up and down. "Did you know her? You look too young to have been a friend of hers."

"My late husband did," she finally admitted, although she wasn't sure it was truly the case. So far, she only suspected he knew her. She could have lied and said she'd known Gwen but if he'd known her too he might ask her questions she couldn't answer. "I guess my curiosity got the better of me."

Chase was giving her a strange look but she was determined to stay tight-lipped. Unburdening her soul about a hiccup in the universe was not on the agenda.

Straightening, Chase pointed to his right. "The papers had it wrong. Gwen was killed on the banks of the James River farther that way."

"Is it far?"

"No, but I'm afraid I'll have to ask you to leave the property now."

Halting, Bailey raised her eyebrows and crossed her arms over her chest. There wasn't anything to steal so what was the big deal if she walked around for a few minutes?

"Or?"

Chase smiled and rubbed his chin thoughtfully. "Let's not go there, shall we? I'd like to stay a gentleman here. Now if you would please follow me. I'll make sure you get back to your vehicle safely."

Bailey sighed and nodded. Arguing wasn't going to get her what she wanted. She needed to come up with another plan but at the moment she was out of ideas. Time to regroup.

"After you, Mr. Jennings."

"I hope you haven't had a wasted trip. You should visit Colonial Williamsburg or Yorktown. People love it."

Actually, it wasn't a waste. She'd learned that the newspapers were wrong about the location of Gwen's murder. Maybe that wasn't the only thing they were wrong about.

Chapter Seven

C HASE LOST COUNT of the number of dogs that vied to lick his face and jump into his lap. His friend and neighbor Joshua Coleman was a veterinarian and there were always a plethora of animals in his home – some just visiting, some actual residents – but tonight was more than usual. All of this love was wonderful but eventually he'd have to get up from the floor. A sharp whistle from Josh had the canines backing off, tails still wagging and tongues lolling out.

"They haven't seen you in awhile," remarked Josh pulling two beers from the refrigerator. "They remember that you'll throw the tennis ball until your shoulder gives out."

Rising from the floor, Chase accepted the beer gratefully. It had been a long day and he'd been looking forward to this. "There's more of them than last time."

Josh shook his head and chuckled. "No, it's the same. Actually, maybe one less. Harley the poodle was adopted by Wanda down at the bookstore."

Chase remembered seeing a dog dressed in a ruffled collar the last time he was in there. Like Shakespeare.

"Still no cats?"

It was a running joke between the two of them.

"Still allergic, so no."

"How can you be a vet and also be allergic to cats? Isn't there some rule about that?"

Josh scratched his head. "Not that I know of. And as I've said before, I didn't know I was allergic to cats until after I decided to be a vet. I'm getting the shots so I'm not having any issues."

Chase opened the pizza box as Josh pulled plates from the cabinet over the sink. The smell of garlic and tomatoes made his stomach growl with hunger. He'd had a lousy roast beef sandwich for lunch around eleven. Far too long to go without food.

"So what did you want to talk about?" Josh asked as they dug into dinner. Chase had met Josh when he'd moved in next door and since then they'd become fast friends, practically living at each other's homes. He felt as comfortable at Josh's place as he did his own. Like so many other evenings, Chase brought the pizza and Josh provided the beer. If they were feeling particularly social they might invite over a few other guys and play poker.

Glancing at the door, Chase hesitated. He didn't want to have to do this twice. Frankly he didn't want to talk about it at all but it had been bugging him since seeing that woman at the camp earlier today. "Is Ellis coming?"

Ellis Hunter was a detective with the local police and that meant he kept strange hours and they never knew if he was going to show up or not. They didn't mind but the women he dated did. About a year ago he'd sworn off relationships for an undetermined length of time.

"Eventually. He'll be late to his own damn funeral with a long list of excuses. He can eat the pizza ice cold. I'm hungry now."

Ellis wouldn't care about the temperature of his food. Chase had seen his friend eat out of Chinese food containers straight from the refrigerator without batting an eye. No food snob, he'd just as soon eat a burger as Chateaubriand.

"I guess I can catch him up later." Chase set his pizza back down on the plate. "I found a woman out at the summer camp today. Had to run her off with a little warning not to come back."

Josh frowned, his brows pulled together. "Nobody ever goes out there. What did she want?"

"She wanted to see where Gwen Baxter was killed. She said her husband knew Gwen but I'm not sure she was telling the truth."

"Do you think she's a reporter?"

"Why would the press be interested in this story after all these years?" Chase shrugged. "They barely reported on it when it happened. I did ask her though and she said no."

Josh took a long swallow of his beer before speaking. "And you believe her?"

"Yeah," Chase replied after a moment. "She didn't look like a reporter. Too skittish and not polished. A reporter would have had a cover story all ready and believe me this lady didn't. It was almost like the visit was a spur of the moment thing she hadn't really thought through all that well."

A smile spread across Josh's face. "Maybe she was there on a dare. Like a double dog dare."

Christ on a crutch. Josh needed to hang out with humans more often.

"Or better, maybe there's something she isn't telling me. It's been bugging me all day."

Josh gave him a shrewd look. "She's been bothering you or the memory of Gwen has been bothering you?"

"Both," Chase answered immediately. "I barely knew Gwen but I saw her dead body that day when they were loading her into the ambulance. Jesus, that sticks with a kid and I'll admit that the fact they never found her killer bugs the shit out of me. How can that be? How can there be absolutely no witnesses and no clues?"

"Just forget about the whole thing. It happened years ago. Unless this woman is pretty. If she is, you should definitely talk to her again."

Bailey Scott was pretty, all right. Just his type with all that long dark hair and dark eyes. Her figure had looked sweet as well in that sundress she'd been wearing.

Late husband.

She was a widow. She seemed so young but that didn't mean she couldn't have lost a husband. Maybe in the war.

"So is she?" Josh prompted.

Chase pulled his head out of his ass. He was daydreaming and it was a bad habit.

"Is she what?

"Pretty. Is she pretty?"

Josh was looking at him like he was stupid, which he had to admit might be the case.

Chase took a big bite of pizza, the flavors exploding on his tongue. "It doesn't matter. I don't know how to get a hold of her."

"So she is nice looking," Josh stated with a grin.

She was but Chase would never see her again. It was just as well because the last thing he needed in his life was to think about Gwen.

Josh was right. It had happened years ago and he needed to stop thinking about it.

Let that poor girl rest in peace.

BAILEY'S PHONE WAS ringing when she stepped into her hotel room. Williamsburg was popular with tourists so she'd had plenty of choice when it came to lodging and food. Pressing a button, she had Willow on the line.

"How's it going?" the other woman asked. "By the way, Peyton's here with me too."

"Hey," Peyton's sing-song voice emanated from the speaker. "So, did you go to the summer camp? What was it like? Did you see anything?"

"It went south quickly," Bailey groaned as she slid onto the bed, her head hitting a down pillow. "I got my ass royally kicked. The land owner was there and he escorted me off his property before I could see anything. Though before he did he said that he knew Gwen but he wouldn't say anything else. What do I do now? I went there with no plan, no cover story. I should have prepared better."

"Tell him the truth," Peyton urged. "Maybe he'll be sympathetic."

"I can't go back there," Bailey snorted. "Orange is not my color."

"How did he even know you were there?" Willow asked. "I thought the place was deserted."

"Apparently he has nosy neighbors. He said there are no secrets around there."

"What's Plan B then?"

Right now, Bailey didn't know what to say. She'd wanted to come here to see if there was any connection between Gwen Baxter's death and Frank's but she didn't have a clue as to what she was doing. She was no amateur detective. This was not her skill set and she'd dragged Willow and Peyton in to her hare-brained scheme. At least she hadn't brought them with her.

"I'm sorry," she said softly. "I don't have a Plan B. I don't know what I'm doing here or even how to go about this."

Willow and Peyton were uncharacteristically quiet.

"None of us knows," Willow pointed out after a bit of silence. "We'll figure this out together. This isn't all your responsibility, you know. I want answers, Bailey. A few days ago, I thought I knew everything about Alex and his death. Now I'm not so sure. Like you, I need to know if his death is in any way connected to Gwen's."

Frustrated, Bailey shook her head, forgetting her friends couldn't see her. "I don't know how to find that out. I came here thinking there would be answers but I wasn't being realistic. They're not going to just fly out of the ground or the trees when I walk by."

"Thank goodness, that would be scary," Peyton giggled.

"Bailey, it's okay. I didn't think you had some super secret decoder ring that was going to tell us what to do. It would have been cool but I figured we'd have to find our way."

"I don't know what to do next," Bailey admitted, feeling suddenly tired and more than a little helpless.

"I do," Willow declared, certainty in her tone. "You have to go back to that summer camp. You need to talk to that property owner. He said he knew Gwen. Maybe he knew our husbands as well."

"The answers aren't at the camp. We know that. I doubt I'll see anything that will tell us what happened."

"But if you go back, the neighbors will tell on you again and you'll get another visit from the owner. Talk to him. Throw yourself on his mercy. Give him the sob story of the century. But for heaven's sake, get him to talk. If he knew Gwen, he's our first clue."

"He might throw me out on my ear."

Willow laughed. "I'm not above offering him money for his information. Find out his price and I'll have a check to him in the overnight mail."

Bailey had a feeling that Chase was the kind of man that couldn't be bought. He had that air about him. Alpha, in charge, and unconquerable. Bossy and annoying. Just the kind of man that she avoided. Men like that were always throwing their weight around and trying to tell her what to do.

"I'll go back right after dinner," Bailey sighed in resignation. "If I get caught again I guess I can say I wanted to see the sunset over the James River."

Bailey wasn't so sure about this scheme. This plan of theirs had more holes in it than a miniature golf course but it was the best they could do. She really did want to see the scene of the crime although she knew it wouldn't help them find the connection. She didn't know why it was important to her but it was. Maybe she thought she might see something there that reminded her of Frank? Not likely.

"He doesn't look like a stupid man," Bailey said wryly. "I think he probably does expect me to try again. He might be on the lookout."

"What does he look like?" Peyton asked. "You have a strange tone in your voice when you talk about him."

Bailey shifted uncomfortably on the mattress thinking about the way he'd looked her up and down. Had he liked what he'd seen? The question shouldn't even come up because that wasn't what she was here for. This was about getting the truth. Besides, she was a shambles when it came to men. She'd been married and now a widow and she was still shy and hesitant when it came to the opposite sex. She'd never really understood men and certainly never felt comfortable being herself around them.

"I don't know what you mean."

Willow sputtered with laughter. "I think you do. But you didn't answer the question. Is he handsome?"

"He's not ugly but he's probably married with six kids and a cocker spaniel."

"What if he isn't?" Willow challenged. "Be nice. Invite him for dinner. Maybe he'll tell you about Gwen Baxter."

"I don't need a date," Bailey denied, feeling the heat suffuse her cheeks. "Least of all some guy who lives a thousand miles from me."

"Hon, you are more uptight than anyone ought to be allowed," Willow declared with a chuckle. "You definitely need a date and soon. Have you dated much since...?"

Bailey didn't even have to answer; she knew the silence said it all. "Have you? What about you, Peyton? Have either of you dated? Because I have a feeling I'm not alone here."

Willow sighed in defeat. "Okay, I haven't either. But I'm not nearly as high-strung as you are."

"I haven't either," Peyton offered softly. "But then I haven't had much luck with men. I think I'm better off without them."

The three women sat in silence for a moment before Bailey made her excuses and ended the call. She had a few things to do before she could head back to the summer camp. This quest had barely begun. There was so much more to learn.

Chapter Eight

CHASE AND JOSH were sitting out on the front porch enjoying the cool night air when they saw it. He shouldn't have been surprised. He might have run the lady off of the property earlier in the day but she'd seemed rather determined.

Flashlight.

"Son of a bitch."

Joshua lifted his feet from the railing where they'd been resting and placed them on the floor, sitting up straight. "Is that a light down there?"

"Yes," Chase growled in frustration. He'd been having a nice evening and now he was going to have to deal with that woman again. She seemed pleasant enough – pretty too – but this time he wouldn't let her get away with that lame-ass story as to why she was here. He wanted the truth. "Dammit, I had a feeling she wouldn't give up."

Both Josh and Chase's homes were built up on a small hill that looked down on the banks of the James River. The sun had just set and from his vantage point, he could easily see the flashlight in the distance.

"You have to admire her determination," Josh laughed as they hurried over to Chase's house to grab his gun. He doubted the woman was packing heat but one could never be too careful in the woods at night.

"I don't have to admire anything. She's a menace to society."

"Want me to come with you?"

Chase nodded and the two headed off down the trail that led to the river, trying to keep as quiet as possible. He intended to give the woman a little scare so hopefully she would learn her lesson. He didn't have the time or patience for this shit.

Well...technically he had the time.

He could hear the crackle of grass under her feet along with the crickets and he paused, raising his hand so Josh would do the same. She might be cute but she also might be crazy. She was muttering to herself and it sounded like a complete back and forth conversation.

"This doesn't exactly match the picture," she said at first.

"But it's been years," she went on. "Things could have changed."

A rustling in the grass and then more talking. "I think this is where he pointed. She would have been found right here. Could they hear your screams up at the camp, Gwen? Or had he lured you all the way out here so no one could hear you? Did you know what was happening to you? Were you scared?"

Chase had heard enough. They were all questions he'd pondered in his own mind. Stepping forward, he swept his own flashlight across the small clearing and over her face.

"Actually, you can hear screams from here all the way to the camp. You can also hear them at my house up on the hill. You can see a flashlight too."

The gorgeous brunette had been quiet so far but she sighed and rubbed the back of her neck, her teeth sinking into her full bottom lip. "I swear I'm really not trying to cause any trouble. I just figured your neighbors would tell you I was out here. I really want to talk to you."

"Why?"

She looked up at him, her earnest expression illuminated by the flashlight. "I'm here looking for the truth about my late husband. I know you have no reason to believe me but I swear I'm not here to cause trouble. I just want the truth."

He looked at Bailey for a long time as she stared at her feet before glancing at Josh who had a smile playing on his lips. For once, Chase was going to trust his gut.

"I believe you."

The brunette's head jerked up and her eyes widened in surprise. "You do?"

"Is there a reason I shouldn't? I heard what you were talking about and it does seem like you are truly interested in Gwen's murder. My question is why. And don't try and give me any stories or half-truths. What does your late husband have to do with Gwen? It's time for the truth or I call the cops and you spend the night in jail. Your choice."

"I'll tell you but you won't believe it."

"Try me."

The brunette smacked at her arm and hissed. Mosquitos. "Can we go inside somewhere? I'm getting eaten alive."

Should he trust her inside of his home?

If he and Josh couldn't handle this little bit of a woman they ought to turn in their man-card. Unless of course she was armed.

"Are you carrying any weapons?"

Bailey groaned and rolled her eyes. "I'm not even carrying any bug spray and I locked my purse in the car. I'm truly defenseless here and I think I'm the one who is being trusting, not the other way around." Suddenly she frowned and looked him up and down. "Are you carrying any weapons?"

Chase patted the back of his belt where he'd tucked the revolver. "Yes, ma'am. But I don't intend to use it except for self-defense."

"I'm harmless. I hope like hell you are too."

That remained to be seen.

WHEN THEY RETURNED to Josh's home, he offered Bailey a slice of pizza, which she declined. Introductions were made all around as she hadn't formally met Josh yet. He then offered her a beer, which she also declined but she did accept a ginger ale as they settled into his living room. She seemed wary and for good reason. She was in a strange man's house with one other man and Chase was certain she was questioning the wisdom of being here.

"Do you want to start?"

Bailey took a deep breath and scooted to the edge of the couch cushion, placing her drink on the coffee table. "I guess I will. It all started at a party for charity a few nights ago. I'm from Midnight Blue Beach in Florida. It's on the Gulf Coast around the Clearwater area and the party was for the local children's charity. Anyway, there was a kitchen fire…"

Chase listened as Bailey explained, interjecting funny but strange details every now and then. As the story progressed he found himself in disbelief. It was too far-fetched to be true but the woman seemed completely serious. Even Josh, who had flicked a glance or two Chase's way, was engrossed in the tale. But could it possibly be true? What were the odds? They had to be astronomical.

Bailey looked around the room as she began to wind down her story, her gaze finally resting on Chase. "So I decided to come here. I guess you could say we hadn't thought it through much, if at all. I– I mean, *we* just want the truth. It seems to be too much of a coincidence that they all died on the same day. If our husbands' deaths have a connection to hers, we want to know. I *need* to know."

Not sure how to respond, he tried to make sense of what he'd heard. His emotions were all over the place and he didn't quite know how to deal with them. First, there was some shame that he'd admired the attractiveness of a widow. Sure, she'd been single for five years but he still didn't think it was a cool thing to do. Second, it was hard to believe that they'd found each other by accident. Bailey had explained about Chaos Theory and the Butterfly Effect but he still had his doubts. Perhaps their meeting had been planned in some way, by a third party? Thirdly, their husbands' deaths had all been ruled accidents. They were nothing like Gwen's which made any connection suspect at best.

But he had to admit she had a compelling tale. If he'd been in her shoes, he would have been out there looking for the murder scene too.

Chase cleared his throat and stood, playing for time. Josh was watching him closely and he had a sneaking suspicion he was only quiet because Chase was.

"That is…something," he finally said, not wanting to appear not to believe them. He did believe them. Her sincerity was clear to anyone but that didn't mean that the whole situation didn't fuck with his head.

Josh scraped his fingers through his hair. "What my friend is trying to say is that is the strangest story we've ever heard."

Bailey slapped the arm of the couch with her hand, her lips pressed together. "Are you calling me a liar?"

Shaking his head, Josh smiled. "No, I am not. For some strange reason, I believe you. Or at least, I believe that you believe it. You know we can check your facts, right?"

Bailey stood and walked to the window. "I do and I invite you to do so. We're telling the truth. Listen, we're having a difficult time with it ourselves if you must know. The only thing that made it something we could deal with at the time was massive amounts of booze. We handled it by being drunk but I'm stone cold sober now and facing the possibility that everything I thought I knew about my husband just might not be true." Her dark brown eyes glistened with unshed tears. "How would you feel if that was your reality?"

Something about the anguish in her tone and expression got to Chase in a way he hadn't experienced in a long time. His chest tightened painfully and he had an overwhelming urge to put his arms around her and tell her everything was going to be okay. What a crock. He had no idea if it would be or not but her plight tugged at what was left of his heart. This woman wanted the truth and if he were honest, that's what he wanted too. He'd wondered about Gwen's death for years, never finding any answers. Now he had a life-size clue standing in his living room. There was a chance these women's husbands were the key to solving Gwen's murder. He'd be a fool to turn them away.

"I'll help you," he said, hearing her gasp with surprise. "I'll tell you about that night and about Gwen."

Chapter Nine

B AILEY TOOK A few deep breaths to try and slow down her racing heart. She hadn't realized how much she'd been hoping for Chase to help her. Frankly, she hadn't known where to turn or what to do and any information that he gave her could put them one step closer to finding the truth.

"My family has owned this summer camp since the 1950s," Chase began, settling himself into a chair across from Bailey. "As long as I can remember I spent my summers here first with my grandparents and then when I was ten or so, my parents took over."

He paused and Bailey had to hold her tongue to keep from urging him to continue. He would in his own time and she needed to be patient.

For once in her life.

"I was fifteen the summer Gwen was killed. It was near the end of camp and there was only a few more days left. I helped my parents out quite a bit. Setting up craft classes, and cleaning up sports equipment, stuff like that so I was around her more than the other kids my age. We weren't friends but she didn't have her nose in the air all the time like so many of those kids. They all came from wealthy families and they all thought they were better than me. My parents were basically servants to them. But Gwen wasn't like that. She treated everyone decently."

"That must have made for a long summer," Josh observed. "Did you have any friends?"

Chase smiled at what were obviously happy memories.

"Two. They came every year and we had a blast. They didn't care that my family wasn't rich and I didn't care that they were. But I learned a great deal attending that camp every summer. The most important thing being that money doesn't give you class, smarts, or manners."

Bailey couldn't agree more. "What was she like?"

Chase rubbed his chin. "Smart. Pretty. Popular. All the boys liked her and I could see why. I had a little crush on her myself. She had long blonde hair and blue eyes, plus she looked good in a bikini, which was the main criteria for a teenage boy. The other girls her age didn't give the younger boys the time of day but she'd always say hello to me. She was...different."

"Did she have a boyfriend?" Bailey asked. "It's always the boyfriend when you see something like this on television."

"She had lots of boyfriends from what I could see but no one special person. At least not that I noticed, but you have to remember that my friends didn't hang around her friends. Even at Saturday dances, the age groups kept to themselves. And my group of friends were pretty much ostracized from everyone else."

Josh leaned forward, his elbows resting on his knees. "What happened the night she was killed? What do you remember?"

Chase stood and paced the small area between the chair and the kitchen. "I've thought about this again and again through the years but it was just a night like any other night. We'd all had dinner in the dining hall and then down to the campfire for s'mores and music. The couples were dancing and the singles were hanging out talking about who knows what. School in the fall or some shit like that. I don't even really remember. Eventually it got late and the couples wandered off down to the river. That was the make-out spot. They'd all go there after the adults went to bed."

Bailey took a sip of her drink, her heart still beating way too fast, wondering if he would say something that would link Gwen to Frank. "Did Gwen go with someone?"

"She must have although I don't know who. She was dancing with several guys and then when I noticed later she was gone. The official story was that she went back to her cabin with her friends but I doubt that. The older kids didn't go to bed early and her girlfriends were all with the boys. I think they were covering for her and themselves. They didn't want the adults knowing what they were doing."

"Maybe she didn't feel well," Bailey suggested. "If she had a headache or something she might have gone back to her cabin and then out for some fresh air later."

"That's possible," Chase conceded. "The last time I saw her was at the campfire. That's all I know. The next morning her cabinmates alerted the staff she was missing. A search was carried out and they found her body down by the river. I remember this part like it was yesterday. My dad was white as a sheet and he told me to stay in the dining hall with the other kids. They'd gathered us all there to keep us out of the way but being the little shit I was at the time I didn't listen. I'd never seen my father that upset and I wanted to know why so I snuck down to the river and hid behind some trees. I saw them put her into a body bag. She had been wearing white shorts and a light blue shirt and they were both covered with blood. There was blood on her legs and in her hair too. It was gruesome and believe me it made an impression on a fifteen year old boy."

"Did the police talk to everyone?" Josh asked. "Did you make a statement?"

"We all did but no one saw her after midnight."

"Everyone had an alibi?"

"As far as I know." Chase drank a long swallow of his beer. "I do know they talked to all the teenage boys and even all the counselors and coaches. I remember my dad and mom talking about it that fall and how they didn't have any suspects. People were even beginning to believe there was a roaming killer in the woods. All those horror movies, if you know what I mean."

"Do you remember the names of the boys that liked her?" Bailey asked. "Maybe we could start with them? Maybe they knew Frank."

"I'm bad with names but I have photos stored away. My parents did a little booklet every year, sort of like a memory book. People passed them around and signed them. I have one for every year from about 1985 forward. I'm sure I could point the boys out. Her friends too."

Bailey had seen dozens of Frank's friends over the years at parties, weddings, funerals, and the occasional reunion or fundraiser. If there was a picture of them in the camp, she would find them. For the first time since she'd arrived, she allowed herself to feel hope.

AFTER THEY ALL moved over to Chase's place, Josh helped him carry down the dusty boxes from the attic into the living room. This was the first time Chase was glad his parents had been packrats. They'd saved everything from their time running the camp and he'd shoved it all up in the attic instead of going through it.

His laziness regarding organization and clutter had finally paid off.

Chase handed the last box down to Josh who stood at the foot of the ladder. "That's all I can find. Hopefully the years we want will be in one of these."

Josh used a rag from the kitchen to wipe away the layer of dust on the top of the two boxes. "Do you think you can recognize someone from twenty years ago?"

Chase climbed down the ladder and closed up the entrance to the attic. "I'm getting older but I'm not ancient. I may not remember names all that well but I have a memory for faces."

"And Bailey," Josh pressed. "Do you think she'll be able to recognize anyone? I know you want to help her but this may be a wild goose chase all around. I'm still not sure I even believe her story. I think we should check it out for ourselves and make sure they're telling the truth. The dates of their deaths have to be public record."

While not completely comfortable with the idea of delving

into death certificates, Chase had to concede that what Josh proposed was wise. He'd call their friend Ellis in the morning and let him do the detective work.

"I can't imagine that she'd lie about something we could easily verify but I see your point."

Chase turned to head back into the living room but Josh caught his arm. "You need to be careful, my friend. You're already in deep here."

Frowning, Chase shook his head. "What are you talking about?"

Josh sighed and leaned a shoulder onto the wall. "The girl. I'm talking about Bailey. Don't think I haven't noticed the way you look at her because I have."

"And just how do I look at her?"

Josh chuckled and an evil smile bloomed on his face. "Like she's the greatest thing since sliced bread and pizza with extra cheese. Not that I blame you because she looks damn fine but don't let your little head do the thinking for you. I don't want you to get played. For all we know, she's a reporter or a writer or worse, some sort of whack-a-doodle who has delusions about murders. Don't let her talk you into doing something you wouldn't normally do."

Chase was many things but a pushover for a woman wasn't one of them.

"Thanks for the warning but I think I have this handled. I'll be careful, okay?"

That seemed to be enough for Josh. He headed back to his own place to feed the dogs and get ready for the next day. Chase joined Bailey in the living room again where she was scrolling through her phone. She looked up when they entered and smiled, showing off a perfect set of dimples and even white teeth.

She could be a crazy person. I have to remember that.

He arranged the boxes on the rarely used dining room table. He wasn't sure if there was any link between Bailey's late husband and Gwen but if there was, it just might be among these photos. For the first time in twenty years, there might be an actual clue in the murder.

Or this could be a cruel hoax perpetuated by the woman in his living room.

If it was the former, he'd thank whatever part of the universe pushed her into his life.

If it was the latter, she'd wish she'd never come here and stirred this up.

Chapter Ten

IT DIDN'T TAKE long for Chase to locate the boxes from the years that Gwen Baxter attended the summer camp. Old and faded, the memory books were really just regular white paper folded and stapled together, probably assembled at a copy center. The pictures of the campers were in black and white and often not that good. Some were posed but many were candid shots of the kids at play – swimming, riding, and generally having a good time.

"This is Gwen." Chase pointed to a young blonde in a photo with three other girls sitting at a table eating ice cream. "Those were her cabinmates. They stayed together every year so I'm guessing they were close. They did everything together."

Bailey studied the girls, fresh and young, smiling as if they hadn't a care in the world. So much like Frank's yearbook picture. The cruel world hadn't touched them yet and she couldn't help but be a little envious. She barely remembered those days and they seemed so far away.

"She's pretty," Bailey remarked, peering at the photos more closely to see if she recognized any of the females. "All of them are."

None of the girls looked familiar so she turned to the next page. More happy teenagers but none she recognized. With each page it was more of the same. She didn't recognize anyone. Chase held up another booklet.

"The one you're looking at was two summers before. This one is the same summer. My parents had created the book a week ahead of time since there was only a few more days of camp left but because of the murder they didn't hand them out. I don't know if it was by choice or they simply never had a chance. Everyone's parents came to get them early so the camp cleared out within twenty-four hours. No one wanted their child in a place where there was a killer."

If she'd been in their shoes, she would have had her kid out of that place in a heartbeat so that news didn't surprise her. But...what happened to Chase's parents was sad.

"I feel sorry for your mother and father. They had this family business and in a second it was gone. They must have been devastated."

Chase smiled and shook his head. "You'd think that but you'd be wrong. They were relieved. They had a real estate business that they ran full-time and they never really enjoyed the outdoors. They only did this for my grandparents who loved it. They would have retired anyway once my grandfather and grandmother passed on."

"I guess I just assumed... You held onto it. Never changed anything. I assumed it was for sentimental reasons."

"In a way, it was. I enjoyed my summers here but it was more than that. I get offers on the property all the time but just haven't been able to part with the place. Not while Gwen's murder is unsolved. Maybe if he's ever found I could put this in the past, sell the place and move on."

Bailey took a sip of her soda. "It sounds like it was more than a crush on her."

Chuckling, Chase handed her a booklet, taking a copy for himself. "I can assure you it was just a passing fancy. Seeing her dead was what got to me. So full of life the night before and then suddenly gone. And in such a gruesome fashion. Those images have haunted me for years."

That had never occurred to her. "Haunted? Are you saying the camp is actually haunted by Gwen?"

His eyes widened and this time he laughed. "Hell, no. The *thoughts* haunted me. There are no ghosts here. At least none that I know of. Why? Are you a ghost hunter too?"

She shuddered delicately. "No. What I am is a big wuss. I don't like anything scary. Just standing in the camp tonight as the sun went down freaked me out. Every branch in the wind, every cricket and frog. That's why I made so much noise when I showed up and that's why I was waving that damn flashlight around hoping your neighbors would tell on me."

He was really laughing now, rich and deep and quite attractive. "Why didn't you just come directly to me?"

"Because I didn't know where you lived," she explained as if to a child. "How was I supposed to find you? You had to find me."

"All you had to do was go into town and ask anyone. They would have sent you here. Standing in the dark by the river wasn't required."

Well, crap. She hadn't thought of that and she was supposed to be smart.

"That never occurred to me," she finally admitted. "Peyton and Willow suggested coming out here and I guess I didn't think any further. I'm an idiot."

"You're not an idiot. It worked, didn't it? Here you are. Now let's look through this book."

Only a few pages in, Chase pushed a picture in front of her. "Right here. These boys. They all liked Gwen. Especially the one with the dark hair. I saw them kissing one night."

Studying the photo, Bailey could understand why Gwen couldn't make up her mind about which boy to choose. They were all handsome, each in their own way.

"The night of the murder?"

"Not that night but other nights. I saw her dancing and kissing a lot of boys actually. As I said, she was popular."

Hmmm...

"When you say popular do you mean something else?"

"If you're asking if she was sleeping with these boys I don't know. I do know that there was a great deal of...fornication going on that summer. Hell, every summer, but I was too young to know the details. The kids that came to the camp were pretty wild and Gwen was no exception."

He'd been fifteen that summer. Plenty old enough to be getting into trouble. Why she needed to know she didn't understand but she found herself asking.

"What about you? Were you wild? Did you have a summer girlfriend?"

Sputtering with laughter, he shook his head. "Not even close.

Those stuck up girls wouldn't give me the time of day. I was *poor* according to them. Never mind that we were actually upper middle class—to them I was practically Oliver Twist at the orphanage. My two friends might have gotten lucky – they were wealthy – but me? No way. I had to do without female attention while I was here. That's why Gwen stood out from the other girls. She didn't treat me or any of the staff with the usual disdain."

"I grew up middle class too. We had a few rich kids in our school or what we thought was rich. Doctors and lawyers kids. My mother was a nurse and my father owned a bakery that supplied the restaurants in town. I worked there every summer and after school. That's where I learned to bake." She frowned, realizing he didn't really know anything about her. "I opened a bakery after Frank died. I needed something to concentrate on."

She didn't mention that the bakery idea had been a constant bone of contention between her and her husband. She'd wanted to go into business for herself shortly after they were married but he'd objected, saying her job was to take care of him. If she had a business, she wouldn't be able to travel with him at a moment's notice or might be too tired to attend the multitude of parties and functions that were a part of his life.

It was on one of those impromptu vacations to Turks and Caicos where he'd had his scuba diving accident. She'd been in the spa getting a pedicure when she'd heard the news. To this day, she couldn't smell nail polish without getting nauseous.

"You mean like cakes and pies?"

She didn't imagine the excitement in his voice. "Just like that. Everything sweet and decadent."

Groaning, he closed his eyes and grinned. "You just became my best friend. I have a huge sweet tooth."

"If you play your cards right, maybe I'll make something for you while I'm here if you give me the use of your kitchen. It's the least I can do for you since you're helping me."

"Consider it yours, and I'd like to think we're helping each other."

Bailey shrugged, trying to suppress a smile. "Then I won't bother baking anything."

"On the other hand, I am doing you a big favor."

She couldn't keep a straight face. He was almost pouting and it looked hilarious on a grown man. "Don't worry. I'll bake something. It's not a chore—it's something I really love. What's your poison?"

His eyebrows shot up. "Pardon?"

"Your poison," she repeated patiently. "What kind of sweets do you like?"

"I'm not fussy. I like red velvet cake and I also like coconut cream pie. But truly, I won't turn down anything you make."

Typical bachelor. Bailey had a few that frequented her bakery and she loved trying new recipes out on them. They'd eat anything and give her honest feedback.

"Neither of those are difficult." She paged through the book and a picture caught her eye. Bringing it closer, her heart stopped for a moment and her breath caught. She had to force herself to inhale and exhale before she could speak. "Chase, I think I've found something."

Chase put down his own book to look over her shoulder. "What have you got?"

She set the booklet down and pointed to the smiling teenager holding a tennis racquet surrounded by what appeared to be friends.

"That's Frank. That's my husband."

Chapter Eleven

I T SHOULDN'T HAVE been a shock. After all, that's why Bailey had hopped an airplane from Tampa to Virginia, leaving her manager in charge of the bakery. This was what she'd been looking for but now that she'd found it she wasn't so sure she wanted to know. Her imagination was working overtime and right now she had a picture of Frank pledging his undying love to Gwen, never getting over her death.

It would explain so much about their marriage.

"Let's see if he's in any more photos."

Bailey heard Chase speaking but she was still having her out of body moment. It was as if this was happening to someone else and she was simply a spectator. Rubbing her fingertips together, she realized the blessed numbness had returned.

"What?"

Chase placed his hand on her shoulder, the warmth seeping through the thin material of her shirt. "I said we should see if he's in any more photos."

She nodded mechanically and reached into the box, her hands shaking. She furled her fingers into tight fists and took a deep breath to get control of her body. This was no time to reveal her jumbled emotions. She barely knew this man, and she'd already told him too much.

They sifted through each year he could have attended, finding photos of him in four of the years with a gap between the third and last year. Bailey couldn't stop staring at the pictures, taking in every detail as if her life depended on it. Frank looked so different, so happy and relaxed.

"Did he change much?" Chase asked softly.

Rubbing at her temple, she shook her head. "Physically he didn't change all that much. A few lines around his eyes and a few gray hairs but I could have picked him out of a crowd." She ran her finger over the picture of Frank, tracing the outline of his face and shoulders. "What changed was who he was inside. This man has joy inside of him. He's smiling and optimistic about his life. He's…happy."

Shifting in his seat, Chase turned so he was facing her. "And your Frank was different?"

Like night and day.

"My Frank," she began, having trouble with the phrasing. Even after they'd married, she'd never felt like they belonged to one another. They'd been separate people living parallel lives in the same house. "Somewhere between here and meeting me he lost some of this spark. This man looks open and free. The Frank I knew kept a large portion of himself closed off from everyone, even me. He only let me in part of the way. No matter how I tried to break down those walls, I just couldn't. Eventually I stopped trying."

Her hands were clenched tightly, the knuckles white with the effort not to howl with leftover pain. He'd rejected and hurt her so many times. She'd believed that she was immune but this was bringing up all the old feelings of inadequacy. She'd never been enough for Frank and in his own subtle way he'd let her know.

"I'm sorry."

Such simple words but Chase made them sound heartfelt. She didn't like the idea of comparing the two men but she couldn't stop herself from thinking that Frank wasn't much for figuring out how other people were feeling. He was too self-involved. Not in a mean way. He hadn't been a cruel man but he had been an indifferent one.

"Me too," she finally said, too many memories crowding around her at once. She needed space to breathe. To think. "I tried hard to make my marriage work but in the end I was exhausted. I doubt we would have made it, if I'm brutally honest. Whatever brought us together in the beginning was long gone by the end. I failed."

His fingers pressed into the flesh above her knees insistently, keeping her anchored to the here and now. "I've been married and divorced and if I learned anything it's that it takes two. Two to make it good and two to make it bad. I'm sure you both did the best you could at the time."

She lifted her head, their gazes colliding. "You were married?"

He smiled and groaned. "In full technicolor glory. Young love and all that. Cheryl is a good person but we grew in different directions. She's remarried now and has a couple of kids. I'm genuinely happy for her. Maybe that's what happened to you and Frank. As time when on, you went in different directions."

"I didn't fight hard enough."

His fingers captured her chin, not letting her look away. "You both had to fight. You could have fought all day long but if he wasn't as committed as you were…"

"I know what you say is true. It's not the first time I've heard it. I just wish things had been different."

"I wish that all the damn time."

A smile curving her lips, Bailey let a little laughter escape although it wasn't all that funny. "I thought I had moved on. Life has a funny way of showing you the truth."

"You've experienced a great trauma, Bailey. Maybe you should give yourself a break and stop thinking that you shouldn't be affected. Your husband died while you two were having marital difficulties. I imagine there's a great deal of guilt inside of you but I'm telling you now that you need to release it. Just let it go. You're not doing Frank any good and you sure aren't helping yourself either."

"Are you some kind of shrink?"

It would be just her luck if he was a psychiatrist.

"Not at all. Actually, I'm self-employed." A grin bloomed on his face. "So I guess you could say that I analyze people as a hobby."

"Take up fishing. Or get one of those machines that find metal at the beach."

He sat back in his chair, and she felt bereft at the loss of warmth and comfort from his hands. There was something about Chase that made her feel safe, as if he was a beacon in a storm. That shelter a person runs to when the wind, rain, and lightning become too much.

"Tell me what you're thinking right now."

No way.

"You're nosy."

"You're running," he shot right back. "Seriously, tell me what's on your mind. What are you afraid of?"

So many things.

Of liking Chase too much.

Of letting go of the guilt. It had become so much a part of her these last five years she wasn't sure what to do without it.

But mostly she was afraid of…

"Finding out something about Frank that I don't want to know."

"Such as?"

Shrugging, she stood and wandered over to the window, looking out at the darkness. From this vantage point, she could easily see where she'd stood with the flashlight hoping to gain someone's attention.

"What if he was lying to me the entire time I was married? What if my life was all one big lie?"

Chase also stood but he didn't crowd her, content to stay a few feet away, somehow aware that she needed her space at the moment. "And if it was? You can't change the past. You can't yell and scream at him because he's gone. All you can do is deal with the here and now. The fact is you don't have to do anything more. You can get on the night flight back to Tampa and put this out of your mind forever. But I think you're braver than that, Bailey. It took guts to come here and dig up the past. I don't believe you want to live in some fantasy world. I think you want the truth whether it hurts you or not."

She'd like that to be true but she wasn't as certain as he was. "I think you're full of shit."

"What if I call your bluff?" He reached for his phone. "I'll book your airline ticket right now. My treat. Is that what you want? To go home and pretend good old Frank didn't have any secrets? Because, woman, everybody has things that no one else knows. I bet you've got a few and I know I do."

"I've told you all my secrets and I don't want to hear yours."

Maybe not all of them.

He held up his phone, his brows raised in question. "What's the verdict? Are you going home or moving forward? It's your choice."

Choices. They were a luxury she hadn't always had in her life but he was correct. She had one today and it was in her power to make it. She could walk away and go back to living her life. Or she could keep digging and find out the truth. It might be nothing. It could be a completely innocent reason Frank had kept those clippings. There might not be any connection to Gwen's death and Frank's.

A total, weird and wacky coincidence.

"I think you know my answer."

Because she didn't believe in coincidences. Not one like this anyway.

"I'd like to hear it."

She turned so she could look right into his eyes, that blue gaze that seemed to see way too much. "I want the truth."

"Then we better get back to work."

FOR A WHILE there, Chase was sure Bailey was going to cut and run. He wouldn't have blamed her. After all, she probably hadn't truly thought through what her investigating was going to mean. It was one thing to wonder if there was a connection. It was a complete other thing to uncover that connection and then dig deeper to find out what it meant. If there was more.

Her husband Frank – a man she swears wasn't sentimental – kept a stack of newspaper clippings regarding Gwen's death. It could be a simple case of clutter. He'd been interested at the time but forgotten all about them as the years passed. They might have been meaningful once but that time was gone.

With Chase's help, they scanned in the pages of the booklets and emailed them to her friends in Florida so they could look for their own husbands. Bailey wasn't as sure the men would be in the photos but they needed to cover all the bases.

She held up one of the pictures and pointed to Chase in the background. "I guess you knew Frank."

And she didn't look particularly happy about that.

"I remember his face but I don't remember anything about him. I couldn't have told you his name until you pointed him out. He was older than me so we weren't friends. But I do remember him hanging out with these guys. I know a couple of them that live in this area and I see them maybe once a year." Chase pointed to the other young men in the photo. "They were all the same. Spoiled brats with too much money and not enough common sense. Arrogant little SOBs."

A funny look passed over her face and too late he realized what he'd said. Trying desperately to backpedal, he kept talking even when he should have shut up. "Don't pay any attention to me. I'm sure Frank was different. Hell, he was probably going along with his friends. Peer pressure and stuff like that. Plus teenage boys can be a real pain the ass. I'm sure I was too."

Somebody wrestle me to the ground and slap a gag over my face.

Holding up her hand, she looked down at the picture again. "No, I think you pretty much nailed it the first time, although it sounds like he was much less subtle in his youth. Frank came from an incredibly wealthy background and I didn't. Believe me, his family and friends never let me forget that I was from a middle class family who lived in the cornfields of the Midwest. Frank wasn't overtly a snob but he had his moments."

A sour taste in his mouth, Chase studied the features of Frank Scott. He didn't even know this guy but he didn't like him. Anyone who made Bailey feel less than wasn't the type of person Chase wanted to be around.

"Tell me he defended you."

She folded the booklets and tucked them back into the box, one by one. "He defended me although I think that eventually he was tired of fighting my battles with his family. I guess he thought I should have joined them by then but instead I couldn't shake my blue collar roots. Honestly, I think he was baffled as to why I wouldn't embrace the whole money and conspicuous consumption thing. But it didn't matter. After awhile his family's disdain became less overt and more passive-aggressive and I became less concerned with what other people thought of me. Frankly, I didn't give a rat's ass if they liked me or not. Not one of them has tried to keep in touch with me since Frank died so I'm happy about that. At least I don't have to keep up the facade of pleasantness and family unity."

The Scott family didn't deserve Bailey. Chase hadn't known her long but he could tell she was a strong, determined woman who believed in honesty.

"It's their loss."

Her lips turned up. "Thank you but I'm not sure they see it that way. It was quite ugly at the reading of the will."

It hadn't even occurred to Chase that Bailey was a wealthy widow. She acted so down to earth. Not that he hadn't met normal, nice people with lots of money. He had. Many of them, in fact, and he was proud to call them his friends. But his early years had made an impression on him and he was well aware of how the one-percenters *could* act.

"They were upset?"

Bailey rolled her eyes and laughed. "Upset? They were livid. Frank's brother threw a hissy-fit right there in the lawyer's office like he was a two year old. I didn't even want the damn money but the attorney insisted that Frank wanted me to have it. He gave me a letter that Frank had written that basically said that and also took responsibility for the marital issues we'd had."

Maybe Frank Scott wasn't so bad after all.

"It takes a big man to admit when he's done wrong."

Nodding, Bailey picked up her phone, which had begun to vibrate. "There was a lot of good in Frank. He wasn't a perfect man but I've never been accused of perfection either. We had some good times and that's what I try to remember." She frowned at the screen. "Willow and Peyton looked at the pictures we sent them. Their husbands are in the photos too. It looks like they might have been friends with Frank. That's strange because I don't ever remember meeting them or Frank even mentioning them."

The case for a connection between the three men's deaths and Gwen was growing stronger, although at this point Chase was baffled as to what it might be. But Bailey was right – this was no coincidence.

"Do they ever remember their husbands mentioning Gwen?"

Shaking her head, Bailey tapped out a text back to her friends. "They don't but they're going to go through what they have left of their husbands' possessions. They might find something although Peyton said she doesn't have much of Greg's things. They also are strongly suggesting that they come here to help."

"How do you feel about that?"

Chase regarded Bailey closely, looking for any sign in her expression that this whole situation was more than she could handle.

"It would be nice to have their support, especially as it's not just Frank involved, but I don't want them to drop everything and come here without knowing how they could help. There might be things we need done in Florida. We just don't know yet."

"There are definitely things we need done down there," Chase replied. "Specifically, we need to know if your husbands had any contact with each other after they left summer camp. That might give us some insight into how they're connected."

Bailey frowned, her fingers poised over the cell phone. "How would we be able to find that out? I don't remember seeing any of those men. At least I don't think so."

"They should talk to family and friends if they can. Maybe business associates too. Perhaps your husbands had something financial in common."

Busily she tapped out the text. "I'll let them know. Hopefully they can find something. What are we going to do in the meantime?"

Chase had already been working on that plan. His mental list was getting longer by the minute and he was optimistic for the first time about Gwen's case.

"I have a friend who is a detective for the local police. I'm going to ask him to get a copy of the case file. I'd like to see if the cops ever talked to your husbands. I also think we should talk to Gwen's friends and family from that summer. They might have a better memory than I do of Frank."

"They might not want to talk about it," Bailey warned. "If something like that happened to a friend or relative of mine, I wouldn't be all that thrilled about rehashing it twenty years later."

He'd thought about that too.

"That's why we're not going to tell them."

At least not yet.

Chapter Twelve

" I CAN'T JUST give you the file," Detective Ellis Hunter protested. "They'd have my ass in the unemployment line."

The next morning Chase had stopped by the police station to talk to Ellis before he met Bailey for breakfast. His friend, a pessimist by nature, was not being as cooperative as Chase had hoped.

"I don't expect that," he explained patiently, letting his gaze sweep the small office at the back of the police building. They'd stuck Ellis – lead detective for their little town – as far away from everyone as possible. He didn't work well with others. "I want you to take a look at it and hopefully answer some questions."

Ellis waved his arm toward a stack of files on the corner of the desk. "Do you see that pile of unsolved cases? I don't have time to look through a twenty-year old cold case file because you're obsessed and can't let it go. As your friend, I'm trying to help you. Just forget about that summer, bro. That case is colder than the Arctic Circle."

All business, all the time. That was Ellis's motto. At thirty-five he was the youngest head of detectives this town had ever seen and few crimes went unsolved under his watch. He'd run a tight ship for the last six years and Chase respected the hell out of him.

But sometimes he could be a real pain in the ever loving ass.

"Will you get that stick out of your butt and help me? Things have changed and I've been trying to tell you about it but apparently you haven't had enough coffee or something. This case needs to be looked at again. There's more out there. Trust me."

Ellis sat up straight in his chair and scowled. "I do not have a stick up my butt and I've had two cups of coffee. I'm just trying to save you from more heartache, my friend. That case is nothing but trouble."

"So you haven't been listening to me," Chase sighed, rubbing the back of his neck. "I have new information that might make a difference. You keep interrupting and we're not getting anywhere but pissed off at each other."

Playing with a pencil between his fingers, Ellis nodded. "Fine, I'll listen. You talk."

Chase slowly explained all that he'd learned in the last twenty-four hours to his friend and waited for the explosion of disbelief when he came to the part about the four deaths on July twenty-first. To his shock, Ellis didn't seem fazed in the least.

"You don't seem surprised. I'm waiting for your cynicism to kick in and tell me that I'm full of shit."

Ellis grinned and gave an evil laugh. "I love to shock and surprise my friends. You might not believe this but as a cop I've seen some weird shit in my time and some of it defied logical explanation. You say that the women think the universe is fucking with them? Well, I have to agree. Of course, this could have a perfectly reasonable explanation. Honestly, I'm less concerned with how these ladies got together than I am as to what this new information means. Let me ask you a question. Do you believe that there is a connection between Gwen Baxter's death and the supposedly accidental deaths of these three men?"

Chase had thought long and hard about that very question but there was only one answer. "I do. It's clear they knew her and it's simply too much of a coincidence that they died on the same date fifteen years later."

Pinching the bridge of his nose, Ellis reached for the phone on his desk. "There have been stranger ones but I think this is enough to make me take a second look. I'll call central files." One quick conversation later, he was hanging up the phone. "They're going to dig out the case file and send it over. I know what I'm looking for but is there something specific you think might be in there?"

"I want to know if they talked to Frank Scott, Greg Nelson, or Alex Vaughn. If so, what did they say? I also want to know what suspects they had at the time. I'd like to see if those suspects had any connection to the three men."

Frowning, Ellis sat back in his chair. "Do you think whomever killed Gwen had something to do with the other deaths? You said they were ruled accidental."

Chase stood and paced the small room. "That's something else that needs to be investigated. Were they ruled accidental because of the circumstances, because of their wealthy families wanting to bring any investigation to a close? I'd like to see what the local officials have on those deaths."

It wouldn't be easy. Bailey's husband had died in a diving accident in Turks and Caicos, which would make any paperwork regarding the death almost impossible to get. Peyton's husband had died in France so the same impediment applied. Only Willow's husband had died in the States and his accident had been alcohol and drug related. There had to be a coroner's report at least.

"I doubt you'll be able to get your hands on that," Ellis replied. "If there is something funny going on here and we have a killer on the loose, they certainly aren't stupid. In fact, they might be a genius."

Chase stopped and shook his head. "How do you mean? They did this all on the exact same day. Not exactly trying to hide their tracks, are they? It was almost like they wanted to be caught."

Ellis drummed that damn pencil against the wood of the desk making Chase's head hurt. But he'd seen that expression before. His detective friend was deep in thought and nothing was going to make him speak until he was ready.

"Christ, just say something," Chase finally groaned as the silence stretched on. "I know you want to."

Standing, Ellis leaned against his desk and crossed his arms over his chest. "So here's the thing. The reason I say they might be a genius is because if the men's deaths were foul play the killer planned them perfectly. Two of them were out of the country. Think about that. There's nothing a tourist destination wants to close out faster than the case of a person who had a bizarre accident. Shut it down and keep it out of the press. Nothing to see here, folks, move along. Then the third death was a nasty accident with someone who was known to abuse alcohol and drugs. But let's face it, anyone could have slipped him something and no one would know. Whatever showed up on his toxicology screen wouldn't even be questioned. If these deaths were murder, then the killer isn't stupid."

There was one thing his friend wasn't thinking about though.

"The killer might not be stupid, but is he a time traveler?"

"What are you talking about?"

Chase leaned on the desk and looked his friend right in the eye. "All the deaths were on the same damn day. Unless this killer can travel through time, how in the hell was he in three places at once? Tell me that."

Ellis fell back into his leather chair with a groan. "I don't know. Are we now postulating that there are multiple assailants? A conspiracy? Jesus Christ, Chase. This gets murkier with every passing minute."

"Welcome to the last twenty-four hours of my life. Do you see why we need to look into this again?"

There was a look of resignation on Ellis's face. Chase didn't know whether to feel sorry for his friend or tell him to snap out of it. There was work to be done and Chase wasn't a cop. He needed his friend's expertise.

"I'll help you," Ellis said with a shake of his head. "We'll look at the file and see what's there. What else do you want me to do?"

"I need the names and addresses of the people Gwen knew well that summer. I want to talk to them."

"About her murder? What makes you think you aren't going

to get the door slammed in your face?"

"You sound like Bailey," Chase grinned. "I have an idea actually. A way to get them to talk about that summer without letting them know I'm looking at the murder."

"Whatever crazy scheme you've come up with probably won't work."

What would Chase do without his glass-half-empty friend? "All I need it to do is get me in the front door."

"It's going to get you thrown out on your ass and I want to be there to see it."

"With friends like you, who needs enemies?" Chase laughed.

Ellis held up his hands in a sign of surrender. "Just be careful, okay? The last thing we need is any more deaths. You do realize July twenty-first isn't that far away, right?"

Chase glanced at the calendar on the wall. It was exactly four weeks from that date and he sure as shit didn't want to end up a strange coincidence.

That no one could explain.

BAILEY HAD NEVER been a morning person. She loved staying up late reading or watching a movie, then sleeping in until the sun shone brightly in the window. A luxury she rarely experienced. In her line of work, mornings were an important time and even when she'd been in school she'd scheduled classes early in the day so she could work at a part-time job in the afternoon and evenings. But those days she could sleep in felt better than anything in the world.

Today wasn't one of those days.

Apparently Chase was an early bird, the annoying bastard, because he'd scheduled their breakfast for eight in the morning. For a male, that meant he rolled out of bed at seven-thirty, took a quick shower, brushed his teeth, maybe shaved, ran a comb or his fingers through his hair, threw on clothes he barely glanced at, and then walked out the door. By seven-forty-five. An eight o'clock meeting wasn't a big deal.

For a woman it was completely different.

There was hair to wash and blow dry, legs to shave, makeup to apply, clothes to select. Sometimes being female was exhausting. This was why she spent so much time in yoga pants, tank tops, and flip flops. She didn't stop to ponder why her appearance was so important when she was around Chase. She wasn't necessarily ready for the answer she'd get.

Finding the restaurant didn't take long however and she was sliding into the booth at one minute till eight. Punctuality was important to her. Chase, however, seemed surprised she was on time. He looked up from his menu, his brows lifted.

"You're here. I guess you didn't have any trouble finding the place."

The cozy restaurant was off the beaten tourist path, down the highway from Colonial Williamsburg, which was fine with her. She liked people but too many at once wasn't her preference.

"Did you expect me to get lost?" She held up her phone. "I have the knowledge of the universe in the palm of my hand."

Smirking, he signaled for the waitress to bring Bailey some coffee. "With all that wisdom at your fingertips, you must also know that this place makes amazing waffles."

"It seems like every corner has a pancake or waffle house on it. I didn't realize our Founding Fathers were so breakfast-centric. I must have missed that day in high school history class."

The smells coming from the kitchen were amazing and her stomach growled softly in case she was planning to deny how hungry she was.

"Now you know," he laughed lightly, and she noticed the crinkles next to his eyes when he smiled. Chase Jennings was – by any measure – a handsome man, a kind man, a smart man. She hadn't dated much since Frank's death. It was her choice and one she was comfortable with. She hadn't met anyone that had captured her interest until now. But romance wasn't what she was here for and getting sidetracked wasn't a good idea. This was about finding out the truth, not flirting and kissing.

"So what do you recommend?"

"Everything's good but the waffles are great. I eat them with maple syrup but they have a whole slew of toppings if you want to get wild. They also do a nice traditional bacon and eggs if you don't want something sweet."

He didn't know her at all. She'd crawl buck naked over hot coals to get to a chocolate cupcake.

"I always want something sweet. I'm a baker."

The waitress came to take their order and Bailey decided on the blueberry waffles and a side of bacon while Chase selected the traditional buttermilk waffles with a side of hash browns and bacon.

"Tell me about this bakery."

She sipped at the coffee and let the warmth seep into her

bones and muscles, swearing she could feel the caffeine beginning to work. "I love it. Now if I want red velvet cake I simply whip one up. Every day if I so desire."

His gaze raked her up and down as she sat across from him, his scrutiny making her warm and tingly like she was back in high school and he was captain of the football team.

Focus, for heaven's sake.

"I don't think you ever mentioned what you do."

He didn't answer at first, instead playing with the handle of his coffee cup and looking out of the window. Perhaps he wasn't going to answer which seemed odd, although he might be unemployed and too ashamed to tell her. Geez, she needed to keep her curiosity under control. Making Chase feel badly about his financial situation was a crappy thing to do when he'd offered so nicely to help her. In fact, it should have occurred to her before this. Who else would have time to assist her other than someone without a job? She made a mental note to pick up the check.

"I have…investments," he replied, sounding way too hesitant to be believed. Now she really felt lousy. He turned and smiled at her as if he didn't have a care in the world. "I keep busy here and there. Always something to do."

Probably odd jobs, and she was keeping him from working while he was helping her. Maybe there was a way to get him to let her pay for his time?

"That's great," Bailey said, anxious to change the subject. "What do you like to do in your free time? Do you have any hobbies?"

"Not really. I run every morning, weather permitting. I like watching sports and I do some kickboxing with my friends Josh and Ellis. Sometimes we go camping or fishing. I guess you could say I like to be outdoors."

Not one thing he listed was anything she enjoyed doing. Dear Lord, he was *outdoorsy*. As in he liked being outside. In the heat, the cold, the sun, and the rain.

"You have a funny look on your face. Don't you like fishing or hiking?"

Artifice wasn't Bailey's strong suit and she didn't use it now. "I have no idea. I don't hang out around the outdoors very often. I'm allergic to pretty much everything out there. Pollen, grass, ragweed. And as for running? There'd have to be someone chasing me. Plus it's outside so to go back to my earlier objection…I do things that I can be inside for. It gets awfully hot and muggy in Florida."

He was looking at her like she wasn't quite right in the head. "Didn't you tell me you live at the beach? Are you saying you don't go there?"

She shuddered, remembering the last time she'd spent the day at the beach. "Maybe once a year when my friends come down from the cold north and drag me there. Too much sun, way too much sand, and last time I got stung by a jellyfish and one of my friends wanted to pee on me. That's enough of the outdoors for at least a year."

To her chagrin, Chase burst into laughter causing a few heads in the restaurant to swivel their direction. "I can see why you feel the way you do. Did you let your friend pee on you?"

She slapped her cup on the table at the unpleasant memory. "I most certainly did not. I made them take me home and we looked up the treatment on the Internet which was relatively simple and straightforward and involved baking soda, not urine."

"Good for you," he approved, but he was still laughing. "I do like the beach but I'm sure I might like it a lot less if I was stung. But you should try running. I do it in the early morning or sometimes the evening as the air is cooling off. It's great exercise but mostly I use it to clear my mind and think things through."

"It sounds boring. You just…run."

"It depends on where you run. I should take you in the early morning before it gets hot."

The waitress came back with their breakfast plates and if Bailey's meal tasted as good as it looked, she was in for a treat. Chase had excellent taste in restaurants.

"We'll see. I don't have any sort of workout gear with me. Besides, aren't we supposed to be working on the case?"

"We will but we can't go see Stephen Baxter until tonight. That reminds me, did you bring a cocktail dress with you?"

The first bite of waffles was like heaven with a full angel choir and harp music in the background. Light, fluffy, and melt in your mouth. Damn, these were good.

"I can tell by the look of bliss on your face that I chose wisely." Chase took a hearty bite of his own breakfast and hummed in approval. "I eat here at least once a week."

"These are criminally good. I wonder if they'd give me the recipe." She took another bite and closed her eyes to savor the flavor. It was nice that he enjoyed eating as much as she did. "And no, I don't have a cocktail dress with me. I wasn't planning on attending any parties."

"You are now," Chase declared. "We're going to one tonight

so after breakfast we'll head out to get you something to wear."

"Does this party have anything to do with Gwen?"

Chase popped a bite of hash browns into his mouth with relish. "It has everything to do with her. The country club is having their usual weekly cocktail hour tonight and Stephen Baxter and his ilk will be there. So will we. You're going to ask Stephen about Frank, not about Gwen. Pretend you're just trying to find out more about your late husband's life before you."

"I am trying to do that."

Chase smiled. "Then it should be easy."

"Just how are we going to get into this country club party? Crash it?"

Chase took another bite of waffle and gave her a playful wink.

"Piece of cake, honey. I'm a member."

Now that she hadn't expected.

Chapter Thirteen

BAILEY SMOOTHED HER hands down over her hips and regarded herself critically in the full-length mirror back at her hotel. She hadn't thought much of this dress when Chase had plucked it off the rack and urged her to try it on but she had to admit he'd chosen well. Normally she wore black, white, or red. Clean, classic lines. This was something altogether different.

Bright flowers on a cream-colored background had made her skip over the dress when she'd been browsing but the halter-style bodice and the flowing skirt that fell just about her knees was feminine and flattering. She'd paired the frock with red high-heeled sandals and purse. Her jewelry was simple as well to go with the summer theme – a plain gold chain around her wrist and gold hoop earrings.

The buzzing of her phone let her know he was downstairs waiting. She couldn't delay this any longer. She was of two minds about this evening. One part of her desperately wanted to speak with Stephen Baxter, find out if he knew anything about Frank. The other part, that portion of her that was shying away, was trying to scare her with all sorts of thoughts about what the truth could do to her. That part was currently being squished under her heel like a bug.

"You look gorgeous."

Chase didn't look so bad himself. The suit looked like it could have been made for him, the way it fit his broad shoulders and tapered to his slim hips. The trousers were dark gray and the jacket was a lighter shade of gray, which he'd pulled over a white shirt and black and gray striped tie. This was not the wardrobe of a man who was unemployed. She'd seen expensive, hand-tailored suits and this had all the signs.

"You look good too. Nice suit."

He pulled a face and helped her into his car. "I'd prefer my usual shorts or jeans but they have a dress code at these things."

The drive was short and they spent the time discussing the strategy for the evening although she couldn't shake the feeling there was something he wasn't telling her. Trying to calm her nerves, she took several deep breaths and touched up her lip gloss with a shaky hand. So much was riding on tonight and she didn't want to mess it up.

"Just relax. Everything is going to be fine. You look amazing and everyone is going to be charmed by you. You'll be the belle of the ball."

His pep talk helped slightly but her heart was still racing as he handed the keys to the valet and then took her arm in his, escorting her to the wide front entrance. From what she had seen so far, this had all the markings of the snooty parties she'd attended in the past and for the life of her she couldn't imagine this man being there of his own free will.

"You said you're a member here?"

The doors whooshed open and they entered a large atrium type foyer with soaring ceilings and plants everywhere. "I am although I rarely come to any of these functions. Mostly I use the membership to play tennis with Josh."

They glided through the atrium and into a larger room with a grand chandelier hanging from the middle of the ceiling and sconces along the walls. A long buffet table with finger foods took up one side of the room while a four-piece string quartet played boring music on the other side. A bar stood at the wall furthest from the door. They made you work for your booze.

"They do this every week?"

Heading straight for the bar, Chase didn't break stride. He must need a drink as badly as she did. "Cocktail hour every Friday night. It's a tradition."

"So don't question it," she murmured under her breath, taking in the subtle and not-so-subtle displays of wealth.

Note to self. Ask again about those investments. There's no way Chase is unemployed.

"Did you say something?"

She looked up at him, this man she clearly didn't know well at all. As late as this afternoon, she'd thought he was a simple man who lived a normal life. A working stiff. The kind of males she grew up with.

But this... This was far from that image. This was what she'd been dealing with since meeting Frank.

Grabbing his lapel, she tugged on it so he had to lean forward to hear her.

"Just who in the hell *are* you?"

BAILEY HAD ASKED him a straightforward question but the answer was anything but. He liked to be taken at face value but that wasn't always possible.

"Will you trust me?" he asked instead, his head bent low so only she could hear him. She smelled like vanilla and springtime and damn if his heart didn't lurch in his chest. The more he was around her the more he wanted to be. "I'll explain later and answer every single question but for right now I'm asking you to extend just a little trust."

Those brown velvet eyes were wide with curiosity but to her credit she let go of his lapel and smoothed it down, stepping back to put some space between them. "I can but I think it's clear that a whole lot is going on here that I don't know about."

"I didn't keep it from you on purpose. Honestly, I sometimes forget all about it."

Her brows rose a few millimeters but she was also smiling. "That's some memory loss. You should see a doctor about that. Now how about you buy me a drink?"

Exhaling slowly with relief, he placed an arm around her shoulders and walked up to the bar. Bailey Scott ordered a dirty martini and he had a whiskey neat. Moving to the perimeter of the room, he surveyed the guests with a smile of satisfaction. Everyone who needed to be here had arrived.

"Which one is he?"

Chase smiled and nodded as someone walked by before nudging Bailey to the left. "The tall blond man over there in the blue pinstripe talking to the older man with glasses."

He hadn't seen Stephen Baxter in over a year but he looked exactly the same. All the men here looked pretty much alike. Or maybe they acted alike. Hell, it was probably both. Chase had never quite fit in with this crowd but then he'd never tried all that hard.

"So do we go up and say hello…?"

Chase shook his head. "Absolutely not. We have to be much more subtle than that. Someone is going to come over and say hello here in a moment or two. We won't be able to avoid it. Then we will start circulating through the crowd until we eventually end up talking to Stephen. When we do, you know your lines, right?"

She nodded, clearly nervous. Her fingers were white holding her glass and she kept biting her lip. Hopefully she wouldn't take up playing poker professionally. She'd be slaughtered. But in this crowd she'd be fine. She was beautiful and charming enough that it would blind most people to anything else.

"So we just stand here—"

"Chase, my boy. I didn't expect to see you here tonight. It's been ages." A balding man with a slight paunch slapped Chase on the back. He scanned his memory quickly and surprisingly came up with a name. Norman Aldridge. "Are you going to introduce me to your lovely date?"

Chase certainly was planning to do just that.

"Norman, this is Bailey Scott. She's visiting the area. Bailey, this is Norman Aldridge, president of one of the local banks."

Norman shook hands with Bailey, his admiring gaze sweeping her from head to toe. Chase felt a twinge of jealousy and before he could stop himself, he had put his arm around her waist. Like she belonged to him. He was sure he'd hear about it later from her and he'd deserve it. They weren't even an item and he hadn't kissed her yet.

Yet? What the hell was he thinking? Just because he was attracted to her didn't mean his feelings were reciprocated or that he had to do anything about them. She was a widow and he needed to act respectful. They were adults for fuck's sake and that meant they could simply be friends.

Except that was a depressing thought.

"Have you been to the Colonial area yet?" Norman asked proudly. "It's something you don't want to miss, also Yorktown and Jamestown."

"Norman is on the board of our historical society," Chase said, deciding to keep his arm around her since she hadn't decked him in the jaw or even given him a dirty look. If anything, she'd moved slightly closer as if meeting new people made her uncomfortable. He made a mental note to ask her about that later.

Bailey smiled at the older gentleman. "That must be very rewarding. I'm afraid I haven't visited yet but I do intend to. Is there any must-see that you can suggest for me?"

Charming, beautiful, and smart. She knew just how to handle men like Aldridge. Clearly, this wasn't her first cocktail party.

"You don't want to miss the Governor's Palace." Norman wore a huge grin on his face. This was his favorite topic. "There's also a wonderful folk art museum that I highly recommend. Really, there's so much to see and experience."

If they weren't careful they'd be hearing about it all evening and circulating was a must. Luckily, Norman's wife decided to join them and that sent them off on the merry-go-round of guests. It took less than an hour but they found themselves standing in front of Stephen Baxter.

Show time.

Chapter Fourteen

THE RESEMBLANCE BETWEEN Stephen Baxter and his sister Gwen was slight but Bailey put it down to aging and bad photographs. They did sport the same blond hair which Stephen wore short on the sides but curly on the top, sort of a subtle quiff. He smiled easily when they were introduced, shaking her hand and welcoming her to Williamsburg. She desperately hoped her palms weren't noticeably sweaty because this was her moment. No screwing up allowed.

Chase opened the conversation exactly as they'd discussed. "I'm hoping you can help Bailey, Stephen."

Stephen frowned slightly but nodded. "I will if I can."

Sucking in a breath, Bailey knew her time had come. Now or never. "I'm trying to find out about my husband – I mean, late husband actually. I'm finding that I never really knew much about him at all."

"I'm not sure how I can help with that." Stephen glanced at Chase. "Why talk to me?"

"You knew him," Chase replied smoothly. "Frank Scott. He was at camp the same time you were. Same age. Same friends.

Bailey originally came to me but being younger I didn't really know much about him."

Shrugging nonchalantly, Stephen grimaced and took a drink of his whiskey. "That was a long time ago, Chase. I'm not sure that I remember anything."

Where before Stephen had been open and relaxed, he wasn't anymore. His shoulders had tensed underneath his expensive jacket and his gaze was darting around the room. He wanted to be anywhere but here.

"Any little thing you can remember would be helpful," Bailey urged. "Even things that don't seem important. My husband passed away young and unexpectedly and he never told me much about his youth. It would be a great comfort to me to hear some stories about him."

It wasn't a lie. She did have good memories of him. She also had bad ones but that wasn't any of Stephen's business.

"I'm so sorry for your loss but I'm not sure I can really help. I did know Frank but I wouldn't say he and I were all that close. He was best friends with some other guys. They had a real tight group." Stephen smiled awkwardly. "I do remember that he was a good guy. Always happy and friendly. I never heard a bad word about him."

Bailey wasn't ready to give up yet. "I don't suppose you remember any stories or little anecdotes? Did he play a sport or was he in a band? Did he have any summer romances?"

Paling, Stephen shook his head. "I really don't remember anything like that. I do think he played on the water polo team."

"You said he had some close friends. Do you know their names? Maybe I could contact them?"

"You should do that," he said, more than eager for her to go away. "Let's see. There was Guy Eckley. Um…Danny Ford. There was Greg Nelson—I think he moved to Europe or something. And, one more…let me think…Alex Vaughn. He's in Florida with his family last I heard."

The room spun and she had to grab ahold of Chase's arm so she wouldn't collapse.

"Thank you," she said breathlessly. "I appreciate your time. I hope we didn't bother you too much."

Stephen Baxter had recovered his easy charm and smile. "You didn't bother me at all. I'm just sorry I couldn't help more. Now if you'll excuse me, there's someone I need to say hello to."

Bailey watched him retreat to the other side of the room before turning to Chase. "That's confirmation. I mean…I know we saw the pictures…but this confirms it. Frank, Alex, and Greg didn't just know each other. They were close friends."

Fumbling with her purse, she pulled out her cell phone. She had to tell Willow and Peyton.

What had started as a strange coincidence was turning out to be something much different.

"ARE YOU OKAY?"

Bailey didn't turn around but then she didn't need to. It was Chase coming to find her after she'd told him she needed a few minutes to herself and some fresh air. He'd agreed but she'd known he wouldn't let her be alone for long. He'd actually done pretty well. The fifteen minutes he'd allowed was about ten more than she'd expected.

"I'm okay. I'm not surprised but I guess there was a part of me that was hoping he'd say that this was all my imagination. That Frank never went to the summer camp and those pictures were of someone that just looked a lot like him."

Chase came to stand behind her, placing his hands on her shoulders. The heat from his skin sent a bolt of electricity up her spine and tingles to her fingers and toes. She couldn't remember the last time a man's mere touch had made her react this way and she closed her eyes and savored the warmth that was beginning to build in her belly. She shouldn't want Chase but would it be so bad to enjoy him for just a moment?

It had been so long since anyone had touched her. Truly touched her.

Like she mattered.

She didn't mind being single most of the time but every now and then she longed to be held, kissed, and touched by a pair of strong arms. She wanted a deep voice to tell her she was beautiful.

"They knew each other although I didn't realize they were such close friends. I'll get in touch with Guy or Danny to see what they can tell us. I've talked to Danny a few times over the years."

His fingers were playing with a strand of hair as his fingertips brushed the sensitive flesh at her nape. A sigh escaped her lips and she found herself leaning back on his broad chest as he tenderly rubbed the tight muscles of her neck and shoulders.

"When he said Danny Ford did he mean the same person as Senator Daniel Ford? Is that a coincidence too?"

She felt rather than heard Chase's chuckle rumble against her ear. "One and the same. My parents' summer camp was known for attracting the rich and connected. Many of them went on to successful careers. Doctors, lawyers, politicians, captains of industry."

"All of them?"

"Not all," Chase conceded, his breath close to her cheek. "There are always exceptions."

"Are you going to ask me which side Frank was on?"

She held her breath waiting for an answer but the one he gave was typical Chase. Firm and completely certain. "No. The last person I want to talk about right now is your late husband."

His hands had glided down her bare arms raising gooseflesh on her skin before he turned her so she was facing him, her eyes still closed. His fingers tipped up her chin and his forehead rested against hers.

"Are you going to look at me?"

That was not the plan. If she did she was afraid she'd chicken out of what appeared to be happening between them. The growing attraction was something she'd thought she could ignore but if she were honest she didn't want to. They would both move on with their respective lives but that didn't mean she couldn't enjoy what they had in the here and now. She wasn't normally the casual type but this was no ordinary situation.

Chase was no ordinary man either. He'd already proved himself to be solid, steady, and trustworthy. He was helping her when he didn't have to. He could have turned his back and sent her away but instead he was spending his time digging into the past.

"No, I won't open my eyes."

Chuckling, he ran his thumbs over her eyelids. Funny, how she could swear she heard him smiling. "Any particular reason or am I simply too hideous to behold?"

She snorted indelicately but kept her eyes tightly shut. "Hardly. I just like it like this. It's dark and peaceful. Simple. If I open my eyes it makes everything complicated."

She didn't expect him to understand but he didn't push. Instead his fingers caressed her lips before moving to her jaw and then down her neck to that spot where her pulse beat rapidly under the pad of his thumb. "Have you? You know…since?"

His question was vague but to her quite clear as if their minds had somehow linked up and were talking to each other in a silent language. Or maybe there were words in his touch, saying what he couldn't out loud. "Not really. A few dates since Frank passed on. Most of the time I'm quite happy on my own."

If he was alone as well, she didn't have to tell him about the times it wasn't all right. He'd have experienced them too.

"And if you open your eyes?"

"I'll see you and all the reasons that I shouldn't do this."

The tang of his aftershave teased her nostrils along with the scent of freshly mown grass and the delicate fragrance of Virginia bluebells. She could feel heat radiating from his body and feel his soft breaths against her hair.

"I'm not sure I like the sound of that."

He didn't understand and she wasn't sure she could explain it correctly. "If I open my eyes, I'll see everything. You. The world. All the issues I have to deal with. I can't block any of it out. It's there hanging over my head like an executioner's axe.

But with my eyes closed…"

"You can pretend it's just the two of us," he finished. "The world falls away and we're not trying to solve an anomaly of the universe."

She nodded. "And that's why I'm not going to open my eyes. I'll have to eventually but I'm in no hurry."

He moved a step closer, one arm sliding around her waist while the other tangled in her hair.

"Neither am I. I intend to take my time."

His voice was a soft whisper and so was the kiss at first. His lips brushed Bailey's as delicate as the wings of a butterfly but then grew more needy, more passionate, and so much more ardent. The already warm summer night air steamed with every gasp of pleasure as his mouth trailed across her jaw to gently nibble on her earlobe before traveling down her neck to lave her collarbone with his tongue.

Her head had fallen back and she sighed as her fingers tightened on his biceps. It felt so good. So amazingly wonderful to be touched, held, and kissed. It had been so long. Too long, really. Those first few years she hadn't been ready but for the last year or so she'd wondered if there was maybe someone out there she could care about. Now here she was with Chase and it was good.

If you didn't count all the crap she was trying to get to the bottom of.

She must have stiffened or flinched when that thought flitted through her brain because Chase lifted his head and her lids fluttered open. His face was inches from her own and his blue eyes had turned dark, his pupils blown wide. Some of her lipstick had smeared on his face and she reached up to wipe it away with her thumb, his stubble scratchy against her skin.

"It's all back, isn't it?" he asked, his voice gravelly. "You shouldn't have opened your eyes."

"I couldn't stay in the dark forever." No matter how much she might want to. She was here for a reason and it wasn't to be romanced by a handsome but mysterious man. "I haven't forgotten that you owe me an explanation."

His lips quirked up in a half smile. "Nor have I. How about we get out of here? We can go back to my place, have a glass of wine, and I'll answer any questions that you have."

Bailey let Chase lead her through the throng of people, his hand at the small of her back. They were halfway through the atrium when an excited female voice called Chase's name.

"Pamela, it's good to see you."

Tall, willowy, and blonde. Designer dress, shoes, and handbag, plus dripping with diamonds. This Pamela was also quite familiar with Chase. She was pressed up against his side, her hand on his arm as she looked up at him adoringly.

Ick. Be a little less obvious, Pamela.

"Chase, I had no idea you'd be here tonight. You've been hiding out from everyone."

"I've just been busy that's all."

Doing what? Oh yeah, he's going to tell me when we get to his home.

"All work and no play make Chase a dull boy," the blonde cooed before she finally seemed to notice that he wasn't alone. "Are you going to introduce me to your…friend?"

Chase wrapped an arm around Bailey. "I certainly am. Bailey this is Pamela Gray. Pamela, this is Bailey Scott." He leaned down to speak closer to the woman's ear but Bailey could still hear what he was saying. "You may have known her late husband, Frank Scott. You remember him, don't you?"

Now it was clear as to why Chase had allowed Pamela Gray to waylay them on the way out of the door. She'd known Frank back in the day.

The blonde's eyes widened and her hand flew to her mouth in shock. "Frank's dead? I'm so sorry for your loss. He was such a wonderful man. So much fun and full of life."

It was time for Bailey to speak. "It was an accident five years ago. He was diving in Turks and Caicos."

"I had no idea," Pamela whispered, her gaze falling to the floor. "So young."

"You know, Pamela, you might be able to help Bailey. She came here to learn more about her husband's younger days. He never told her much about his youth and she was hoping to meet some of his friends. That's how she and I met. She found some photos from our summer camp days."

Pamela lifted her head and smiled. "Those wonderful summers. Such good memories. Frank was so much fun. He had a real zest for life. People loved him, you know."

No, she didn't know. It was hard to reconcile the man she was hearing about with the man she'd married. He'd always been reserved but as time had gone on he'd become colder and more remote with every passing day. He hadn't been happy married to her.

"What about his friends?" Chase queried. "Who would you say he hung out with the most?"

Her smiled widened and she batted her eyelashes. "That's an

easy question. They were like the five musketeers. You rarely saw one without the other. There was Alex, Greg, Danny, Guy, and of course Frank. They were like brothers. They played together and competed against each other."

"You knew Frank well?" Bailey asked eagerly.

Pink colored the pretty woman's cheeks. "I had a crush on Frank for a few years but ended up dating Alex. Now he was a wild one. Frank was more intellectual. He would quote Shakespeare to soften the girls up. Alex would take you on a motorcycle ride and almost get you killed."

Frank had liked Shakespeare. And Keats as well.

"So you didn't date him? You can tell me if you did, I won't be upset," Bailey assured Pamela.

"I didn't although I wouldn't have turned him down. He was with a lot of girls over the summers. He didn't like being tied down. He must have fallen hard if he married you. He told me he never wanted to get married or have kids."

Well, he'd stuck to one of those. Bailey had agreed not to have any children when he'd proposed.

"Did he date Gwen?"

Chase's question dimmed Pamela's smile and she swallowed hard before she answered.

"Yes, he did. That last summer they spent a lot of time together. But Gwen spent time with other boys too. She was wild that summer. It seemed like she was trying to prove something, although I don't know what. But she flirted and kissed a lot of guys, including Frank." Pamela pulled a tissue from her purse and dabbed at her tearing eyes. "Shame on me, I haven't thought about Gwen in years. She was such a sweet girl."

"So you were friends?" Chase asked, reaching for the blonde's hand and giving it a reassuring squeeze.

"Yes and no." Pamela laughed nervously. "I was a year younger so I wasn't in her inner circle but we were allowed to hang around the campfires with them and listen to music and dance. That sort of thing. I guess you could say that we were friends once removed. She let me borrow a skirt once but I didn't hear her deep, dark secrets. That's what I told the police all those years ago. It's so sad that they're both gone now. It's hard to believe. They were so full of life."

"Alex Vaughn and Greg Nelson are also gone," Bailey revealed. "They died five years ago too."

Pamela frowned, her brow wrinkled. "All of them? There's no way they could have died together."

It wasn't phrased as a question.

"No, they weren't together when they died," Bailey replied. "You seem awfully sure about that though. Why?"

"Because on the day after Gwen was found I saw the three of them arguing. They even took a couple swings at each other. I didn't see them speak another word for the next two days. Then when I went to Danny's wedding I expected to see all of them there, but according to one of the bridesmaids the five of them weren't friends any longer. The strain of the summer took its toll on all of us I guess but in different ways."

They were friends and then they weren't. The only thing that had changed?

Gwen Baxter had been brutally murdered.

Frank had more secrets than Bailey had ever imagined.

Chapter Fifteen

B AILEY HAD BEEN quiet the entire drive to Chase's house and
he hadn't tried to force her to talk. Instead he let her absorb
all that she had learned about her late husband knowing she
needed the time and space to process the information.

Plus the kiss.

He hadn't been planning to kiss her when he followed her
outside. He'd been worried about her state of mind, but then
when he'd placed his hands on her silky skin and breathed in the
light fragrance of her hair he'd been powerless to stop himself.
And damn if her lips weren't the softest he'd ever felt in his life.
The breathy little sounds she made when his tongue had explored her mouth had him hard and ready but it was way too
soon to be thinking carnal thoughts. This relationship – assuming there was going to be one – needed to move slowly. She was
ready to move on but she had business from the past that had to
be tended.

It didn't help that they lived hundreds of miles from one another. He wasn't a casual kind of guy and if he slept with Bailey,
it was because he had real feelings for her. He wasn't the hit and

run type. If he fell for her, was he willing to make compromises for her?

Shit, too soon. Way too soon.

They'd had one kiss. Maybe he could stop planning their life together. Enjoy the moment and see where things led. In a couple of days he might be completely tired of her company. For all he knew she snored, had bad table manners, and drank like a fish. Or even worse, worshipped money and all that came with it. That would be the worst thing he could imagine.

No time like the present to find out.

"Why don't you relax on the patio and I'll get us some wine?"

The evening air had cooled from the heat of the day and a pleasant breeze was blowing over his back patio that overlooked the river. At this time of night, the purple sky was dotted with stars with only a sliver of moon to light the scenery.

Quickly pouring two glasses of chardonnay, he joined her outside settling onto the love seat glider. It had been one of his first purchases after his divorce and he'd fallen asleep on it more nights than he could count as he listened to the crickets and the rustle of leaves.

He didn't waste any time. She had questions and that's why they were here.

"I'm a member of the club because I like to play tennis and they have the best courts. Otherwise I spend very little time there."

There was a small silence as Bailey took a sip of her wine. "Forgive me for being blunt but I kind of thought you were perhaps unemployed. You seem to have a great deal of free time on your hands that most people don't. You haven't talked about a job or vocation…"

That was true, he hadn't. Mostly because he found it dull as dishwater and whenever he had spoken about it he just about put people to sleep.

"I am unemployed in the sense that I don't work for other people. I work for myself. And the reason I don't talk about it much is that I don't find it very interesting. Just because I'm good at something doesn't mean I enjoy it."

Her forehead was all wrinkled and her lips pursed together. "What? I got the first part but then you lost me."

"I buy and sell stocks for a living. That's how I make my money. Before that I was a real estate broker like my parents."

She looked back out over the river. "Like a stockbroker? Or a financial advisor?"

Chase shook his head. "I do it just for me. Turns out I have a knack for picking winners and making money at it. But I find the whole thing kind of boring, honestly. I only did it because I needed money after the divorce. Mother necessity and all that."

She didn't appear all that angry with him for not telling her. Her lips were curved into a wicked smile. "Some people just get a job."

Shuddering, he was reminded of what his own parents had said on the subject. "I've heard that rumor from friends and family but I refused to believe it. You probably figured this out about me eventually so I'll let you in on a not-too-secret factoid about me. I hate to be told what to do. It's a flaw, I know, but that's me. I don't like people bossing me around and I get rather contrary about things and tend to do the opposite. Consequently

I had to find a way to make money without actually being an employee."

Bailey threw back her head and laughed, a musical sound that made his heart skip. "That is the funniest thing I've heard in a very long time. That must have been a hindrance when you were married."

Groaning, Chase took a big gulp of his wine. Ah, the rotten memories. "That's an understatement. But I figured out my issue and then I found a way to make money despite it. I'm actually good at it but I wouldn't say that I have any passion for it. It's a means to an end."

"What do you have a passion for?"

Dare he tell her? He was a simple guy and some women didn't want that.

"I like going running every morning no matter the weather. I run some local marathons and want to run the Boston Marathon someday. I like to fish, hike, and camp. I like to watch sports and drink beer and eat wings. I like to read on rainy days and play poker with the guys on Friday nights. Twice a year I travel for a few weeks and see a corner of this planet I haven't seen before. Mostly I like slowing down long enough to enjoy life. You probably think I'm lazy and I've heard that before. I wouldn't blame you or anything. I know women like workaholic men."

Wrinkling her nose, Bailey shook her head. "Been there, done that. I think your life sounds kind of nice. Except for the camping part. I've never been able to figure out why people want to sleep outside. That's a mystery. But the rest sounds nice. My friends would probably tell you I work too much."

"Then slow down. Don't you own your own business?"

"It's not that simple."

"Sure it is, if you want it."

She didn't speak for a long while and Chase didn't either. Eventually she shifted on the glider to face him. "Thank you for telling me."

"You're welcome. Is there anything else you want to know? My life is an open book although I don't talk about it much."

"Maybe one question."

"Shoot."

Their gazes locked and she moved closer to him, her hand brushing his arm. "Why do you hold onto the summer camp? Why do you live right next to it?"

She had a way of cutting to the heart of a matter. "I live here because some of my best memories are here. Those summers as a kid were good. As for why I don't sell? It's a piece of my parents and I'm not ready to let it go yet. My childhood wasn't exactly Norman Rockwell and my parents had their issues, but for a few weeks in the summer we acted like a family. I guess I'm not ready to let that go yet. I've had offers. Good ones. Someday I will."

"That's it." Bailey shrugged. "I think that's all my questions."

"No personal questions about my marriage or my divorce? So disappointing, Bailey."

She rolled her eyes and set her wine glass on the side table. "I think I'd like to be on a need to know basis there. If I need to know, tell me. Otherwise, I'd like to concentrate on the present when it comes to us. As it is I'm delving in the past too much."

Wise. It was also a relief. He didn't like talking about that time in his life all that much. He'd been young and stupid and in his experience that was nothing to brag about. Least of all to a woman.

"Just know you can ask me anytime. This wasn't a one-time offer."

She sighed, her fingers playing with the hem of her dress. "There is something I want to ask you but it's not about your past. It's about Frank."

His fingers covered hers, his hand encompassing her much smaller one. "Go ahead. I'm listening."

She laughed softly and smiled. "You always do, you know? You really listen to me even when I'm babbling on and on about something."

"I wouldn't call it babbling."

"I would," she retorted, her smile dying and her chin quivering. "Pamela said that Frank and Gwen dated that summer. Do you–do you think–Damn, I can barely say it. I came here because I thought that the person who killed Gwen might have some connection to Frank's death, even though it was supposed to be an accident. But now, hearing what Pamela said, do you think...Frank might have been a suspect?"

Chase had been avoiding that subject but the short answer was yes. "There were over a hundred people in that camp and every one of them was a suspect in the beginning. Yes, even me until I could prove I had an alibi. We'll know more when Ellis gets us a copy of that file and we can see the statements from any witnesses. I wouldn't go borrowing trouble when we already have plenty of our own."

"You're right," she murmured, mollified at least for now. "It sounds like Gwen dated lots of boys. I can't help but wonder though what Frank, Alex, and Greg were arguing about. Was it Gwen or something entirely different?"

"That may be something we'll never know. But I'm going to try to get us in to talk to Danny Ford. He might know or know of someone else who can tell us. We need to talk to Guy as well. I'll use some of my contacts and see if I can get a number for him."

He ran a finger down her bare arm until she looked up at him, their gazes colliding. The tension and heat that had been simmering between them all night was in full force again and he cautiously – slowly – lowered his head to press his lips to hers, giving her the chance to pull back if she wanted to.

She didn't.

Her mouth blossomed under his and he pulled her closer, his hands gliding down her back to rest at the base of her spine. Her fingers were digging into his shoulders and his ears rang as the blood pumped through his veins.

Her palms flattened against his chest and she tore her lips from his, their breathing ragged and labored. "Are you expecting anyone?"

What the hell was she talking about? He dipped down to capture her lips again but she moved away quickly. "The door. Are you expecting anyone?"

Only then did he realize the ringing in his ears wasn't from the kiss, although it had been sizzling hot. Someone was laying on the doorbell like their life depended on it.

Lumbering to his feet, he straightened his shirt as he plotted the demise of whomever was on the other side of that door.

The doorbell rang again and now that Chase's brain was beginning to function again he knew that ring quite well.

Ellis.

It better be damn important. He'd better have the file he promised.

"Can you wait here for a moment while I go beat the hell out of my friend?"

Chapter Sixteen

E LLIS HUNTER WAS tall, handsome, and obviously a good friend to Chase. He'd strode into the house as if he'd been there a million times – and he probably had – asking for a cold beer before handing over the thick manila folder in his hand.

"Is that a folder in your pocket or are you just happy to see me?"

Chase reached for the file but Ellis held it back.

"I shouldn't even be giving this to you."

Arching a brow, Chase snatched it out of his friend's hand. "Right. Because the local cops give a shit about a twenty-year-old murder that they weren't able to solve. I'm sure they want to draw everyone's attention to that as often as possible. Give me a break. They'd like that file to get lost in the incinerator in the basement and never be seen again."

"I'm told it was a black eye to the department at the time."

"Do they have anyone working this cold case even if it's only now and then?"

Ellis twisted the top off the beer bottle and tossed it in the trash. "The low man on the detective totem pole works cold cases so he might have looked through the file or the evidence. All I'm saying is don't go telling anyone I gave that to you."

"Who would I tell? Josh?"

Ellis laughed and settled onto the couch. "That asshole will tell all his dogs and cats and you know what gossips domesticated animals are."

Chase turned to Bailey who had been watching the back and forth with interest. "Josh is a veterinarian."

"We should have him meet Willow. She loves animals."

Bailey made a mental note that she needed to call both Willow and Peyton. So much had happened since she'd last spoken to them. It might indeed be time for the two women to travel up here.

Bailey took a seat on the recliner and Chase sat on the other end of the couch. "Can you give me the summary? I'll look through every piece of paper but I'd kind of like to know the end of the book before I read it."

"Cheater," Ellis taunted, stretching out his legs and taking another draw on his beer. "Hmmm...where to start? By the time the cops got to the crime scene it had been contaminated by people trampling all over any evidence that might have been left there. So forensically we were shit out of luck for the most part. They did find a few stray hairs on Gwen's body and they believe that the killer was left-handed, which narrows the suspect pool down to a mere ten percent of the human population."

Chase tapped his chin. "Stabbing is a messy method. Was there any other blood there besides Gwen's?"

"It's messy but according to the coroner's report Gwen was probably incapacitated by a blow to the head before the killer began stabbing her. A detail the cops kept to themselves. Everyone else only knows about the knife wounds. As for other blood, there was no other blood found on her. There was other blood in the area but it was inconclusive as to whether it belonged to this incident or someone just getting hurt a day earlier."

"The camp nurse was kept pretty busy," Chase conceded. "We were always getting into trouble and that meant a lot of Band-aids. What about suspects?"

Bailey was beginning to lose hope with every question and answer. It didn't look like there was any concrete evidence as to who killed Gwen Baxter. So even if they had a strong suspect, they wouldn't be able to link him or her to the crime.

Or to Frank's death.

This entire trip might have been a fool's errand. Was she crazy for wanting the truth?

Ellis flipped open the folder and leafed through the pages. "They never had a strong suspect, to be honest, but a few people did catch their eye. The first adult was the swim coach, Martina Dowell. There was some scuttlebutt that Martina was having an inappropriate relationship with one of the teenage boys…one Alex Vaughn. Anyway, Alex was also kissing and flirting with Gwen and a few people pointed fingers at Dowell for the murder. However, she's right-handed and your mother saw Martina enter her cabin at ten-thirty. So she was struck off the list."

A myriad of emotions washed over Chase's face but in the end disgust won out. "I do believe Coach Dowell was having a relationship with some of the boys. There was talk and I'd heard it even at my age but I don't think she was a killer."

Ellis's smile was mocking. "And just what do killers look or act like? Some of them are the most mild-mannered people you'd ever want to know. They generally don't wear signs."

Bailey was still processing Ellis's statement that Gwen was with Alex. It corroborated Pamela's story.

"Was Frank Scott mentioned in that file?"

Shuffling through the folder, Ellis nodded, his gaze on the papers in front of him. "I remember that name. He made a statement to the police and there were others who mentioned him as well. Apparently, he and Gwen were making out near the lake and then they headed back to the camp. He went in to his cabin and she was not far from hers but she never made it. Technically Frank Scott was the last person to see Gwen alive."

Nausea washed over Bailey and she had to press her hand to her mouth and swallow the bile that had rose in her throat. "He was a suspect then?"

She was shocked at how normal her voice sounded when her world was slowly melting into a big pile of crap.

Ellis held out a piece of paper to her but she couldn't seem to command her arms to reach for it. Instead, Chase took it and quietly perused the contents before setting it on her lap. With shaky fingers, she lifted it into the light and began to read Frank's statement of what happened that night so long ago. It was basically as Ellis had described it with more detail thrown in but it didn't change the outcome.

"His cabin roommates vouched for him and said he was in bed by midnight and never left the cabin until morning. He was questioned and then removed from the suspect list."

"Good. That's good."

Not very eloquent but the relief was real. The idea of her husband being a killer wasn't a pleasant one. But she'd already figured out she didn't know everything about him. She'd come to the conclusion that knowing someone didn't mean knowing everything. There was always something hidden. Sometimes it was small and sometimes it was big and ugly.

"Who were the roommates that vouched for him?" Chase asked. "We might need to talk to them."

More combing through the file but finally Ellis found what he was looking for. "Here it is. There were four people… Danny Ford, Alex Vaughn, Guy Eckley and Greg Nelson."

"No one else?" Bailey asked faintly.

"Not that I can see. It was enough for the detectives to mark these boys off the list of suspects though."

Bailey could feel Chase watching her – perhaps waiting for some sign of distress – but the welcome numbness was back and she didn't fight the cold feeling as it spread through her extremities, all the way down to her toes.

"We're planning to talk to Guy and Danny," Chase said. "I'm also thinking we should talk to Gwen's friends as well. Teenagers are notorious for not telling adults the whole truth. There might be more to the story that they didn't reveal to the cops."

Ellis set the file down on the coffee table. "Did you get a chance to talk to Stephen Baxter? Or did he kick you out on your ass?"

"We talked to him," Chase retorted. "He actually gave us some good information that jives with yours. That's why we need to speak to some of the kids that knew Gwen, that were her age. I wasn't part of that crowd so there's only so much I can do."

"I'll leave this file tonight and tomorrow but then I need to get it back to the station before anyone realizes it's gone."

Chase laughed and shook his head. "Why would they even be looking for it?"

Grinning, Ellis shook his finger at his friend. "Because you're about to stir up a hornet's nest on this old case. You're fixing to ask a sitting United States Senator about a murder twenty years ago and whether he was involved or perhaps covering for a friend, are you not? Shit like that gets people's attention and that's what pushes the brass to yell at the rank and file like me. Then we go pull these ancient, dusty files and see if anything's changed. That means that folder needs to be back in the file room before you start pissing off every millionaire and billionaire that ever went to that summer camp. Money equals power and influence. They can shut you down before you even get one question answered. I have a feeling from looking through this file that's what happened back then and I doubt any of these families want to revisit this. They had the power to make this all go away."

Chase reached over and patted Bailey's knee. "What my old friend is trying to say is we have an uphill climb ahead of us. There may be people that don't want this murder solved."

Ellis nodded. "You better have a strong stomach because this is going to get ugly, and real fast too."

"Rich people don't scare me," Bailey said, resolve in her tone. "I won't let them deter me from the goal here which is the truth."

Snorting, Ellis stood and moved toward the front door. "Whose truth would that be? If I've learned anything in this job it's that the wealthy can buy their own facts. Ask Chase. He can tell you the same."

Bailey lifted her chin. This man didn't know anything about her and was making more than a few assumptions. "You don't know me very well if you think I'll just run back to Midnight Blue Beach with my tail between my legs."

Ellis's eyes widened and then a smile spread across his face. "You're right and I humbly apologize. I don't know you at all. But I think there's some information in that file you might want to read. It's about Midnight Blue Beach. Interesting stuff. It's late so I'll bid you both goodnight. Chase, I'll call you tomorrow about getting the file back."

Bailey frowned and reached for the thick file, her curiosity piqued. Why would her hometown be mentioned in the file other than that it was where Frank grew up? It wasn't even an important detail, let alone interesting.

She was paging through the file when she heard Chase's voice. "Should I make some coffee?"

"A whole pot. I think we're going to be up late tonight."

Chapter Seventeen

B AILEY REREAD THE page for the third time but was having difficulty truly comprehending what it was telling her. It was too strange and frankly farfetched to be real.

"The Evandria Council," she said slowly, scouring her brain for any previous references in her past. Surely if what this paper said was true then Frank or someone else would have mentioned this before now.

"You've never heard of them?" Chase asked as they sat at the kitchen table poring over the file. They only had a short time to review it all. "Really? I thought everyone had but that it was some sort of urban legend, like cutting out people's kidneys and leaving them in a bathtub full of ice in a hotel."

What in the hell is he talking about?

"Pardon? Who is getting their kidneys cut out?"

"It's just a story. A guy meets a pretty girl in a bar. They go back to her hotel room and have another drink. He gets sleepy and blacks out. When he wakes up the next morning he's sitting in a hotel bathtub with ice. He's had surgery and they took a kidney. You've never heard that urban legend before?"

Bailey shook her head. "Apparently I didn't need the moral lesson not to pick up strangers in some bar. So you've heard of the Evandria Council? Who are they?"

"A powerful and secret organization. I've heard they're part of the Illuminati, but who really knows except its members? And that's assuming that the Illuminati actually exist in the first place. Many people – including myself – think that's an urban legend as well. Anyway, it's an old group of wealthy people and they have their own rules and hierarchy. I never knew it had a stronghold in Midnight Blue Beach but then I'm sure I wasn't supposed to. Supposedly they're serious about keeping their organization under wraps."

"How could I have lived in that town all these years and never heard about this?"

"Because it simply may not be true. The detective who put together this report added this information because he was told by one of the kids that their parents were in the Evandria Council and that parent was an attorney who showed up while we were all being questioned by the cops. I do remember that guy, believe it or not, and my parents couldn't figure out how he knew to come in the first place. But that doesn't mean he was part of some conspiracy. Personally, I don't prescribe to all that tinfoil hat bull. The wealthy are powerful, that's true, but I don't think they are plotting against the government or some shit like that."

Bailey wasn't much into conspiracy theories either but it still felt strange that she'd never heard of this organization. "So how did he know to come after Gwen had been killed?"

Chase shrugged. "I'm guessing one of the kids snuck up to

the office and called their parents. I snuck out as well to see Gwen, remember? It wasn't all that difficult. The adults were all distracted."

The explanation made sense and she didn't want to make a mountain out of what was essentially a molehill. "I'm going to call Willow and Peyton. Tell them what we've found and see if they've ever heard of this Evandria-whatever. Peyton's family has lived in Midnight Blue Beach all her life so if anyone would know about it, it would be her."

Chase nodded and smiled. "Good idea. I'm going to keep reading these statements and reports. Afterward we can fire up the laptop and see what else we can find out about the Evandria Council. If it's a secret, it's on the Net."

"And every crazy theory right along with it," Bailey laughed. "Do you mind if I use your back porch for the call so I don't disturb your work?"

Plus she wouldn't mind a little privacy for this.

"Help yourself. Do you think they're going to want to come up here?"

Bailey was pretty sure they'd have their bags packed and be on their way before the sun came up. "They wanted to come with me but I persuaded them to stay there, so I don't think there's any doubt they'll head here immediately."

She was surprised they hadn't already. Settling into a chair, she scrolled through her contacts until she found Willow. If Peyton wasn't there as well, they could always conference her into the call.

Willow picked up after two rings. "We've been waiting for you to call."

"Hello to you too," Bailey laughed. "I don't suppose Peyton—"

"She's here. We've been drinking margaritas and waiting for you to call. I'll put you on speaker. What's happening up there?"

"We talked to Gwen's brother Stephen and he says he knew our husbands but he wasn't part of their group. Apparently they were like most teenage boys and were quite...active if you know what I mean when it came to their love life."

Willow snorted through the phone. "Sounds like my Alex."

"My Greg too. He liked to have a woman in every city. I think it made him feel secure."

"About Alex... When we read through the file, it seems he was having an affair with the swim coach that summer at the same time he was romancing Gwen. They even questioned the swim coach about killing Gwen out of jealousy."

"That sounds like Alex, may he rest in peace. He had a zest for life."

Thank goodness neither woman seemed surprised or bothered by the revelations. If anything, they were amused by their late husbands' youthful antics. Bailey filled them in on the rest of what they'd learned, finally bringing up the Evandria Council.

"Have you ever heard of it?"

There was silence on the phone and then a long, heavy sigh. Peyton. "I have. Greg was a member. I found out sort of by accident the night before the wedding. They threw him a bachelor party and all the men had lapel pins that matched. I asked Greg what it meant but he quickly changed the subject. When he came home drunk later I asked again. This time he answered in a half-ass way. He said it was the Evandria Council.

A club. Then he passed out. When I asked him about it a third time in the morning he said it was like a fraternity or brother-hood. I didn't ask anything else as I didn't think it was a big deal. I guess it is, though."

Greg had been a member. Interesting.

"Willow?" Bailey asked. "What about you?"

"Alex was too," Willow admitted, reluctance in her tone. "He never told me. The only reason I know is that when I was dancing every now and then some big spenders would come into the place and throw around high dollars. When I was new, another dancer told me that the men had just come from an Evandria Council meeting and that I should be nice to them. One night Alex came in with them. The rest is history, of course."

If Alex and Greg were members it was almost certain that Frank had been. Politely, Willow and Peyton didn't mention the obvious that was staring all of them in the face.

"You never asked him about it?"

"I assumed it was something like the Freemasons and he wouldn't be able to tell me anyway. He never mentioned it and it never came up or was important."

Another dead end. Fantastic. Maybe Senator Ford or one of Gwen's friends could shed some light on whether Frank had been a member and if so, what did membership mean? Did you get a lapel pin and dinner once a month? Did they make dona-tions to worthy causes or just play poker and get lap dances?

Willow and Peyton filled Bailey in on what they'd found – or not found – in their own local investigation. As far as they could find Greg, Alex, and Frank hadn't communicated or done business with each other after they left summer camp that year. But of course, if they were all members of this super-secret-no-girls-allowed club then they might have met up on the sly.

"So do you still want to come up here? Or do you want to stay down there and investigate this Evandria Council?"

"There," both women said in unison, giggling following as Willow said, "Jinx. You owe me a Coke."

Peyton cleared her throat. "Seriously, it sounds like it's time for us to come up there and lend a hand. The more of us there are the more quickly we can talk to not only Gwen's friends but also our husbands'. I remember that Greg had a college buddy that lived in Washington D.C. Maybe I can look him up and ask him about the secret council thing."

In the meantime, Bailey and Chase would continue their snooping in Williamsburg. She wanted to know more about this organization and Frank's past, including Gwen.

"I'll call now and have the jet gassed up for us. We'll leave early in the morning," Willow said. "Where should we meet you?"

They decided Willow and Peyton would rent another car and meet her at the hotel. They would call her when they arrived. She disconnected and rejoined Chase in the kitchen.

"Their husbands were members so I'm guessing Frank was too," Bailey said as she sat down at the table. Resting her chin on her hands, she searched her memories from their early marriage. She simply couldn't remember Frank having regular meetings at the same time or even him mentioning anything remotely like that.

Chase looked up from the file, his brows drawn together.

"Listen, that whole Evandria Council thing probably is a red herring. Yes, the file mentions it but that's all. They didn't pursue it as a lead because I'm guessing it wasn't important. If you have a room full of people who love Star Wars for example and one of them ends up dead, it doesn't mean that George Lucas was in on it. It's probably just a coincidence."

Bailey groaned and slapped her hands over her eyes.

Not another coincidence.

Except that this one looked plausible. Of course, a bunch of rich kids who went to the same summer camp every year would be involved in the same extracurricular activities. Really, it was almost a given. Time to get back to the real work. Talking to Gwen's friends.

If anyone knew a teenage girl, it would be her teenage friends.

IT WAS AFTER one in the morning when Chase and Bailey called it quits. There was more to review but by then they were yawning and cross-eyed. They needed sleep and maybe some bacon for breakfast. Chase offered her a spare room but she wanted to be taken back to the hotel. She tried to call a taxi but Chase insisted on driving her home. He wasn't enough of a gentleman not to be thinking about another kiss but he wasn't so bad as to send her into the dark night in a cab.

Pulling up to the front of the hotel, Chase put the car into park and escorted her upstairs, ignoring her protests that she was fine on her own and she didn't need a bodyguard.

"Do you have a high crime rate around here?" she joked, key card in hand as they approached the door to her room. "Should I be scared and checking around corners?"

"We don't and you shouldn't, but my mother would have boxed my ears if I didn't see you to your door. It's the right thing to do."

She gave him a smile and slid the card into the slot, the door light flashing green. "Then I thank you and your mother. And thank you for getting me in to talk to Stephen Baxter. Without you I know I would be spinning my wheels."

"It's all about who you know around here." Chase leaned in, the fragrance from her shampoo swamping his senses. The kiss from earlier was still fresh in his mind and he wanted to do it again as soon as possible. Preferably right here and now. A goodnight kiss to hold him over until tomorrow. The more time he spent with Bailey the more he liked her. Straightforward, honest, smart, and pretty darn good looking too. Frank Scott had been an idiot to ignore her. "I'm glad we're working together on this."

Abruptly Bailey stepped back, almost banging her head against the door. "I am too. So I guess I'll see you in the morning."

She moved quickly but he had good reflexes as well. His hand reached out and held the door in place, forcing her to turn around and look at him. "Is everything okay, Bailey? Are you angry with me about earlier? I thought we both enjoyed it but maybe I was wrong."

He hoped he wasn't.

She sighed and leaned against the door frame, staring down

at the carpet for a long moment before looking up at him. "I'm not angry at you, Chase. You've been great. I'm angry at me."

He let go of the door, his arm falling to his side as disappointment crashed through him. It was two steps forward with her but now three steps back. He'd thought they were making progress and that she felt the same attraction he did.

"You're angry at yourself because we kissed?"

"I can't start anything up right now. The timing is bad, you have to admit. Plus the whole long-distance thing. At first, I thought I could just be casual about it all but I think I might not be the casual type. I think I'm the relationship type."

Swallowing hard, Chase didn't respond right away. "You want a relationship? You mean like marriage?"

Bailey half groaned and half laughed. "Oh hell no. I can't see myself getting married again but I don't also see myself having a casual fling with a handsome guy while I'm here. I'm looking for something in between those two extremes."

That didn't sound as scary as matrimony and until-death-do-us-part.

"That's not out of the question."

Her lips quirked up in a gentle smile. "Is that what you want? Really?"

"I don't know," he admitted. "In my defense I've enjoyed being single and you and I have just met recently."

"All the more reason to move slowly. As I said, the timing of this sucks because I'm here to do something important. Maybe when I'm done…"

"We can talk about it again," he finished for her.

"I'm not going anywhere, Chase. I'm not seeing anyone else

or even looking to date anyone else. I know that tonight didn't come out of nowhere. We've been working up to it and it was amazing. But to be honest? It scared the hell out of me. I didn't expect this when I came here and I'm not sure I'm emotionally prepared to go any further."

He didn't bother to argue that it had been five years or that she was still young and beautiful. That she deserved happiness and fulfillment. Bailey was an intelligent woman. She knew all of that already. Plus, arguing her point seemed pushy and that was the last thing he wanted to be with her. He wasn't a man that had to convince a woman to share his bed. He wanted it to be just as much her idea as it was his.

"Fair enough," he conceded, moving away from her so he wouldn't be tempted to try those full lips again. "We'll do this at your pace. But I want you to know one thing, Bailey."

"What's that?"

"I liked that kiss a hell of a lot and I want to do it again. I think you're gorgeous and funny. You make me laugh and you challenge me in a way I haven't been in a long time. I'd like to see where this goes but I understand if you don't. I'll respect that because I respect you and everything you've been through that's brought you to this point. But if you change your mind, I'm right here."

Her mouth hung open and her eyes were wide with shock. She hadn't been expecting his moment of truth. Good, she was a woman who needed surprises. Often. She'd become complacent with her life, which was easy to see.

"Okay."

One word. Simple and to the point.

"Okay?"

She nodded. "Yes, okay. It means that I'll keep that in mind. You've given me a lot to think about here, Chase. I'm sure I'll have to thank you at breakfast for a sleepless night."

"Alright then."

Whistling as he walked down the hall to the elevator, he smiled to himself and waited for the fear or trepidation to set in but it didn't come. Instead, there was a rightness to what he'd told her. Bailey Scott wasn't just any woman and that kiss hadn't been a fluke.

At least he wouldn't be the only one awake all night.

CHASE COULDN'T SLEEP, so instead of tossing and turning he dragged his fatigued carcass out of bed and went straight back to the case file. Leafing through the papers, he found what he was looking for. The Evandria Council. Since he couldn't sleep he might as well do some research. He settled into his recliner, only the glow from the laptop screen lighting the room.

One Google search later, he'd learned quite a bit but nothing that helped.

The Evandria Council was founded in 1861 by a group that broke off from the Freemasons, although why wasn't clear. Sources said it was a power struggle but there were rumors that it was a separation due to differing opinions on the role of the federal government. The rules and ceremonies were secret and even the Internet couldn't shed much light on that. It did say that the code of behavior was strict and punishment for infractions was harsh. Blackballing a member was considered worse than death.

Membership dues were astronomical with a yearly fee in the seven-figure range, plus they had to promise to leave thirty percent of their estate to the group when they passed on. But the benefits of belonging were lavish. The council owned a huge parcel of land in Central Florida that included an estate, horses, tennis courts, a golf course, and a swimming pool. Parties were held at least one weekend every month and members were encouraged to network and play. Billion dollar business deals were made on the eighteenth putting green or during cocktail hours.

Midnight Blue Beach, however, was where the official meetings were held in a building called The Clubhouse. Those meetings were only for the highest officials of the group and to attend one had to be invited.

The Evandria Council was rumored to part of the Illuminati, who were supposedly responsible for the French Revolution. The Council's mission statement said it was created to uphold social justice and free the world's citizens from oppression.

Worthy goals, depending on how they planned to do it. One person's good deed was another's evil action.

"I'm a cynical bastard," Chase muttered under his breath as he scrolled through the website, taking note of the long list of charitable efforts of the group. Hospitals, youth outreach, food pantries, just to name a few. Hundreds of millions were donated in their name every year. Yet few people had heard of them. Either they had a lousy publicist or they were trying to keep their actions under wraps.

Snapping the lid of his laptop shut, Chase sighed and closed his eyes, letting the tension drain from the tight muscles in his shoulders and neck. More information that didn't help at all but it didn't hurt either. So what if all the men were members of the club? They were friends, so it wasn't any kind of a shock. It did explain how the families would have enough powerful connections to get the investigation shut down though.

Now he was going to dig it all up again, and probably pissing off more than a few people.

It was one of his favorite things to do.

Chapter Eighteen

B AILEY DIDN'T EXIT Chase's car even though he'd opened the passenger door and was standing there waiting. Frankly, she wasn't sure she wanted any part of this and was puzzled as to how he'd talked her into it. She could only blame it on the lack of caffeine in her system. She didn't make good decisions until after her second cup of coffee.

"Maybe this isn't such a good idea."

Chase didn't reach for her or in any way pressure her. He simply stood his ground and smiled indulgently as if he'd expected her protests.

"You'll love it. It's the perfect way to start the day and really get the blood pumping. We're killing two birds with one stone here this morning. A run in Colonial Williamsburg. You'll get your exercise and see a historical landmark."

She did want to see the delightfully restored district but she didn't want to do it while running. Her boobs were too big for this despite lashing them to her chest with two bras tightened to the second hooks. When he'd asked her if she had shorts and a t-shirt she should have known he was up to something. She should have lied and told him no.

She tried another tactic. "I'll just slow you down and it will be no fun for you."

"I'm in the mood for a nice, light jog. We'll go slow and stop anytime you want to take a closer look at something or just need a break."

This time he held out his hand so she inwardly groaned and took it, letting him help her out of the vehicle. Her mind was already working on ways to get even with him. Maybe she'd teach him to crochet.

"You know I hate you for this, right?"

Laughing, he led her to the uneven sidewalk. They'd parked in the merchant's part of the village and it was so early in the morning none of the shops were open yet. When he'd said he wanted to get an early start she thought that meant a big breakfast.

"It's okay if you hate me." He pointed to his right. "The restored area is this way. We're going to stay on the road which isn't open to traffic. Don't step in horse poop."

Wait. What?

He began a few stretches and she followed suit, not really sure if it would do any good. Surely she would be nursing sore muscles and possibly two sprained ankles by the end of this. With any luck he'd have a big knot on his head where she'd hit him after she tripped over her own feet.

They started off at an easy pace despite his much longer legs. He wasn't even breathing heavy or sweating despite the humidity while she was becoming short of breath. She wanted to stop and buy a coffee and a cinnamon roll.

"Don't think about your feet or your body. Look at the scenery and think about what it might have been like over two hundred years ago. I'm going to take you right down the main drag which is the Duke of Gloucester Street."

Maybe it wasn't so bad after all. His advice was spot on and soon she was too absorbed in the beauty of the historic area to notice the aches and pains from the unaccustomed physical exertion. The little houses were darling and she breathed in the sweet air perfumed with flowers...and the past. She was a woman of the modern era but she could see herself running her bakery and talking to the townsfolk, indulging in gossip or debate over whether to declare independence from Britain.

"Beautiful, isn't it?" Chase grinned. "Let's go up the Palace Green so you can see the Governor's Palace. We need to come back so you can take a tour. The original home burned down and it was reconstructed in the 1930s on the original site."

If the inside of the house was anything like the outside, it was amazingly impressive. The lawns were carefully manicured and the facade was well-maintained. If it wasn't original, they'd done a good job of making it look that way. But even a beautiful home couldn't stop the stitch in Bailey's side. She gasped and stopped, holding her ribs and bending over to catch her breath.

"I need a minute."

Or fifteen. Or a leather recliner and an umbrella drink.

To her surprise, his hand settled over the exact spot and began to lightly massage the cramp. Now her problem wasn't a stitch in her ribs but a man this close that was making it hard to breathe. She stepped back and held up a hand.

"I'm fine. I just need to rest."

She didn't imagine the look of hurt that crossed his features but he nodded. "What you need to do is walk around. Standing won't help. Why don't we head down the street and you can see more of the district?"

It would have been churlish to refuse and she'd already hurt his feelings, so she followed him as he showed her points of interest – a tavern, the courthouse and magazine, even a shoemaker.

"You really love this."

His cheeks were a ruddy shade but it could have been from running rather than embarrassment.

"I do. I love history and I especially love Revolutionary War history. I think I've read every book ever written about it and the Founding Fathers."

"I love it too," she admitted. It was strange to realize they had more in common than just the past. "One summer during college me and a friend took a trip to Boston and did all the touristy stuff. I loved it."

His face lit up with a wide smile. "I did too. As I looked out on Boston Harbor I could actually imagine crates of tea being thrown overboard into the water."

Bailey shook her head and grinned. "Such a waste of good tea, too."

"All for a good cause. How about we start jogging again?"

Sighing, she agreed but this time she kept a slower pace that honestly wasn't much faster than an energetic walk, but Chase didn't complain. When they reached the end of the street, they crossed over to another main road and jogged that way, enjoying the morning air and saying very little. Every now and then he would point something out but for the most part they were quiet until they reached the car.

Stretching her tired muscles, she couldn't help but admire Chase's physique as he bent over to touch his toes. He was well-built but lean too, his muscles defined but not bulging. She'd never gone for that type. He lifted the hem of his shirt, waving it to let in some cool air and revealed a perfectly formed six-pack. *Damn.*

"See?" he said, digging the car keys from his pocket. "It's a great way to start the day. Fresh air and physical exercise. It gets the blood flowing to the brain, plus you can feel smug all day long knowing you did something good for your body."

"My body wanted a stack of pancakes with maple syrup. Or maybe a bear claw."

"Both of those things can be arranged. Do you want a shower first?"

What she really wanted was to have her head examined. She'd been so sure last night that they shouldn't be going any further in this relationship – or whatever it was – but this morning she wasn't as positive. She liked this man, dammit. She liked him a lot and it wasn't fair that she had all this baggage hanging around her when in her heart she was ready to move on.

And yet he was standing there as if last night never happened. Like they were simply two friends out for a side-splitting run. No kissing. No touching. No desire. It was kind of pissing her off. She didn't answer his question, instead posing one of her own.

"Do you do this a lot?"

His brows furrowed at her query. "Do what? Run? About

five or six times a week. When the weather's good, every day."

"No, *this*. Kiss a girl and then the next day act like it never happened. Do you do that a lot?"

A smile spread across his face. "Not often, no. I'm doing this because I thought it was what you wanted me to do. You slapped me down last night. I remember that part quite clearly."

Bailey regarded the pavement, not able to meet Chase's eyes. "Well...yeah. I mean, I'm right. It's terrible timing and I've got all this crap I need to figure out. None of this screams *start a relationship*. But I don't know...you're acting like it didn't happen at all."

"So are you."

She lifted her head so their gazes met. "I'm confused if you can't tell. I haven't dated since college and I wasn't all that good at it then either."

Chase leaned against the car, playing with the keys in his hand. "I like you, Bailey. A whole lot. I think you like me too. I understand protecting your heart because I'm not anxious to get hurt either, to be honest. But I'm not sure we have much choice about this. We have feelings for each other and if we try and deny them we're going to be miserable."

It had only been a few hours and she already was unhappy. "So what do you suggest?"

His hand reached out and tucked a strand of flyaway hair behind her ear, caressing her cheek with his fingertips. "Take a chance. On digging up the past. On me. Close your eyes and jump, Bailey. We just might be worth it."

He didn't know how much he was asking. Her entire life had been about structure and discipline. It had been what had pushed her through school and snagged her a scholarship to one of the best universities in the country. Then later it had served her well during her marriage and when she'd started her bakery. It was safe and predictable. Comforting.

"I'm not sure I'm capable of that. It's not that I don't want to. It's just...I may not literally have the ability."

He held out his hand in offering. "You don't have to do it alone. I'm here."

"I'm afraid to fail. Then we both get hurt and I don't want to do that."

But her hand had a mind of its own and she found their fingers curled together.

"How about we take this one step at a time. A date. One simple meal. Bailey Scott, can I buy you breakfast?"

That wasn't too scary. Food and lots of daylight. People all around them. It wasn't dancing in the moonlight with candles and champagne. Like last night, and look where that had led them.

She held his hand tightly, her inner demons fighting a battle to the death. It would be so easy to say no and stay in that spot where she didn't have to worry or try. But that place was becoming less hospitable with every passing day. She couldn't stand back and watch from the sidelines. She had to play the game.

She wasn't a wuss. She was a survivor and she had ample proof.

"I can do that."

Chapter Nineteen

T AYLOR RICHARDSON LIVED in the cul-de-sac of a tony neighborhood outside of Washington D.C. Graceful brick mansions and long, sweeping driveways conjured up images of ladies in white gloves sipping mint juleps on a white-columned front porch.

Bailey glanced down at her simple flowered sundress and sandals. "I think I may be underdressed."

Chase plucked at his own cotton button down that he'd paired with khaki cargo shorts. "They'll probably mistake me for the gardener but it's over ninety degrees out here. No way was I going to wear a suit and tie." His gaze swept her head to toe, leaving a heat in its wake that had nothing to do with the temperature. "I think you look just fine. Very fine, in fact."

"What did she say when you called her?" Bailey asked as they approached the front door. "Is she okay talking about Gwen?"

Ellis had managed to dig up Taylor's number and address but it was left to Chase to contact her and ask for a meeting. The police were not officially active in the investigation although the case had never been solved.

"Surprisingly she is. I told her about how you're trying to find out more about Frank's life before you met him but I didn't mention the date connection of their deaths. She thinks this is just about Frank and his past friends and girlfriends."

"She was one of Gwen's best friends?"

Chase pressed the doorbell before answering. "And one of the cabinmates who said that Gwen went to bed early that night."

"When we know from the statements that she was making out with Frank down by the river until almost midnight."

There was no time for Chase to answer as the door swung open and a gorgeous brunette stood there, a welcoming smile on her face. Dressed in a cream-colored pantsuit, gold Jimmy Choos, and a huge diamond on her left hand she looked much like the women Bailey saw and talked to every day in Midnight Blue Beach. Most of them were smart, beautiful, and friendly with way more money than average folk. Some of them came from regular middle-class backgrounds such as hers but most were old money.

"Chase," she exclaimed, stepping back so they could pass into the house. "It's so good to see you after all these years. Please come in, you and your friend."

Bailey followed Chase and Taylor through the luxurious home – all marble floors and mirrors – and onto a glassed-in back patio that had been set with lemonade and several kinds of cookies and cupcakes. Things were officially looking up. She welcomed sweets in any form into her life.

Introductions were made and they settled at the table as the ceiling fan above twirled lazily. Taylor poured three glasses of frosty lemonade and Bailey helped herself to a few cookies and a mini-cupcake that might just be salted caramel.

Taylor folded her hands in her lap, her smile disappearing. "First let me say that I am so sorry for your loss, Bailey. Frank was such a great guy and to go so young… It must have been quite a shock for you."

"It was," Bailey agreed, for a moment going back to that day when a police officer had shown up at her hotel to deliver the news. "I guess that's part of the reason I'm here. Frank didn't mention his years before me very often and I'm trying to piece together his youth by talking to some people who knew him."

"He didn't talk about it? At all?" Taylor frowned, a V forming between her brows. "That seems so strange. He would have had such funny stories. I remember a time…I think we were thirteen…we all went skinny dipping in the pool after the camp counselors went to bed. It was quite scandalous at the time since it was boys and girls. I was pretty innocent and I got quite the education that summer. I always laugh and say that my parents received their money's worth."

Bailey bit delicately into a shortbread cookie that tasted of lemon and thyme. "These are exactly the kind of stories I was hoping for. Something to help me create a more complete view of Frank before we met in college. It sounds like he was the life of the party. When I met him he was much more serious and quiet."

"Frank was serious and quiet? That doesn't sound like him but college can change a person," Taylor conceded, although it was clear she was having issues with Bailey's description. "He and his friends were wild and loud, always dancing around and having fun. At one point, I think they even organized a rock band. Alex was the lead singer." The brunette giggled. "And the ladies' man. The girls sure loved him. I wonder if he ever settled down? I seriously doubt it."

"Actually," Bailey began carefully, watching Taylor's reaction closely. "Alex did get married but he passed away five years ago in a car crash. Greg Nelson is also gone. An allergic reaction."

Mouth slack and eyes wide open, Taylor's hand flew to her throat. "My God! That's…macabre. All three of them and so young."

Taylor's eyes glistened with tears and she sniffled delicately as she reached for a box of tissues hidden discreetly behind a lamp.

"It's tragic," Bailey agreed quietly. "I heard they were such good friends too, almost like brothers, but I have to admit that Frank never spoke of them. Do you know what caused their falling out?"

Taylor fidgeted in her seat for a moment, her expression growing even sadder. "They fought. It was the last summer of camp before college. They'd fought before so we didn't think this time was any different but then…" Burying her face in the tissue, she blew her nose before looking up at Chase. "You know what I'm talking about, don't you?"

Chase nodded. "Gwen."

Taylor gave them a sad smile. "I used to think about her every day. For the longest time I did but then it became every other day. Then every other week. I still think about her but it's different now. I thought about her on my wedding day and how she would never get married. I thought about her when I had my first child and how she would never get to be a mother. I thought about her when I buried my father and how no parent should ever have to bury a child. I know this sounds strange but I like it when I think about her. It makes her feel closer. I still miss her, you know."

Bailey was acutely aware of all the pain this conversation was digging up and she didn't feel great about it, but they couldn't make any progress without reopening a few wounds.

"You and Gwen were best friends?" she asked.

"The best of friends. Now they would have called us BFFs," Taylor laughed, wiping a tear from her cheek. "She was sweet and funny and she could keep a secret. I knew if I shared my deepest fears with her no one would ever hear about them. She was that kind of person."

There wasn't a delicate way to pose this question. "She and Frank? They were an item?"

Her cheeks turning pink, Taylor sighed. "They were but I doubt it was serious or anything. Gwen hung around with several boys that summer. She said she didn't want to be tied down and that she just wanted to have some fun."

It was time to challenge Taylor's statement all those years ago and luckily, Chase had volunteered to be the bad guy.

"Someone saw her with Frank the night she died. Right before midnight. They'd been down at the river."

Those pink cheeks turned bright red. "That's true. I know what we said to the police but it's just that we were all so scared. We thought we'd get in trouble and we didn't want anyone to think less of Gwen. We didn't want them to think she was, you know, less than virtuous. Her parents were so strict about that and we didn't want them to be any more upset than they already were. We did it to protect her, you have to believe me."

Chase leaned forward, his elbows on his knees. "Gwen was sleeping with Frank, wasn't she? That's what you were trying to hide."

More tears fell from Taylor's eyes and her hand pressed to her mouth. She didn't say anything for the longest time and Bailey let her battle whatever demons she'd been carrying around all these years. Finally, her hands dropped to her lap and she squeezed her eyes shut, taking a deep breath.

"I wish that's what I was trying to hide. I wish that's all that was going on that summer. But Gwen came to camp determined that summer to have fun and be wild. She succeeded." Taylor's eyes opened, her expression anguished. "Gwen was sleeping with Frank that summer. But she was also sleeping with several other boys as well – Alex and Greg included. I think she slept with Danny and Guy as well. She said she was going to have as much fun as she could and she wouldn't be tied down to one boy. She said she was going to be free and live the way she wanted to. We tried to talk her out of it and tell her she was going to get a bad reputation but she said she didn't care."

Bailey wasn't someone who made a habit of making moral judgments about people. Gwen's actions weren't something she herself would have done but if the young girl was happy and wasn't hurting anyone? Then there was a whole societal double standard of boys being school heroes when they screwed around but girls were sluts. It wasn't fair and it looked like Gwen wasn't going to allow herself to be dictated to by others. The only question was did her behavior get her killed or was it something else completely?

"I'm sorry that we're putting you through this," Bailey apologized. "This must bring up painful memories and I do apologize."

"Some painful and some good," Taylor agreed. "As I said, I kind of like remembering Gwen and the fun times we had. I've learned as I've gotten older that happiness and pain can go hand in hand. I can't have one without the other in this situation."

"The night Gwen was killed…is she what Frank, Alex, and Greg were arguing about?" Chase asked. "Is that why they were fighting? Jealousy?"

"I don't know for sure but I would assume so. They all knew about each other since Gwen didn't bother to hide it and the tension built with each passing week. I think it just blew up that night. Not sure who started the fight but I know that when their parents came to pick them up the next night they wouldn't even look at each other. I guess I assumed they'd repaired their friendship somewhere along the line but they didn't. Sad."

The husband Bailey had known would never have ended a friendship over a girl, but then this Frank wasn't the man she'd married. Not at all.

Chase rubbed his jaw, his expression tight. "Taylor, I have one more question. Have you ever heard of the Evandria Council?"

Taylor's brows shot up and her lips curved into a small smile. "Of course I have. That's a silly question, Chase."

He glanced at Bailey and then back at the other woman. "Is it? Do you know many members of the group?"

She'd been about to take a sip of her lemonade but instead set the glass back down. "I think just about everyone I know is a member. I've been a member since I turned eighteen. My husband, father, mother, brother, sister, grandparents, and all my friends. Chase, everyone that attended your summer camp became a member as far as I know."

Apparently, it wasn't a boys only club after all. An interesting development.

Bailey found her voice, wanting confirmation of something she'd only suspected so far. "So Frank was a member?"

"His whole family was for generations." Taylor's brow knitted in confusion. "You didn't know? You're not a member?"

Bailey shrugged as if it was no big deal. "He wasn't active in the group while we were married, so no, I didn't."

Taylor relaxed back into her chair. "I wouldn't say I'm active either. I haven't been to the retreat in years, before my kids were born."

Chase popped the last piece of a cookie in his mouth. "I read about the group and I found myself intrigued by The Clubhouse. Have you ever been inside?"

Laughing, Taylor shook her head. "I'm afraid not. It's only for officers of the Council. My father was an officer one year and he got to go inside but he wouldn't tell us anything about it. Of course we've all heard stories, each one wilder than the last. I assume most of them are untrue. It's just a building, after all."

"So you're okay with all the secrecy?" Bailey asked, twisting her napkin between nervous fingers. "It doesn't bother you?"

"Why should it? Evandria is about doing good things for our world. The fact that they want to keep it a little bit mysterious is half the fun. Sure, we could all just have bake sales and blood drives but where's the excitement in that? This way people get to feel like they're a part of something big and they also do charitable works. It's a win-win for everyone in my opinion. Why do you ask about it?"

"No particular reason," Chase assured her. "It was mentioned that the lawyer that came to the camp was a member of the Council and I was curious."

If the families were all members it only made sense that the attorney was also.

Bailey dabbed at the corners of her mouth with her napkin. "I want to thank you so much for taking the time to speak with me today about Frank. I've learned so much about him and I'm very grateful."

"I have more stories if you'd like to hear them," Taylor offered with a laugh. "I have more of those lemon cookies as well."

"How can I say no?" Bailey smiled.

Every detail she learned about her late husband might be the one piece of information she needed to understand his death and those of Alex and Greg.

The cookies were good too. Maybe she could get the recipe.

Chapter Twenty

CHASE WASN'T SURE what he'd been expecting but Peyton and Willow weren't at all as he'd pictured them. Perhaps it was the widow moniker that made him think they were older than they actually were or maybe it was the way Bailey had vaguely described them. Peyton was petite and blonde while Willow was taller with dark blonde hair. Those adjectives were only the tip of the iceberg.

By the time they had finished dinner at his place – takeout Chinese – he'd learned that Peyton was something of an artist who believed in reincarnation, psychic energy, and the power of a damn good book on the reader's general mood. Willow wasn't a run of the mill female either. She quickly revealed that she'd been an exotic dancer and that's where she'd met her late husband. She was considered quite scandalous by the good citizens of Midnight Blue Beach and seemed to revel in her role if the grin on her face was any indication. She also had a mischievous sense of humor. Chase liked both of the women immediately.

He shouldn't have been surprised that the females were on

the young side and quite attractive. Bailey, after all, was only thirty-two and he thought she was gorgeous. He'd found his attention gravitating toward her all evening as she laughed and joked with her friends. Even when the conversation grew more serious and somber, he'd had a hard time ripping his gaze away from her soft brown eyes, full lips, and creamy skin. Yep, he had it bad. This woman had him twisted into knots and she hadn't even broken a sweat to do it. He couldn't remember the last time that had happened. Not even with Cheryl.

Willow sat back against the cushions of the couch and patted her stomach. "That was just what this girl needed. Now all I want is a long, hot bath and a nap. I can never get to sleep on a plane."

Peyton elbowed her friend. "Then after that? It's still early in the day."

"Then I'll be ready to tackle whatever it is that Chase and Bailey need us to do."

He shot a sideways glance to Bailey and she nodded. They'd talked about this after leaving Taylor's house. "How do you ladies feel about New York City?"

Willow's brow arched in question. "Just in general? I think it's a great place to go on a shopping spree and see a few shows, but somehow I don't think that's what you had in mind."

"It's not. The last address Ellis was able to get for Guy was in New York and I was wondering if you two would like to head up there and talk to him."

Peyton and Willow nodded in agreement but the latter tapped her chin as her gaze darted back and forth between himself and Bailey. "Sure we can. We came to help. What might you two be doing while we're up there? Anything…interesting?"

The way Willow dragged out the last word told him that she'd noticed how he was looking at Bailey. These ladies didn't miss a trick. Or perhaps he was simply that damn obvious. Or both. But he wasn't the kiss and tell type. If Bailey wanted to give them the story it wouldn't bother him but he was a private kind of guy.

"We're headed to DC to talk to Danny. Not sure if I'll even be able to get in but we need to try."

Peyton stared down into her glass, shifting uncomfortably where she sat on the floor. "My family knows some people who know people. Maybe I could make a few calls ahead of time. I don't want to see you waste a trip."

As much as Chase hated the old friend-of-a-friend network that seemed so important in these circles he couldn't argue with the logic. Even though he'd spoken with Danny more than a few times in the last several years at the club, it didn't mean that an audience with the senator would be automatically granted.

"I'd appreciate that," he found himself saying. "There is plenty of work to do here and spending it on a wild goose chase isn't a good use of time."

"I'll make a few calls."

Peyton stood and excused herself, heading for the back porch while Willow pulled out her phone. "I guess I'll send a text to the pilot and let him know we need to leave for New York City as soon as he can get the jet ready. We'll need a hotel room as well."

"You can just take the train."

That's how he planned to get to Washington DC.

She was typing something and didn't even glance up. "It will be faster this way plus we can travel on our own schedule, not somebody else's."

Couldn't argue with that. Must be nice to have a plane.

Chase cleared his throat and threw a nervous glance at Bailey before plunging forward. "Willow, I was kind of wondering about your thoughts on all this. It must have come as a huge shock to you when you found out about Frank and Greg, and then Gwen of course. Do you think it's a weird coincidence or do you think there's a connection?"

The smile fell from Willow's face. "I do. I wouldn't be here if I didn't, but I'll tell you that even if I didn't believe I'd be here to support Bailey and Peyton anyway. We're attached in some strange way by the universe and that's something that I simply cannot turn my back on. No matter what happens I'll be right here with them to help."

Bailey's eyes were bright with tears. "I feel the same way. I know I wanted to run away when we first met but I don't feel like that now. You're stuck with me."

Willow's mouth fell open in mock horror. "Oh, the tragedy! I'll find a way to endure. Seriously, we found each other for a reason. Whether or not we find what we're looking for here, well, we may never find the truth. But that doesn't mean we walk away from each other. You're stuck with me too, honey. Get used to being friends with the town harlot. I hope you like being gossiped about."

"I think we should give them something to talk about."

Chase looked up and saw Peyton standing there with a gleeful grin on her face.

"Any suggestions?" Willow asked, laughter bubbling up. "Be careful because I just might do whatever your idea is."

Bailey held up her hands in surrender. "Easy there, let's slow down. We have work to do. Once we're done we can go scandalize the pearl-clutching biddies of Midnight Blue Beach. But let's stay focused here."

Peyton waved her phone in the air. "You make a good point so I'll table that discussion for awhile, but just know I have some ideas. What I want to talk about is the conversation I just had with the senator's top aide. The senator is willing to meet with you at eight o'clock tomorrow morning. It has to be then because he's going out of town on a business trip. At first I got a resounding no but then I threw my dad's name around along with Chase's name, and then Frank, Greg, and Alex's name in the pot along with it and suddenly he's available. Can you do it?"

Bailey nodded, her chin lifted in determination. "Wild horses couldn't keep me away. I'll be there."

Peyton's gaze shifted to Chase and he also nodded in the affirmative. Nothing would keep him from this meeting. He wanted to know what Frank, Alex, and Greg were arguing about that night. Was it about Gwen? Could she have been killed because of jealousy? He hadn't wanted to say anything to Bailey or the other women but there was certainly motive there for all three men to want Gwen injured, if not dead.

Not to mention each other.

If they held grudges for fifteen years, that is. Chase wasn't the type but the men might have been.

"I'll be there."

Hopefully Danny would have answers. Chase was getting tired of running laps and getting nowhere. It was time to make some progress for a change.

Chapter Twenty-One

T HE NEXT MORNING at 8:04 Bailey and Chase were ushered into Senator Daniel Ford's palatial office. Danny had stayed in shape and with his expensive suit and haircut might even be called handsome. He sat behind a large, dark oak desk in a room lined with bookshelves, a thick carpet on the floor, and photos of the current and past presidents on the wall. A young woman fluttered around the senator placing a stack of files on his desk along with a cup of coffee.

My tax dollars at work.

Lowering herself into a guest chair, she could smell the power and money of Washington. It was an actual physical awareness that she'd felt practically the moment she stepped off the train this morning. It was an energy that she'd only felt a few times in her life. Once in New York. Once in London. And now here.

Danny Ford didn't waste any time. He smiled that handsome, politician smile that she didn't believe for a second as he shook their hands, telling Bailey how wonderful it was to meet her and how sorry he was for her loss. Frank was a great man and so on. She wasn't sure he was being sincere. If Frank was so wonderful then why hadn't Ford been around all those years?

"It's good to see you, Chase. My assistant told me a little bit about why you're here but I'm not sure that I can help you."

They'd had plenty of time to discuss their strategy on the train and they'd decided the bare truth was the way to go.

Chase sat up straighter in his chair. "You may be the only who can help us, Senator. You and perhaps Guy Eckley."

Ford visibly started. "Guy? You've been in touch with him?"

"Not yet, but we're planning to speak with him. Is that an issue?"

"No." Ford drew out the word, uncertainty in his tone. "It's been years since I've talked to him. Give him my regards."

"We will, Senator. I'm sure he'll be happy to hear about you."

Ford waved off the comment. "What's all this *senator* stuff? Call me Danny. You did before I was elected."

Chase let his gaze wander over their surroundings. "Maybe it's the office and all the trappings. I'm sure you have a busy schedule so I'll get right to it. Our first question is simple. What were Frank, Alex, and Greg arguing about the night Gwen Baxter was murdered?"

Ford's throat worked and he didn't answer right away. "I don't know. I wasn't with them when they fought. By the time they got back to the cabin they were all three pissed and looked like they'd rolled around in the dirt. I think their argument turned physical. But no one wanted to talk about it. Then Frank went down to the river with Gwen, and Alex and Greg had dates too. I went for an ice cream with Lorna and then we went for a swim in the pool. We didn't find out about Gwen until the next morning."

"Did Alex meet up with the swim coach that night?" Bailey asked, watching his reaction closely.

Ford's cheeks turned a ruddy shade and he nodded. "He did. They'd had a thing going all summer but it was casual. It was…what do they call it now? A friends with benefits relationship."

"So she didn't care that he slept with Gwen too?" Chase pressed. "That's very understanding of her."

"She didn't care about him that way." Ford shook his head. "I think it was more the excitement of getting caught that was a bigger turn-on for her than Alex was, to be honest. Hell, for all we know she could have been sleeping with other guys as well. I wouldn't say she had the highest moral fiber."

Bailey bristled at the senator's words. "I don't agree with her decision to sleep with a young man when she was supposed to be an adult and in charge but slut-shaming her is also in poor taste."

Ford raised his hands in surrender. "I meant no disrespect. The fact is I wouldn't say any of us were shining examples of morality. There was a lot of naked, naughty things happening that summer and we were all willing and eager participants. Looking back, I think we were trying to redefine the word hedonist to our own specifications."

Relaxing back in her chair, Bailey let out a slow breath. "I'm sorry I jumped to conclusions. This entire situation—"

"Say no more," Ford interrupted, shaking his head. "I can only imagine what you must be going through."

Bailey leaned forward, placing her hands on the edge of the oak desk, the wood smooth and cool under her palms. "When did Frank become a member of the Evandria Council?"

She didn't bother asking *if*. It was only a question of *when*.

Reaching to loosen his tie, Ford cleared his throat several times. "You don't become a member. It's by invitation only and Frank was invited when we all were. On our eighteenth birthday."

"Does everyone accept?" Chase asked. "What is the criteria for an invitation?"

Ford smiled at the questions. "I've never known anyone to decline. As for what the criteria is, I have no idea but a strong drive to make the world a better place is certainly part of it."

"And Frank had that?" Bailey questioned, not recognizing her late husband as someone who had that inclination. He hadn't been involved in politics or any charitable organizations in the years she'd known him.

"He did." Ford nodded vigorously. "A strong sense of right and wrong along with a desire to see social justice in our time. I was always surprised he didn't run for office. He would have made an excellent politician and with his family backing him...well, the sky would have been the limit. He could have ended up on the Supreme Court."

Except that Frank hated law school and had complained about it often.

"Social justice? What does that mean exactly?"

She'd heard the phrase several times in conjunction with the Council but she wasn't sure what they meant by it.

The senator's expression grew sober, lines appearing in his forehead. "People don't know where their next meal is coming from. They can't find good jobs and the cost of everything goes up every day. People are working harder and getting further behind. We want to change that."

It sounded great. "Just how are you doing that?"

Ford smiled and slapped the desk in excitement. "I'm glad you asked that. Outreach programs to disenfranchised youth. Food banks and programs that help working parents. Groups that assist abused women with finding a job and a place to live. I can't begin to tell you the satisfaction I feel when I see a success story. It's life changing not just for them, but for me as well. It's why I do what I do."

"It sounds wonderful. But I have to admit I never saw Frank involved in any of this."

It was Ford's turn to be surprised. His brows shot up to his hairline and he scratched his freshly shaved jaw.

"That does surprise me but there's more than one way to support our mission statement. By simply paying his dues, he was helping. Maybe he didn't want to brag to you about his philanthropic endeavors."

"Possibly." The subject of the Evandria Council had been beaten to death and frankly, it didn't seem to be a factor in Gwen's murder, nor Frank's. Time to change the subject. "Senator...was Frank serious about Gwen? Enough to be upset if she slept with another boy?"

His face went pale and he swallowed hard before speaking. "What you're really asking is if Frank was jealous enough to kill Gwen. Well, the answer is an unequivocal no. They were having fun but he wasn't in love with her or her with him. But even if he had been, she left him at the door of our cabin very much alive. He was with us all night. End of story."

"You saw Gwen then?" Chase jumped on that statement. "You saw her right before she was murdered?"

"I didn't actually see her but I heard her outside the door. They were saying goodnight and she was heading to her cabin."

"It could have been someone else's voice."

"It could have but it wasn't," Ford countered. "I know because Guy and I razzed Frank about what he and Gwen had been up to. If it had been another girl he would have said so. It was Gwen. I'm sure of it."

"You didn't tell the police that. Why?" Bailey queried.

Ford shrugged carelessly. "I'm sure that I did. I answered what they asked me and then my parents came to get me and Guy that afternoon. I never talked to anyone after that but I'm sure I told them."

That little tidbit never made it into the case file. Interesting.

Chase was punching something into his phone. "When did Alex and Greg come back?"

"I'm not sure. Maybe around two. I fell asleep and only woke up for a moment when they came in."

"Did they come back together or separately?"

Ford rubbed the back of his neck and sighed. "Jesus, Chase, that was twenty years ago. I don't really recall but I think it was at the same time. I don't think I woke up twice but hell, I might have. I'm not sure."

"I'm just trying to get all the facts straight."

"That's good. Now I've been very cooperative but I want some cooperation in return. My assistant said that you were looking into a possible connection between Frank's death and Gwen's. I was going to ask you when you sat down but we got off track with talk of Guy. Just what is this supposed connection?"

Chase flexed his fingers and weighed his words. "Gwen was murdered on July twenty-first."

"And? Does that have some significance?"

"My husband was also killed on July twenty-first. Fifteen years later," Bailey piped up. "A strange coincidence."

Ford's eyes narrowed as he contemplated their revelation. "It is a coincidence and a weird one, I'll give you that, but I doubt there's anything nefarious going on here. I doubt there's any connection. It's a—"

"Fluke," Bailey finished his sentence. She knew exactly how it was going to end before he'd said anything. "Yes, you could make that argument except for one thing."

"And that is?"

It appeared that Senator Ford was losing his patience. His fingers drummed on the surface of his desk rather loudly.

"Greg Nelson and Alex Vaughn also died on exactly the same day," she said, schooling her own features carefully. "That's some coincidence, huh?"

Looking like the breath had been knocked out him Ford sat back in his chair, his skin pasty and green-tinged. He looked as if he might be physically ill.

"Are you alright, Danny?" Chase stood and reached across the desk, placing his hand on Ford's shoulder. "Do you want a glass of water or something?"

"No. No... I'm okay. I'm fine." Clearly he wasn't, though. Sweat had popped out on his forehead and his breathing was labored, his voice hoarse. "I'm just shocked, that's all. Alex and

Greg are gone too? Jesus H. Christ. I had no idea."

"You and Guy are the only ones left," Chase replied quietly. "Are you sure I can't get you a glass of water? You don't look well."

Bailey didn't imagine the sheen of moisture in the senator's eyes. No matter how the men had drifted apart in the intervening years, he was still deeply affected by the information. "I'll be fine. The news was just...dammit, how did they go? Were they...murdered as well?"

Bailey wasn't sure how to answer that question. A few days ago she would have said no but now she wasn't so sure. It was better to simply give facts not opinions or conjecture.

"Frank died in a diving accident. Alex in a car wreck, and Greg with an allergic reaction."

Shaking his head, Ford pulled a handkerchief from his pocket and mopped at his brow but his color was coming back. "Jesus, that's terrible."

Chase had moved to stand by the windows looking out on the green lawns. "It is, but all of them dying on the exact same day is a little strange, don't you agree? And on July twenty-first, just like Gwen. I'm not sure we can call that a coincidence anymore, Danny."

"What else could it be?"

"That's what we intend to find out," Chase said, turning back to his friend. "If there's any connection we'll find it. Bailey and the other wives deserve to know what happened to their husbands and Gwen deserves to rest in peace."

Tucking the handkerchief back into his pocket, Ford seemed to have gathered his emotions and was looking much more in control. "Just what do you think you'll find after all these years? It's been so long, Chase. Does it really matter anymore? We've all moved on with our life." The senator nodded to Bailey. "Forgive me, but I have to say I don't think this is a healthy quest for you, Mrs. Scott. My mother always said to keep looking toward the future and she was usually right."

Bailey and Chase exchanged a glance before he spoke up.

"It matters a hell of a lot, Danny. We want the truth. Whatever it may be."

"I can't encourage this."

"I'm not asking for your permission, Senator," Bailey said quietly. "Or your approval. I want the truth about my husband's death. My friends want to know what happened to their husbands as well. I think we're entitled to that."

"Your friends?" Ford asked sharply. "Alex and Greg's wives are a part of this too?"

"Yes, they're my friends and we're supporting each other through this time."

It felt good to call Willow and Peyton her friends. They would be there for each other no matter how difficult and ugly this became.

The senator stood, indicating the meeting was over. "Please give my condolences to your friends. I'm sorry I didn't realize Greg and Alex had passed away. I'm sorry I couldn't help you more but as you can see I know very little about the situation."

Bailey stood, gathering her handbag as Chase moved to stand next to her. They headed for the door but just before they exited, Chase paused and turned to Ford.

"Just one more question, Danny. Who all had Gwen slept

with that summer?"

The man flushed and shifted on his feet. "Lots of guys, Chase. Gwen was sowing some wild oats that summer. It was like she had something to prove. She was wild and almost uncontrollable."

"That isn't an answer."

Ford sighed and stuck his hands in his pockets. "Frank, Alex, Greg, Guy…"

"Anyone else?"

The senator looked down at the floor and Bailey instantly knew there was one more person.

"Me." He looked up, his expression agonized. "I slept with Gwen, okay?"

Chapter Twenty-Two

BAILEY'S PHONE WAS going off as they entered Chase's front door. She moved the bag of takeout food to her other arm so she could answer but Chase smoothly lifted it from her hands despite the fact that his own were filled with groceries they'd purchased on the way here.

She'd promised to bake something for him.

"Peyton, how's New York?"

Chase disappeared into the kitchen and Bailey fell back into the soft couch, her feet aching from all the walking they'd done that day. She shouldn't have worn these heels but they went so well with her dress. She'd wanted to look good for their meeting with the senator.

"It's good. Crowded and energized, as usual. We're going to get some dinner in a little while but I wanted to touch base with you. Did you meet with Daniel Ford?"

"We did but he swears he doesn't know what Frank, Alex, and Greg were arguing about that night, nor did he know that they were dead. He seemed extremely shook up about that, more so than the discussion about Gwen. I guess they were good friends although he said they drifted apart, which seems strange to me. He also said they joined the Evandria Council when they were eighteen. He said you need an invitation. I'm going to go out on a limb here and say that there probably isn't an application process."

"I bet there's an initiation process though," Peyton laughed. "Don't most of these secret groups have some sort of ceremony along with funny hats?"

Frank had never worn a hat in all the time she'd known him. Not even a baseball cap when it was sunny.

"Did Greg have a funny hat?"

"Not that I know of but it's a secret, remember?"

Not likely that she'd forget. How many other secrets did Frank have?

"Did you speak with Guy Eckley yet?"

"That's one of the reasons I'm calling. He's not here."

Bailey levered up from the comfortable sofa to head into the kitchen where Chase was putting away the groceries and delicious smells were wafting from the take out bag. "Ellis's information was incorrect?"

"Kind of. Eckley did live at that address at one time. We talked to a former neighbor. But he moved up to Vermont a few years ago. He said he wanted to get away from the city and get some peace and quiet."

Bailey reached for a pen and scribbled a note to Chase before pushing it his way. He looked at it and frowned before writing something back.

I'll talk to Ellis. He'll get the new address.

"Chase will have Ellis find Eckley's whereabouts, Peyton. In the meantime, are you headed back here?"

"Actually he doesn't need to bother. The neighbor had the forwarding address and often sends a piece or two of mail up there." Peyton rattled it off while Bailey took notes. "Ellis also called us today with the address of the swim coach. It turns out she's right here in the city so we thought we'd stop in and talk to her tomorrow since we're already here."

"That makes sense. Maybe Chase and I can head to Vermont in the morning while you speak with the swim coach."

Chase slipped the eggs and milk into the refrigerator. "We can do that. I haven't been up there in years. It will be nice and cool, I bet."

"It sounds like a plan." Bailey could hear Peyton's indrawn breath even through the phone. "By the way, what is it with Chase's friend Ellis? What's his deal?"

"I've only met him briefly so I'm not sure what you're talking about." Bailey raised her eyebrows at Chase, lifting the phone slightly from her ear so he could listen in. "Did Ellis do something to make you upset?"

Chase leaned forward, shaking his head, a smile playing on his lips. He didn't seem shocked that the subject was being brought up.

"Not really." Peyton paused as if collecting her thoughts. "He's just...different. I'm not sure how to describe him really. Okay, actually I do know how to describe him but I didn't want to. He's abrupt, rude, and fucking condescending. I think he thinks I have the intelligence of a bag of hammers. He acted all sweet but then he kept asking if he needed to repeat anything. Asshole."

Throwing back his head, Chase howled with laughter. "That sounds like Ellis. It's not personal, Peyton. He thinks everyone is an idiot and he doesn't mean to come off that way. Once you get to know him he's absolutely the most patient and loyal guy you'd ever hope to find."

"So is a cocker spaniel," Peyton said dryly. "He thinks I'm stupid, Chase. Does he have a low opinion of women or something?"

"Not in the least. He reveres his mother and sisters. It's just his way of dealing with people. He's not exactly an extrovert with a personality-plus. He works alone and doesn't cooperate well with others but I swear that he's a great guy. He'd take a bullet for you."

"Let's hope that doesn't get tested," Peyton muttered. "It's no skin off of my nose anyway. From now on Willow is going to deal with him. She says she'll have him eating out of the palm of her hand in no time."

Of that, Bailey had no doubt.

They talked some more and then promised to call tomorrow when they had more news. Bailey was anxious to talk to Guy Eckley and she also wanted to hear what the swim coach had to say. After all, she'd been a suspect at one point. By the time they ended the call Chase had filled two plates with steaming lasagna and garlic bread.

"Your friend Ellis is a real piece of work."

Chase laughed and pulled out her chair, his fingertips briefly brushing her arm as he rounded the table to his own seat. "You don't know the half of it. He's an ornery son of a bitch but he really is a great detective. And a good friend too."

At this point, they couldn't have too many of those. They needed every one of them they could get.

Chapter Twenty-Three

"**I**S IT DONE yet?"

Bailey sighed and rolled her eyes as Chase paced around her, practically wearing a hole in the kitchen tile. She was putting the finishing touches on a salted caramel cheesecake that she was sure wouldn't survive the night despite the big meal they'd eaten not that long ago.

"Almost." She sprinkled the shaved salt on the top of the caramel and stepped back with a happy smile. "All done. This is one of my favorite recipes. Classic yet modern at the same time. You were a good helper too."

She'd given him a few small jobs when he'd offered to assist. "Can we eat it now or do we have to stand here some more and admire it? I can take a picture with my phone."

Smacking him on the arm, she gave him a mean look. "Of course we can eat it. I was simply taking a moment to appreciate the result of our hard work. Get the plates and I'll get the forks."

Two plates appeared quicker than lightning and she cut two pieces — a small one for her as she was still full, and a larger one for him. He could go back for seconds and thirds if he was still hungry. She didn't dig into hers immediately, preferring to watch him take his first bite. His eyes closed and his face went slack as a groan of delight was torn from his lips.

"Heaven on a plate."

Chase wore a big grin as he tore into the cheesecake as if he hadn't eaten in days instead of a few hours.

"Slow down. I don't want you to get sick. There's plenty more if that's not enough. I made this for you."

She took a bite of her own and enjoyed the delicate balance of sweet and salty on her tongue. Chocolate was her absolute favorite but every now and then she wanted something a little different. This fit the bill perfectly.

Scraping his plate with his fork, he patted his stomach. "Damn, that was good. I am going to have another slice. You're one hell of a baker. Your business must be booming."

"We do fine." She cut him another slice just as large as the last one. "And thank you. It's nice to have my baking appreciated so enthusiastically."

Chase shoveled another bite into his mouth, although slower than the first piece. "You can bake for me anytime."

"Good to know. Now what time are you picking me up in the morning?"

"Early again. Our flight leaves at eight-thirty so we'll need to be there a few hours early to get through security."

"Hurry up and wait. Maybe I should have asked Willow to send the jet for us."

Chase laughed and popped the last bite into his mouth. "Is that how you usually fly?"

He had a strange idea of what her life was like and it was

time to set him straight. "Absolutely not. I admit I've been on a private jet before but it was hardly the norm for me. Honestly, the trappings of high society make me a little nervous at times. I can navigate my way around the country club or a cocktail party but I'm equally as comfortable with a few friends at a dive bar. Money's never been a big thing in my life although Frank left me plenty of it."

He picked up both plates and set them in the sink. "I'm glad to hear that. I would never want to get involved with a woman who likes money more than me."

Jerking her gaze away, she stared at the wine glass still in her hand as if it held the secrets of the universe. Sadly it didn't. "Involved? Is that what we are? What happened to giving me time and space?"

He was standing too close to her. Much too close. She could feel his warm breath on her cheek and the heat from his body made her want to run her hands down his torso. She finally looked up at him from under her lashes only to find his bright blue eyes staring intently at her. Not in an unkind way. Far from it. There was admiration and more than a hint of desire. She could have him here and now if she wanted to. It wasn't vanity that told her that but the way he touched her, spoke to her, gazed at her when he thought she wasn't looking. She'd ignored it all day; after all, they'd had important business to attend to. But now that they were here alone...

Did she want him tonight?

More than a little attracted to him, she was scared of her own emotions. She'd thought at first they might have something casual. A fling but clearly she was feeling too much for him to sleep with him and walk away when this was all over. If she was going to do this she had to be all in.

All in was scary.

"Okay, I admit I'm not giving you much space," Chase chuckled, his chest rumbling with the sound. "Physical, that is. But I am giving you time. You can have all the time you want. But…"

"But?" she prompted as she turned on the island stool to face him more fully, searching his features for a clue as to what he expected of her. Was he pressing for them to make love? Could she resist him if that was the case? Doubtful. She wanted him and it had been too long since a man had made his intentions known.

His fingers found her chin, tilting her face up so she was looking up into his eyes. The mere touch of his skin against hers sent a quiver through her body and a sigh escaped from her lips. It felt good to be desired, wanted. For a moment she allowed herself to revel in it. Later she'd be more rational and practical.

"But does that mean we can't kiss? I've wanted to hold you in my arms all day and taste that sweet mouth. I bet you taste better than the cheesecake. Leaving me wanting like this would be downright cruel, Bailey."

Staring at his well-shaped lips, she almost swooned at his soft tone and sweet words. She wanted to kiss him so damn badly and that little voice inside of her head that warned her when things were a bad idea was nowhere to be found. That bitch was never around when Bailey needed her and now she'd bailed again.

"Don't you think you're being overly dramatic?" Bailey

teased. "It would be just a kiss."

Chase shook his head as his strong arms lifted her from the stool and onto the island so they were almost at eye level. "Kissing you could never be described as just anything. Are you going to take pity on me? Just one."

What would it hurt? It wasn't like she didn't want this.

"Just one," she whispered, wrapping her arms around his neck and pulling him down. "But I'm not ready—"

His fingers pressed against her mouth. "I know that and I meant it last night when I said I wouldn't push. I just really want to kiss you. No further. Not unless you ask me to."

She didn't bother to reply, instead pressing her lips to his in a kiss that took her breath away. They started out slow and tender, his tongue exploring her mouth as if he had all day and night. Then his arms tightened around her body and the kiss deepened into something far more. It was a promise of much more to come; maybe not tonight, but eventually and soon. By the time he lifted his head she was ready to beg him to do more. Asking didn't even begin to cover the need she felt.

A bar of arousal had taken up residence in her abdomen and a shiver of pleasure ran down to her toes as his lips explored her jaw and neck, coming to rest right at the spot where her pulse beat frantically. His tongue snaked out and licked at her collarbone and then nipped at the sensitive flesh, causing a low moan to tear from somewhere deep inside of her.

So it was a shock when she felt him move away, his heat suddenly gone, leaving her cold and bereft. She reached for him again and he caught up her wrists in his hands, turning them to place a soft kiss on each palm.

"I made you a promise and I keep my word, Bailey. You're in charge here and you make the rules. We do this on your timetable. Just don't ask me not to touch you every now and then. I need to kiss and hold you. I need to tell you how goddamn beautiful you are, not just right now but every moment of every day."

Chase certainly was good for her ego. Her late husband hadn't been effusive with the compliments, although she'd known he thought she was attractive. But she was shallow enough to enjoy the warm rush in her heart when he complimented her. She wanted to say something in return but she didn't know what.

You make me feel safe.

You make me feel special.

You're amazingly handsome.

And sexy.

You're the best kisser. Ever.

You treat me like I matter.

It all sounded stupid and rather like a teenager with her first crush so she didn't say anything at all, simply jerking him back to her and fusing their lips together. There was no tentative exploring this time. Just passion and carnal lust. Heat swept through her veins like lava from a volcano, but instead of running from this feeling she welcomed it. No more numbness. She felt incredibly alive. It was terrifying and wonderful all at the same time.

She was sucking oxygen into her starved lungs when they finally pulled apart. She raised her fingers to her lips, fully expecting them to be singed off. Surprisingly they were intact, albeit slightly swollen from their efforts.

"You have lethal lips, lady. You ought to be outlawed in all fifty states."

She loved this playful side to him. Laughter wasn't something she was used to at moments such as these. "How do you know I'm not?"

He dropped a kiss on top of her head but his arms holding her closely didn't budge an inch.

"I'll take my chances. You're worth it."

Those words sobered her up quickly. Was she worth it? She had a mountain of baggage she was dragging behind her and he did too, but not nearly as much. She wanted to move forward but the past kept beckoning to her, pulling her back.

Would she ever truly be free?

"I'm not so sure about that."

"I am, so you'll have to trust me."

Which seemed to suggest he dated quite a bit, which was a little intimidating. "Have you dated a lot of women since your divorce?"

She wasn't jealous. She was simply curious. Just curious.

"How do you define a lot?"

She pushed at his shoulder and groaned. "Really? We're going to play those games? More than two and less than a hundred. How does that sound?"

"Definitely more than two and well under a hundred." He tugged her back into his arms and leaned down to briefly kiss her lips. "I didn't keep count but it doesn't take that many females to realize that finding someone that you're attracted to and can have fun with isn't easy. Add in the great kisses and the cheesecake and I'm sold."

"I think you might like my cheesecake more than the kisses."

"Not in this lifetime. I'd give up the cheesecake if I had to."

"What will happen when all of this is over? I'll go back to my home and you'll stay here. Are you willing to do the long distance thing?"

He led her back into the living room where they could both relax on the couch, snuggled together. "Considering that less than twenty-four hours ago you were telling me this relationship was a no-go I think we're making progress. You're actually talking about a future."

Scowling, she tapped his nose. "Don't think I didn't notice your non-answer, because I did."

"I didn't answer because I don't have an answer except that I'm willing to do all sorts of things for the right woman. Didn't you say that you had a manager to run your bakery? Williamsburg is a lovely place to live."

He was suggesting she move? For someone she'd just met?

"First off, I do have a manager and she's amazing but I'm not sure I'm ready to pull up stakes and start all over again in a new city for a man I've known for a week. Call me crazy…"

He shook his head and smiled. "I meant eventually, not right away. I'm not crazy either. But I have a very flexible schedule with the work I do so I can travel down there quite a bit. You never know, you might get tired of me being around so much."

They'd spent practically every waking moment with each other these last few days and she wasn't sick of him yet. In fact, she enjoyed his company immensely. They talked about more than just the case. They talked about politics, sports, books, movies, and whether dark chocolate was better than milk chocolate.

It totally was.

"I think the important thing is that we're willing to make compromises for each other," Chase said. "That's how I always pictured how it should be. Two people working as a team, compromising and even sacrificing for each other."

That's what she'd hoped for as well but it wasn't to be. Sadly not with Frank.

"I sacrificed a cheesecake for you, what more do you want from me?"

His expression was perfectly serious when he answered. "Red velvet cake. That's all I'll ask for right now."

That was a request she could handle.

Chapter Twenty-Four

GUY ECKLEY'S HOME caught Chase by surprise. He'd remembered Eckley as a spoiled rich kid who sneered and smirked his way through camp, barely cognizant of anything but his own selfish wants. Chase hadn't been all that excited about visiting him, to be honest, but this was completely unexpected.

"What a lovely little farm. Is that sheep back there?"

Chase squinted into the distance and shook his head. "I think it's alpaca. I never thought to see the day that Guy Eckley raised alpaca. Or any animal, to be honest. Last I heard he planned to be an investment banker."

The two-story white farmhouse was charming and well-cared for, as were the grounds all around. The window boxes had bright pink flowers and the front porch featured two wooden rocking chairs. It looked homey and inviting and not at all like the Guy Eckley Chase had known.

People can change. I have too.

"Maybe he's married and his wife likes alpacas."

That sounded plausible. They parked the car and walked up the stone path to the house where a dog barked in the distance.

A cool breeze blew through the trees, setting off the tinkle of wind chimes. The air had the slight aroma of apple pie and patchouli. A strange combination.

Chase had raised his hand to knock on the door when it flew open, a woman about his own age on the other side. Dark-haired and attractive, the woman wore worn blue jeans, a white blouse, and a welcoming smile.

"Hello, I saw you drive up. How can I help you?"

He and Bailey had already discussed how they were going to handle this meeting. He held out his hand and gave the woman his most charming grin.

"I'm Chase Jennings. I knew Guy years ago when we both attended the same summer camp and I was hoping to talk to him. I apologize for not calling first. I should have, of course. Is he around?"

Her eyes went wide and her smile grew. "A childhood friend of Guy's? How wonderful! Do come in. Guy's in the living room reading. He'll be so thrilled to see an old friend. We don't get many visitors up here. My name is Alice, by the way."

Chase introduced Bailey and they all shook hands before entering into the foyer. The kitchen could be seen straight ahead but to the right appeared to be the living room and Guy, who was peering over his glasses as he stuck a scrap of paper into a book to mark his place. He stood and grinned, his arms spread wide in welcome.

"Chase? Chase Jennings? Holy hell, man, I haven't seen you since we were kids. Come on in. Is this your wife?"

Somehow Chase had stepped into some sort of parallel universe. He hadn't expected much of a welcome, although he hadn't expected hostility either. He wouldn't have allowed Willow and Peyton to try and talk to him if that was the case but this was something completely…bizarre. Guy was acting like they were good old friends when they barely knew each other. Chase hadn't even recognized his photo right away from the memory books. It had taken a few days for him to put names to all the faces.

"Not my wife but a good friend. Let me introduce you to Bailey Scott. I think you knew her husband back in the day. She was married to Frank Scott."

No sense beating around the bush. The plan was to be forthright and honest. It had worked with Danny and hopefully it would work now.

The smile vanished from Guy's face and his shoulders slumped in sadness. Chase thought he could see a sheen of moisture in the man's eyes.

"I heard about his passing. I'm so sorry for your loss. I…I should have been at the funeral but I was kind of tied up with a few things."

Guy scraped his fingers through his hair, his gaze directed anywhere but at Bailey.

"It's fine," she said softly. "It was a small service."

"You should all sit down and catch up," Alice cut in, gesturing to the sofa. "Can I get anyone something to drink?"

Chase and Bailey declined the offer but did settle themselves on the sofa across from Guy. The other man appeared to have recovered from his shock at seeing Bailey, the easy smile back on his face although his eyes still seemed sad. Alice excused herself and headed into the kitchen.

Chase didn't waste time and came right to the point. "Guy, we came here today because we need your help. We were hoping you'd know what Frank, Alex, and Greg were arguing about the night Gwen died. Do you remember? Was it about Gwen?"

Guy's cheeks paled but he shook his head. "It wasn't about Gwen, that much I remember. I'm sure it was just teenage boy stuff. No big deal."

Bailey leaned forward. "There were punches thrown."

The corners of Guy's lips quirked up in a half-smile. "That wasn't all that unusual. We were all wild back then, to be honest. Tempers were quick and fists were quicker. Once we got it out of our systems we were all friends again. No harm done."

"Except that Frank, Alex, and Greg weren't ever friends after that incident," Chase countered. "As far as we can tell they never saw each other again."

"We were all busy with life," Guy replied awkwardly, clearly searching for the right words. "I'm sure they talked to one another, if not regularly then every now and then. They wouldn't just cut each out of their lives. Not them. They were like brothers."

"How did you know about Frank?" Bailey asked. "Did you two keep in touch?"

Guy scratched his head and nodded. "Not often but maybe once a year he'd call. He was a good friend when everyone else turned their backs on me. I heard about his death from my family."

"Alex and Greg too?" Chase queried. "Did they keep in touch?"

"I talked to Alex a couple of times and got a few postcards

from Greg. He was in Europe or something, I think. Haven't heard from them in awhile, actually."

Chase and Bailey exchanged a look. Guy didn't know about them and Chase was going to have to be the bearer of bad news.

"Alex and Greg passed away as well. They're gone."

Blinking and then shaking his head, Guy didn't seem to be comprehending. "What? No, they can't all three be gone. That's crazy."

"They all died on the same day," Bailey replied. "That is crazy, isn't it?"

Now the man was shaking his head, muttering under his breath. "No. No. No."

It was only when they heard the word *Evandria* that Chase interrupted.

"What about the Evandria Council, Guy? Why do you mention them? Tell me what you know about them. Are you a member?"

Leaping to his feet, Guy stood behind his chair, his hands wrung together. Chase's heart accelerated, beating frantically against his ribs. Perhaps they were finally going to learn something that might help instead of spinning their wheels at every turn.

"A member?" Guy laughed but it didn't sound particularly funny. "I used to be a member. But I was blackballed about ten years ago. That's why it was such a big deal for my friends to still talk to me. Everyone else bailed long ago. Frank, Alex, and Greg were the best. Absolutely the best."

Blackballed? What the hell did a person have to do to get thrown out of a secret society?

"What can you tell us about the Evandria Council, Guy? It's been difficult to get any information."

Guy's fingers squeezed the back of the chair, his knuckles white. "I'll tell you anything you want to know."

Chapter Twenty-Five

BAILEY WISHED SHE had taken Alice up on the offer of a beverage right about now. Her mouth was cotton-ball dry and had to remind herself to breathe when she became light-headed. Guy seemed almost too good to be true. He was willing to spill all the secrets?

Chase started off the questions. "According to what we've been told, Evandria is a secret society dedicated to social justice and philanthropic works. Is that true?"

Guy took a deep breath and nodded. "Yes and no. Yes, they do amazing charity work all over the world. They absolutely make a difference in hundreds of thousands of lives and I was proud to be a part of that. But their mission is more than simply social justice, Chase. They want to run the fucking world."

Sucking in a breath, Bailey's pulse jumped at his statement. What had Frank been involved in? "Run the world? What do you mean by that?"

"Exactly what I said in a literal sense. I mean they want to run the world. They want a new world order, to their specifica-tions of course. They've already infiltrated every facet of the government and our financial markets. Every person with power in this country is in some way attached to Evandria. They believe that only they can bring about world peace and prosperity."

"And how do they intend to do that?" Chase asked.

Guy grinned and laughed and Bailey shivered at the sound. It was a little too maniacal and not at all a happy sound. "By controlling everything. Every decision, every natural resource, every political office, every corporation. They feel that only then can they make the societal changes necessary for true equality and freedom."

"I'm afraid to ask what those changes are," Bailey said faintly. "Are they trying to enslave the working class?"

"Not at all." Guy shook his head. "They want the working class to have better lives, but it's the way they've gone about it that makes me wonder. Their intentions are truly good. They want to eradicate hunger, poverty, and war. They dream of a utopian society where everyone can get whatever they need when they need it. They feel they need to grab onto all the world power to make that happen."

Scraping a hand down his face, Chase sighed loudly. "That's an overwhelming mission for one group."

Guy smiled. "One group? They're the most powerful group of people on this blue rock. With each passing day they get closer to their goal."

"And Frank was a part of this?" Bailey asked.

Guy nodded. "Frank was a true believer, incredibly gung-ho back then. So was Greg and to a lesser extent Alex and Danny. I was the one who had doubts. They'd get pissed off at me for asking questions."

Chase also stood and began to pace the small space behind the couch. "Is that what those three argued about the night Gwen was killed?"

Guy crossed his arms over his chest. "I told you I don't know and I really don't. I wasn't there at the time and only heard about it later when they were giving each other the cold shoulder when Frank came back from his date with Gwen."

"What time did Frank come in that night?" Chase asked. "Do you remember? Did you see Gwen?"

"It was not long before midnight maybe, and yeah, I saw Gwen. I had the top bunk near the window and I saw her walk by on the way to her own cabin. I also heard her voice outside when she was saying goodnight to Frank."

She inwardly sighed with relief. That was two people who said Frank had nothing to do with Gwen's death. "And he stayed in the cabin the rest of the night?"

"I'm a light sleeper. If he tried to leave I would have heard him."

Guy was being so forthright Bailey decided to extend a little more trust. "There might be a connection between Gwen's death and that of Frank, Alex, and Greg. The men all died on the same year and the same day, July twenty-first. Gwen also died on the same day, July twenty-first, but fifteen years before. It has to be more than a coincidence."

Rubbing the back of his neck, Guy frowned in thought. "That's...weird. July twenty-first? I can't even imagine... That can't be the case—you must have it wrong."

"We don't," Chase assured him. "Gwen was killed on July twenty-first and all three men also died on that day. We're trying to find a connection and maybe find Gwen's killer while we're at it."

Bailey shifted in her seat. "Was Frank in love with Gwen? Were all the boys? Could they have been jealous of one another? Maybe that's why their friendship ended."

His brows rising, Guy shook his head. "Are you suggesting that one of them...? Jesus, there's no way. My friends would never have done that. They weren't capable."

Chase stopped pacing. "Maybe it was a crime of passion. Maybe one of them was jealous and killed Gwen."

"No way." Guy was adamant. "There's just no way. They were all in the cabin all night. They couldn't have done it. I mean, yeah, they all really liked Gwen and there was a little rivalry going on but they wouldn't murder someone over it. It wasn't that serious."

"So no one left the cabin all night after Frank came back? No one?" Chase insisted.

Scowling, Guy shrugged. "No one. Danny left for a few minutes to take a leak but he wasn't gone long enough to run down to the lake and stab someone and then get back. He was gone two or three minutes. Tops. I'm telling you they didn't do it."

Chase reached down from his spot behind the couch and placed his hand on Bailey's shoulder.

"What about you, Guy? How did you feel about Gwen?"

Throwing up his arms, he groaned in disgust. "I fucked her, okay? Christ, everyone did that summer. She was out of control. If you're going to suspect every guy who crossed the goal line with her then you're going to have a long list of contenders. I don't know what got into her but she was determined to party all summer long. And she wasn't the only one, by the way. Her friends were right there with her. Especially that Taylor. She made the rounds too and don't think Stephen didn't notice. They fought like cats and dogs about her partying."

Taylor and Stephen?

"Taylor dated Gwen's brother Stephen?" Chase asked. "How long had that been going on?"

Guy shrugged. "For a while. They went to school together and he'd given her a necklace on Valentine's Day. I know because she showed it to just about everyone at camp."

Taylor hadn't mentioned it but perhaps she didn't want to admit that she'd cheated on Stephen.

Guy turned away and paced a few steps before turning back to them. "Listen, I know this sounds bad but there is no way I would have fallen for a girl like Gwen back then. I was just a kid and she was too aggressive. She intimidated me, to be truthful. She was so confident and sure of herself. I was envious but I wasn't in love."

There was several long moments of silence before Bailey piped up, anxious to get the conversation back on track.

"So who do you think did kill her?"

"I'll tell you exactly what I told the police that day. Coach Dorrell was pissed about Alex playing around on her with Gwen. I saw her and Alex arguing about it a few days before and the coach was red in the face, poking Alex in the chest. She didn't look happy in the least. Personally, I think she did it. No one would have thought it strange if she was out and about past curfew, plus she was in great shape. Strong. She could have subdued Gwen while she stabbed her, then thrown the knife into the river before getting cleaned up. That's my theory anyway. That woman got away with murder."

With that declaration, Bailey was even more anxious to hear from Willow and Peyton. Hopefully they'd found the woman and had talked to her about that night.

"So you don't think there's any connection between Gwen's death and Frank's," Bailey asked one more time. She couldn't deal with the thought that she'd come here for nothing and would leave with the same.

"I can't think of one but the date thing is strange." Guy looked at Chase. "You don't think we have a serial killer or something from our camp days? Who else has died these last twenty years?"

That was a good question.

Chase shoved his hands in his pockets. "Guy, we appreciate all your help here and how open you've been. I do have one more question and I understand if you don't want to answer. Why were you blackballed from the Council?"

Guy's cheeks turned red and his lips tightened. Whatever memories he had weren't happy ones. "I got hooked on coke and blew through my trust fund. I liked high-priced call girls, expensive suites, fancy liquor, and high-stakes poker. I thought I deserved to live a life of hedonism because of who I was. I was a walking, talking asshole as I'm sure you remember, Chase. I started stealing from my friends and family to support my bad and extravagant habits. Evandria is ruthless when you don't obey the rules. I'd betrayed my brothers and sisters. When I was finally dragged before the Council I didn't have much to say in my defense except that I was addicted and it wasn't my fault. They voted me out but paid for my rehab. I was shunned by pretty much everyone but Frank, Alex, and Greg. Even Danny never spoke to me again after that. Now I live here quietly with Alice and we live on my yearly allowance from the family. I prefer this life, to be honest. I'm surprised I didn't end up dead in some hotel room with a couple of hookers and a needle in my arm."

"I'm sorry, man. I'm sorry I had to ask."

Guy shrugged, an abashed look on his face. "It was my own fault. I was a spoiled shit. Some lessons have to be learned up close and personal, you know?"

Bailey gathered her purse and stood. "They can do that? The Council? That seems harsh."

"They're ruthless. I was a detriment to what they were trying to build. I can't complain. I knew the rules and I broke them. It's better this way."

Had Frank lived under those same rules? Guy had described him as a believer, which didn't ring true. She'd never seen Frank all that passionate about anything in the years she'd been with him. Had he strayed from the Council? Was it because of her? Is that why he'd never told her or tried to get her to join?

They said their thankyous and goodbyes before climbing into the rental car and heading back to the airport. They had a flight to catch in only a few hours. Thank goodness they had been able to connect with Guy right away.

Bailey pulled her cell phone from her purse to check for messages from Willow or Peyton. She'd turned it off while visiting Guy because she didn't want it to interrupt and now the phone was beeping and chiming as each new text and email came in.

"Looks like you're popular today. Are any one of those from the ladies?"

Bailey scrolled through her phone. "I hope so. Damn, there's a dozen messages here from them. Let me open the first one."

The silence stretched as Chase waited for her to say something and she read and re-read the text from Peyton before reading each of the other ones, the tone becoming more and more frantic. This wasn't some joke the girls were playing on her.

"What do they say?" Chase prompted when she didn't speak. "Did they get to see Martina Dorrell? What did she say?"

Tightening her fingers around her cell, Bailey took a deep cleansing breath. Things had become exponentially more complicated as of that moment.

"She didn't say anything. She's dead. They found her body."

Chapter Twenty-Six

A few hours earlier...

WILLOW CHECKED HER phone for the third time as she and Peyton walked down the busy New York City street. That asshole Ellis had to have given them the wrong address. There was no exclusive fitness center anywhere on this block.

"If I ever meet that detective I'm going to string him up by his balls," drawled Peyton who was walking in high heels. She was sensitive about her height and wore them pretty much everywhere except the beach and bed. "He sent us on a wild goose chase. We don't have time for this and my feet are killing me."

There were a few storefronts but several of the buildings appeared to be abandoned. It was no wonder these businesses closed down if the crappy signage was any indication of how they ran things.

Willow stopped and stared at a boarded-up window. "Maybe we should call Chase—"

"There!" Peyton crowed, pointing down the block where they'd been originally. "Someone just went inside that rickety door and they were wearing workout gear."

Willow groaned at her own naïveté. "We've been living in Florida too long. This is how exclusive clubs work here. It looks like shit on the outside and a million dollars on the inside. Let's go."

Payton laughed and tucked her own phone back into her purse. She had been ready to rip Ellis Hunter a new asshole. "We have lived there too long. It's the same way in some of the other cities I've visited."

Luckily, the door wasn't locked although the stairs looked a bit dodgy. Willow breathed an internal sigh of relief when they reached the second floor – a door to her left and a door to her right. Both unmarked.

"Do you feel lucky?" Peyton muttered under her breath, her gaze drifting back and forth. "What is your intuition telling you?"

"You're the one that believes in psychics. You tell me."

Frowning, Peyton tapped her foot as she weighed her options. "I didn't say I believed in psychics. I mean, I do believe in them but I think real ones are extremely rare. Most are just con artists."

Willow had dated more than her share of those. "So which way is your psychic energy leading us? Right or left?"

Straightening, Peyton pointed left. "This way."

Willow reached for the door handle. "Let's see if you're right. If you are, I'll buy dinner and dessert anywhere in the city that you want. Drinks too."

It looked like Willow would be picking up the check tonight. They stepped into a small room with a dark granite counter at the far end. Comfortable chairs were positioned up against the wall and their shoes sunk into the deep carpeting that covered the floors. Even the air smelled expensive, a subtle perfume.

Vanilla. Espresso. Leather.

Peyton smiled at the skinny woman behind the counter. "Hello. I'm hoping you can direct us to Martina Dorrell."

The woman blinked a few times but didn't throw them out immediately. It was a good sign. Peyton was good at charming people. She looked harmless and it lulled them into a false sense of security. "Do you have your membership cards?"

Another disarming smile from Peyton. "We're not members. We're old friends of Martina's and we're in the city to surprise her. Please don't ruin it. We won't take much of her time, I promise. We just want to see her and then invite her out for some cocktails later tonight. A celebration."

Apparently the receptionist liked surprises because a smile lit up her face and she nodded in agreement eagerly. "She loves surprises. If you go through that door and down the hall, take the stairs at the end up to the third floor. She's in workout room K." The woman checked the clock on the wall. "She and her client should have just finished and she doesn't have another for thirty minutes. Have fun!"

Muttering their thanks, they quickly went through the far door and down the hall, finding the stairs with no problem. Loud music pulsed from a few of the closed doors with small signs indicating that a session was in progress.

"I know I shouldn't encourage you as a liar but damn, you are good. I think you could talk your way into any venue you wanted, maybe even the White House. Or a Kenny Chesney concert."

Peyton waggled her eyebrows. "I feel like a spy from the movies. Call me Mata Hari. I'll tell you a few stories over dinner. The one you're paying for."

Willow was feeling adventurous herself which wasn't a common occurrence for her. She took chances but they were carefully calculated and always well-thought out. This little charade was completely off the cuff.

On the third floor, there was only one door on each side – J and K. J was closed and no noise was coming from the room but K's door was slightly ajar, a pop tune from the 80s drifting into the hall.

"Good, she's done with her client," Willow said as she knocked on the door. "Martina? Can we come in and talk to you for a moment? We only want a few minutes."

There was no answer so Peyton pushed open the door a little more and called out. "Ms. Dorrell, I'm Peyton Nelson and this is Willow Vaughn. We just want to talk to you. Is that okay? Martina?"

Not a sound but the music. "Maybe she's in the ladies room or something," Willow shrugged. "Do you think we should go in and wait?"

Willow didn't like to barge in where she wasn't wanted but turning around and walking back to the receptionist wasn't an option either. They couldn't meet up with Martina in front of anyone. They'd know that Willow and Peyton had lied to gain entry.

"I say we go in. We don't want to miss her by walking around and trying to find her. The woman up front said she had another client in thirty minutes so she's bound to come back here at some point."

That was a good enough argument for Willow. She pushed the door open wide and they stepped into the room, the music much louder now. The beat pulsed beneath her feet as her gaze swept the area. Large red mat in the middle. To her right were a few cardio machines and some aerobic steps in a stack. Willow remembered taking those classes quite well. Good exercise and a lot of fun.

It was Peyton's gasp that snapped Willow's attention from the treadmills and to the other side of the room where a rack with hand weights stood along with a few heavy balls and a couple of jump ropes hanging from the walls.

Plus a body.

Distracted with her own thoughts, Willow had almost missed her. The figure was wearing a red track suit and against the red mat she hadn't stood out. Her body was curled up in a fetal position and crimson blood pooled underneath the head, the hair tangled and matted. The strong smell of metal turned Willow's stomach and she had to swallow the acid that had gathered in the back of her throat.

"Jesus, Mary, and Joseph," Willow breathed, her chest tightening painfully. "Is that...?"

"I think so," Peyton said faintly, her hand pressed to her mouth as if she might be throw up. "Oh God, we should call 911."

Willow had already pulled out her phone. "Go get that woman at the front desk. I'll call 911. Then we need to call Bailey and Chase right away."

Someone else was dead or close to it.

It wasn't even July twenty-first yet.

THE NEXT TWELVE hours seemed to move in slow motion for Bailey as she struggled to come to grips with what had happened. That blessed numbness she had come to know and love was nowhere to be found and she'd had to deal with the maelstrom of emotions that had been evoked by Willow's simple statement.

The swim coach is dead. She was shot in the back of the head.

Another casualty of…what exactly? Bailey didn't know but she was more determined than ever to find out. The universe was fucking with her again but she wasn't about to back down. This wasn't some freaky coincidence. This was murder.

Luckily, her innate practicality came to the forefront when she desperately needed it. She and Chase calmly decided it would be better to meet Willow and Peyton back in Williamsburg rather than in New York City. The two women had spent all evening and most of the night at the police station giving their statements over and over but were finally allowed to leave, mostly due to the fact that the estimated time of death was an hour before they'd arrived but also because the tests for gunpowder residue came up negative. They'd been ruled out as suspects but the police said they might be in touch at a later date and time if they had more questions.

Or their quick release might have had something to do with the high-priced attorneys that Peyton and Willow had phoned when it looked like the police wanted to pin the murder on them. The ladies had magically been allowed to leave less than thirty minutes later. Bailey didn't much care of the reason as long as they were back together again. They had a great deal to talk about and they needed to regroup. The case was getting away from them.

Fiddling with her fork at the table, Bailey sat up as straight as she could in her chair to see the front entrance of the hotel. They were all meeting for a late breakfast and she was getting anxious. Willow and Peyton should have been there fifteen minutes ago.

"They'll be here." Chase placed his hand over hers and squeezed reassuringly. "They sent a text when they landed. They're probably caught in traffic."

Plus exhausted. Bailey doubted that her friends had caught much sleep on the flight back and after they ate would probably want to crawl into bed and get some much needed rest.

"I just— I just can't believe that poor woman is dead. You know it has to have something to do with Gwen and Frank. It can't be an isolated incident."

Chase's expression was more closed than she'd ever seen it. Since she'd given him the news, he'd been a rock of support but he'd also been quiet, keeping his own emotions under wraps. Funny how she'd only known him a short time but already she needed to speak honestly with him and share her thoughts and fears. She wanted him to feel the same way and she couldn't deny that it stung that he didn't. He didn't trust her with what was going on inside of him.

"It could be," Chase said, his words carefully measured and his tone calm. "It might simply be a—"

"Coincidence," she finished for him. "Do you really think

that? Because I don't. It may not be July twenty-first, but come on… What are the chances?"

His expression was far away and she didn't know how to bring him back to where she was. He was gone to another place and time and nothing she said seemed to snap him back to awareness.

"Remote, I'll grant you that. We need to calm down and look at things from a purely intellectual level. We're letting our emotions get ahead of us."

He wasn't, so he must be referring to her. She hadn't realized he turned into a robot when the shit got real.

"Excuse me for having feelings," she snapped, her fingers tightening on the edge of the table until her knuckles turned white. "Just call me the hysterical female and be done with it."

His gaze rounded on her and she had to squirm in her seat as it seemed to bore a hole right through her. It was as if he could see everything she was thinking and feeling.

"You're hardly hysterical, Bailey. In fact, you've been quite calm and logical. But I think that perhaps your imagination is taking you to places that it ought not to. Not yet, anyway. The leap you've taken is a big one."

"What leap is that?"

He lifted her hand and kissed her palm, his expression softening. "You know what I'm talking about."

She sighed and let her head fall back, her eyes closed.

"What if the person who killed Gwen killed that poor woman? What if they killed Frank, Alex, and Greg too? Who else will they kill to cover their tracks?"

She'd said it out loud and a shudder ran down her spine.

She'd known all along that there was a killer out there but somehow she hadn't thought that they would be willing to kill more. Others. But Guy's serial killer theory was looking like a definitely possibility; however, he'd been wrong about his number one suspect.

"It's a possibility, I won't deny it but we have to move slowly here. If we go off half-cocked it might send us in a completely wrong direction. We're looking for a connection between Gwen and Frank's deaths and I'd like to remind you that we still don't have any evidence that his or the other men's deaths are anything but an accident."

"You don't believe that. You know they can't be."

He scraped his fingers through his hair. "I don't know what I think anymore. I'm so damn confused and this case is fucking with my head. We need to get some food in our stomachs and then sit down, preferably with Ellis who is a real detective, and try and lay this all out. We need a new plan of action because frankly I don't know what to do now."

Bailey sipped her glass of water, the cool liquid sliding down her throat and calming her jangled nerves. Sadly, it was too early in the day for a stiff shot of whiskey. That would have hit the spot.

"What do you think about the Evandria Council? Is it just a coincidence that they were all members as well? Guy said they were ruthless. Could they be capable of murder?"

Lips twisted, Chase looked less than enthused about her theory. "Guy is also a disgruntled ex-member with a history of substance abuse. I'm not sure we can count on everything he told us being true. Besides, he didn't seem to think they were involved in any way and you can tell he doesn't like them at all. Also, I doubt the swim coach was a member. The yearly fees are in the seven-figure range and I don't think personal trainers make that much but I could be wrong."

"You ask everyone we talk to about Evandria though," she argued. "If you don't think they have anything to do with this, why do you keep bringing it up then?"

"Is that why you're suspecting them? Because of me?" Chase groaned and leaned down to drop a kiss on the tip of her nose. "This is all my fault. The reason I'm asking is because I'm curious. I was at that summer camp every year and I had no idea. None. Frankly that bugs me. My friends never talked about it. My parents and grandparents never talked about it. How is that possible? That's why I've been asking. Not because I think there's some vast conspiracy to kill its membership one by one."

Slowly exhaling in relief, she slumped in her chair and laughed. "Only the ones who break the rules. I guess death would be one step past blackballing."

Chase stroked his chin, his expression thoughtful. "For some, death might be preferable. I imagine the social and business contacts of an organization like this are the lifeblood of many careers. Without them they're screwed."

A flurry of activity in the corner of her eye caught Bailey's attention and she was relieved to see Willow and Peyton striding through the lobby, heading straight for the restaurant.

"They're here, thank goodness. I can't wait to hear all the details."

Willow had given them the bare bones but there hadn't been time to do anything more.

Peyton stopped in the lobby and dug into her handbag, pulling out her phone while Willow joined them at the table. Collapsing into a chair next to Bailey, she gave an exaggerated groan of relief.

"We're back and can I say I have never been so happy to see two people in my life. That was the worst trip I've ever been on." Willow gulped down her entire glass of water and signaled to the waitress for a refill. "I'm starving. Let's order one of everything on the menu."

Bailey was all in favor of that. She hadn't been able to eat last night. "Is Peyton joining us? We should probably wait for her."

"She got a call. She's in the lobby."

The waitress bustled up to the table and refilled Willow's water before pulling out a pad and pencil. "Are you ready to order?"

"We are but we're waiting for someone who is taking a call in the lobby." Bailey stood to get a better line of sight to Peyton. She could see part of her and the phone being tucked back into her purse. "She's on her way so yes, let's order."

The waitress tapped her order pad. "Let me tell you our breakfast—"

A god-awful, teeth-rattling noise ripped through the air and the earth rolled and pitched violently under Bailey's feet sending her to her knees, flying debris abrading her skin. The sound of shattering glass and cracking wood filled the air along with screams of terror and the pounding of running feet. Her ears rang painfully and her senses were muddled as she struggled to gulp air into her empty lungs.

The acrid smell of smoke made her eyes burn and her throat

seize up. She choked and coughed as her stomach roiled in protest, the acid churning in her gut. She felt herself being scooped up into strong arms, holding her close and safe while a soft voice crooned soothing words that she couldn't quite make out.

Chase. She'd know him anywhere.

"What– What– Chase, what—"

"There was an explosion. Stay down," Chase hoarsely commanded, his tone brooking no argument.

Her arms flailed, trying to find Willow and she sighed in relief as her watery gaze landed on her friend who was huddled close to Chase's other side. Her heart had taken up a staccato beat against her ribs and she could hear the blood pumping through her veins despite the noise and chaos erupting around them. It was as if her world had narrowed to only the three of them as they hid under that table, Chase trying to cover as much of their bodies with his own as he could.

Peyton!

Jesus, Peyton is out there.

Chapter Twenty-Seven

CHASE STARED GRIM-FACED at the double-doors at the end of the hall. Peyton was behind those doors, a team of doctors and nurses working to ascertain the severity of her injuries. In the meantime, he'd tried to keep Bailey and Willow calm when he was sure all they wanted to do was cry. In fact, he might shed a few tears himself later. The sight of some of the casualties in the hotel lobby would haunt him for a long time to come.

Tightening his arm around Bailey, he pressed a kiss to the top of her head. "She's going to be okay. Peyton is a fighter."

A palpable shudder ran through her body and she buried her face in his shirt, a sob escaping her lips. "She was so pale and still. I said her name over and over but she wouldn't wake up."

Peyton's deathly white features had reminded Chase too much of Gwen's all those years ago. Add in the blood that had covered Peyton's face and it had been eerily similar in a way he didn't want to dwell on. It didn't mean she was going to die, however. Unlike Gwen, Peyton was breathing and had a pulse, albeit a weak one. She was going to be okay. She had to be.

Taking a deep breath to calm himself, he inwardly grimaced at the antiseptic smell that seemed to permeate the air. The hospital reeked of rubbing alcohol, bandages, illness, and fear, and he didn't like it one bit. It brought back memories of the night his parents had died. After a nasty car accident, they'd been behind a similar but different set of hospital double-doors, except that time the doctor had come out with horrific news. He'd rather be anywhere else but there was no way he'd leave Bailey to face this alone. She was a strong woman but she'd been through so much since she'd come to town. How much was one human being supposed to endure?

The elevator door slid open and Josh and Ellis spilled out, their gazes darting in every direction until they landed on Chase sitting in the waiting room, one arm around Bailey, her head resting on his chest.

Ellis didn't waste any time. "Any word on Peyton's condition?"

Chase nodded toward the double-doors. "None. They're working on her right now. Any news on what happened? Was it an accident?"

A muscle ticked in Ellis's jaw. "No accident. It was a package bomb delivered to the front desk. The two clerks are dead and the four people in the lobby are injured enough that they'll be admitted to the hospital. Luckily, most people were in the restaurant or farther away and their injuries were much less severe. The worst damage was within a ten to twelve feet radius."

Chase's gaze rested on the butterfly bandages on Bailey's forehead where a flying piece of glass had caught her. The cuts on her arms had only needed cleaning which the EMTs had quickly accomplished at the scene.

"She got a call."

All eyes went to where Willow was standing just behind the two men. She'd been unable to stay still and she'd offered to get everyone a decent coffee from the shop in the lobby downstairs.

Ellis took the tray of scalding drinks from the woman's shaking hands. "What was that, honey? Peyton was on the phone?"

Willow nodded, her demeanor still dazed from what had happened. Sheer exhaustion probably wasn't helping the situation either. "She was going to join us in the restaurant but her phone rang. She said it was her dad. If she had just let it go to voicemail…"

Bailey shook her head, tears gathering in her eyes. "Don't think like that. We can't torture ourselves with those thoughts."

"This wasn't supposed to happen," Willow's voice choked. "We were supposed to eat breakfast and then get some sleep. No one else was supposed to die."

Chase had already brought Josh and Ellis up to date on the swim coach and their meeting with Guy Eckley. He desperately wanted to believe this was only a bizarre coincidence but at this point in the investigation, he was beginning to believe this was no accident.

Ellis was giving him a look and Chase nodded, extricating himself from Bailey's clinging limbs and beckoning Willow to take his place. "Can you stay with her for a few minutes? I need to speak with the guys."

Nodding, Willow sat down next to Bailey and reached for two of the coffees Ellis was carrying, handing one to her friend. "We'll be fine. Go do what you need to do."

Ellis led them farther down the hall so they were out of ear-shot before speaking. "This was deliberate. We don't know the target for sure—"

Josh scoffed, shaking his head. "Come on, we know the girls were the target. I think I speak for all of us when I say I'm getting damn tired of using the word coincidence. This was no coincidence. Someone is trying to keep them and Chase from finding Gwen's killer or any connection to the men's deaths as well. They want them – and us – to run away with our tail between our legs. I don't know about you but that doesn't sit well with me. In fact, it pisses me off."

"It's nothing we can prove," Ellis replied. "So for now we can only make assumptions."

"Assume they want the women and probably Chase dead," Josh hissed, his fingers running through his hair and making it stand on end.

Chase rubbed the pounding hammer that was beating against his temple from the inside. "Christ, can both of you keep it down? My ears are still ringing from the explosion and I have a doozy of a headache." He turned to Josh. "You're right. The women were the target, I guarantee it." Then he turned to Ellis. "But you have a point. We can't prove it. What we can do is keep everyone safe and protected until we can. To that end, I'm going to take Bailey and Willow back to my place to watch over them. They can't stay at the hotel any longer anyway. Ellis, is there a way we can get some police to guard Peyton? If not, I'll hire private security."

Those double-doors that had stayed stubbornly shut for the last hour now swung open and a stretcher was pushed into the hall. Peyton lay there, pale and small against the blue sheets. The wound on her head had been bandaged and the blood cleaned from her face and arms. She looked peaceful and serene as if she were simply taking a nap to refresh herself.

Ellis stepped toward the unconscious woman, his gaze glued to her impassive features and his fists tightening at his side. He said something that Chase couldn't quite make out but it sounded like "… get who did this to you."

Bailey and Willow rushed down the hall to meet the doctor, who had paused even as the stretcher kept on moving.

"Is she going to be okay?" Bailey asked, her voice quivering as the two women huddled together for strength. "Is she going to live?"

Chase held onto Willow and Bailey as the doctor explained Peyton's injuries and what they were planning to do. From what Chase could translate into layman's terms Peyton had some bleeding on the brain and they were putting her into a medically induced coma along with medication to relieve the pressure. The doctor hoped that surgery wouldn't be necessary. If she improved, they would slowly bring her out of the coma in a few days but until then she would be in the ICU. He advised them to go home and get some sleep. They could come back and visit tomorrow.

They were lucky that the hospital was being so accommodating. In the beginning, they'd balked at giving Bailey and Willow any information but then had relented when the women explained that Peyton had no family in Williamsburg.

Chase thanked the doctor and turned back to the women. "You're staying with me, no arguments. I'll go get your things from the hotel and Josh will stay with you while I do."

Willow seemed to have snapped back to reality and the determined female Chase had first met was back in full force. "Actually, Chase, I am going to argue. I need to get back to Midnight Blue Beach. Someone has to deliver the news to Peyton's family and then fly them back here. This isn't something that should be told over the phone."

That pounding in his head was getting stronger. He hadn't thought about how her family would be informed. "I can call them. You need to get your rest. You're practically falling asleep on your feet."

Shaking her head, Willow pulled her phone from her purse. "How would you like to get the news about your daughter over the phone? No way. I'm going to tell them in person and then I can bring them right back here. Besides, I have Peyton's phone and I've been trying to call them since the explosion. No answer. I think the best way is to go to them."

Chase sighed, reluctant to push, but the need to keep these ladies safe overrode his sensitivity.

"I can't let you go," he finally said. "You need to be protected."

Bailey's mouth fell open in shock and even Willow looked surprised.

"Are you saying you think that explosion was meant for us?" Bailey asked faintly. "Are we in danger?"

"I think that the safe way to proceed is to assume that theory is a distinct possibility," Ellis smoothly interjected, the cop in him coming out. Chase was impressed by how well his friend was doing. He hadn't pissed anyone off in hours. "It's imperative that we keep you all safe and that means no going off by your-self. I'm sure you understand."

Willow's finely arched brows flew up. "I'm sure I don't. I can hire a phalanx of bodyguards if I need to but frankly, I can take care of myself. I've been doing it for years."

There went Ellis's record.

Chase was about to interrupt when Josh shocked them all. "I'll go."

What?

Frowning, Willow shook her head. "I don't need a babysit-ter."

"That's exactly what you need," Ellis said, oblivious to Wil-low's or anyone else's mood. He was like a bull in a china shop.

She opened her mouth to tell him off but Chase placed his hand on her shoulder to get her attention. "Would it be so bad having Josh along? Just humor us, okay?"

Bailey reached out for Willow's hand, tears spilling down her cheeks.

"Please take Josh with you. I don't want to have to worry about you when you go. I understand why you're making this trip but I'm not going to sleep right until you're back."

Bailey's plea seemed to do the trick. Willow surrendered, if not graciously, at least quietly.

"Then we need to get cleaned up and go as soon as possible. I need a shower and some new clothes." She pressed a few buttons on her phone. "I'll call and tell them to get the plane ready. Josh, do you want to pack anything before we go?"

"Josh has a key to my house so he can take you there to shower after you stop at the hotel to get your things." Chase turned to Ellis. "Are they going to be able to get inside?"

"They can for a few minutes to pack."

"What about Peyton's and Bailey's clothes?" Willow asked. "Should I get them too?"

Josh held up his hands. "I'll get them while you're getting your things. Then Chase doesn't have to make a trip later. I'll drop everything off at his place. Everyone agree?"

No one dissented so it was a plan. Willow and Bailey hugged again and said their emotional goodbyes, the bond between them easy to see despite not having known each other long. If Peyton didn't pull through it was going to hit them hard.

Chase took the empty coffee cup from Bailey's hand and tossed it into the trash can. "I should get you home as well. You need a good night's sleep."

She was shaking her head before he'd even finished the sentence. "I can't leave Peyton."

Stubborn. "There's nothing you can do for her right now, sweet. Besides, she's in ICU and they restrict visitors. You can't just sit with her all night. You need a meal and some sleep. Badly. Tomorrow morning I'll bring you back here, I promise. But you aren't going to be any good to her unless you take care of yourself."

Her chin quivered and for a moment he thought she was going to give in. "Wait, I can't leave her. She needs protection too, right? If we were the intended victims, her life is in danger as well."

So this tiny little miss was going to bodyguard Peyton?

"I'll call in a private team. We'll have someone on her twenty-four-seven."

"No need. I'm going to protect her myself."

For a moment, Chase thought he heard Ellis say he was going to guard Peyton. The ringing in his ears was affecting his ability to comprehend words. Apparently, Bailey had no such affliction.

"That's so sweet, Ellis. But are you sure? What about when you're on duty?"

So Ellis had said it. That was...unexpected, to say the least.

"I have so much vacation saved up that the chief will be thrilled that I'm finally taking some time off. I'll sit right out here and watch over her. I can get some of the guys from the station as well when they're off duty. They'll be thrilled with some extra pay. She's in good hands, I promise you."

This was a development Chase hadn't seen coming. What was Ellis up to?

Chapter Twenty-Eight

BAILEY HAD SOAKED in a hot tub, eaten as much food as she could choke down, and even drank a glass of wine so she'd fallen asleep rather easily, despite how keyed up her body was. The problem was she didn't stay asleep. The illuminated red numbers on the bedside clock said eleven-thirty. She should be catching up on her rest but instead she was staring up at the ceiling of Chase's spare bedroom and replaying the last several days like a movie in her head, all culminating with the explosion this morning.

Peyton in the hospital. A coma. All because Bailey couldn't leave well enough alone. She'd had to dig through the past and now look where they were. Beaten, bloodied, and unsure where to turn. Stephen thought that the swim coach was the killer but now she was dead. Did someone kill her to silence anything she might say? What secrets, if any, had she been carrying all these years?

Tired of lying there, Bailey threw back the covers and climbed out of bed. Pulling on a pair of yoga pants and a t-shirt, she combed her hair into a ponytail and headed out to the kitchen, her stomach telling her it was time to eat. When she entered the living room, Chase was sitting on the couch paging through the case file again.

"I thought you'd sleep through the night." He folded the file closed and set it on the cushion next to him. "Are you hungry or thirsty?"

"No such luck. My brain won't let me go back to sleep. And in answer to your question, yes and yes. Is there anything to eat?"

Chase chuckled and led her into the kitchen, his hands on her shoulders. The warmth was comforting even as everything was going to shit. She hadn't objected when he'd moved her into his home because she felt the safest when she was with him. He was strong, dependable. A man she could count on when things got tough. She'd always been quite independent, proud of how she could take care of herself and stand on her own two feet, but there was something about Chase. He didn't make her feel weak or less than if she leaned on him, whether for a few moments or several hours. She was there for him too, after all.

"I'm the king of frozen food. Toaster pizzas, chicken strips, burritos. You name it, I've got it. Pick out anything you like and I'll nuke it for you."

"You're such a gentleman." Bailey took a seat at the table. "Have you heard anything about Peyton by any chance?"

Chase opened the freezer and held up a personal size sausage pizza and she nodded. "I called them around dinner time and there was no change. She's resting comfortably and her vital signs are strong. It's all good. We'll go see her in the morning. The nurse said that visitor hours are a little different in the ICU but we could get in as early as eight."

It was a relief to hear that Peyton was stable but she shouldn't have to be there at all.

As if he'd done it a million times – and perhaps he had – Chase popped her pizza into the toaster oven and grabbed a water bottle from the refrigerator, sliding it in front of her.

"Thank you for calling. I can't get what happened out of my mind. The killer must be desperate, Chase, to go after us like that. And that poor woman in New York too. None of this would have happened if I hadn't come here. This is all my fault."

Chase pulled out a kitchen chair, the legs scraping loudly against the wood floors. "Hell no, sweet. You're not going to do this to yourself. Even if Willow and Peyton hadn't come here that doesn't mean they wouldn't have been targeted. The killer simply would have done it back in your hometown."

"What about that coach?" she countered. "What about those two innocent people who lost their lives today? My. Fault."

"No." Chase shook his head, placing his hands on her knees. "You are not responsible, the killer is. Everything that has happened is on them. They decided to do this, not you. You're simply looking for answers and so am I. If it wasn't us, it would be someone else eventually. They couldn't keep this all dead and buried forever."

She wasn't so sure about that. They had so far and quite well too.

Tears stung the back of her eyes and she blinked rapidly, not wanting to give into the wave of emotion that threatened to swamp her well-being. She's always relied on hard work and drive to get the things she wanted, but this might be one situation where all of that didn't matter.

"I can't let this all be for nothing," she said quietly. "It's even more important now."

"That's my girl," Chase smiled. "I'm more determined than ever to give them hell and I'm glad to hear you are too. Let's show them that we're not scared."

She hoped that's how she looked outwardly but inside she kind of was. There was a person out there that didn't care if innocent people died. Ruthless and cunning, they were determined to take their secrets to the grave. Hers or theirs was the only question.

He kept her company as she ate her late dinner. They talked about the case file that he was rereading and they postulated on how Willow and Josh were getting on together. Chase seemed to think they'd be fine and based that on how laidback and relaxed Josh was. Bailey wasn't as convinced, knowing how upset Willow currently was about what had happened to Peyton. She hadn't known Willow long but Bailey had the feeling her friend could be difficult at times, especially when she was emotional.

It was easy to be with Chase, hang out and be herself. She didn't have to be anyone or anything for his approval. He was okay with her just as she was and what a relief. She didn't want to think about carrying the right handbag, wearing the right shoes, or liking the right books. She simply wanted to be Bailey Jean Harris Scott. Lover of sweets, chocolate, old movies, and cute puppies. And weren't all puppies cute?

They were cleaning up the dishes when she couldn't resist asking any longer. "What are we going to do now? Where do we go next? You said you're more determined than ever and so am I but we're at a dead end."

"I've thought about that all day and I think we should go back and speak to Daniel Ford. Guy was a hell of a lot more forthcoming than Danny was and I still think our friendly senator was holding back on us. He was too damn happy to get us out of his office."

"But he was going on a trip, remember? He won't be there."

Chase chuckled and pulled out his laptop, typing something in and then showing her the screen. "About that...looks like he changed his itinerary or maybe he was never going anywhere at all. The photographer didn't care about Ford—he was there to snap a picture of another guy but Danny was in the background. He's here at his residence in Williamsburg. We can go see him tomorrow after we visit Peyton."

The senator's behavior did raise several red flags. He'd been anxious to answer as few questions as possible without actually looking like he didn't want to talk to them.

"Are you going to give him some warning of our impending arrival?"

"Hell, no. I think a surprise is in order, don't you? I bet he'll be thrilled to see us, especially when we tell him we talked to Guy."

"You're a devious man, Chase Jennings."

Winking, he dried his hands on a towel after rinsing the last dish. "I think you like that about me. Do you think you could go to sleep now or do you want to watch some television? I can put on a movie."

Instead her gaze drifted out to the back deck that overlooked the James River. She could use a little peace and tranquility in her life and that spot seemed perfect. "How about we sit outside for awhile? Maybe with a glass of wine?"

Chase's smile widened, his shoulders visibly relaxing. He needed the quiet as much as she did and he'd already told her he liked to sit out there and enjoy the weather.

"Perfect. Go on out and I'll pour us a couple of glasses."

She was settled into the glider with a throw over her legs when he joined her, a glass of cabernet in each hand. He sat as close as possible, their thighs pressed together and his arm around her shoulder as they listened to the crickets and the rustle of branches against the house. Neither one of them said anything, content to simply be together.

She didn't know how much time had passed when he finally spoke. "Does your head hurt?"

"I have a few bruises here and there but I was lucky, really. The headache is gone although I have some sore spots where the glass cut me." She looked up at him, her hand running along a nick on his jaw where a piece of debris had scraped it. He hadn't shaved since this morning and his stubble tickled her fingertips. "You got hurt too. Are you okay?"

"I'm fine. You were sitting closest to the lobby so you took the brunt of the blast."

She didn't move her hand away, too lost in the heat of his body and the smell of his skin, citrus and spice. She couldn't make out his features clearly in the dark but his chest rose and fell rapidly with each breath and she would have sworn that he was staring at her lips.

Awareness vibrated between them, raising the temperature, and she shoved the blanket off of her legs and took a sip of her wine. Her insides quivered with excitement and anticipation as he continued to watch her closely even in the dim light. The thud of her heart sounded loud in her ears as he reached out to run a stray strand of hair through his fingers. His hand brushed her cheek and she couldn't suppress the gasp of arousal that burst from her lips. The simple touch had sent a bolt of pleasure straight to her core and she had to press her thighs together to control the growing ache that was building between them.

Taking her glass from her trembling hand, he set both of them down on the side table before cupping her jaw in his large palms and tilting her head up. He was going to kiss her. She knew that and she wanted it but as usual, Chase didn't do it exactly as she expected.

First, he grazed his lips over the tip of her nose before kissing each closed eyelid in turn. Mouth gliding, he nuzzled her ear, nipping at the lobe before soothing the small hurt with his tongue. He even traveled up to her temple and pressed a supremely gentle kiss to the cut on her forehead. By the time he was finished she was boneless in his arms, completely swept away by the sweet sensuality of his ministrations.

It was then and only then, when she would have given him anything that he'd asked for, that he took her mouth with his own. One hand slid to the back of her head, his fingers tangling into her long ponytail, the other gliding down her spine to the small of her back where it splayed there, pressing her closer to his strong frame.

Bailey wasn't aware of the specifics of the kiss, lips and tongues. The world had gone fuzzy, spinning around, and she let herself drift on a cloud of pleasure as he ravished her mouth, showing her without doubt how he'd pleasure the rest of her body. Thoroughly and well.

Yes. A million times yes.

Sex had never been a big deal for Bailey. Frank hadn't been a particularly passionate man so she'd often wondered if she was missing out. She'd filled her life with other inclinations and until this moment had been pretty content with it all, but now she'd been woken up from her long slumber. Losing Frank had allowed her to bury the physical side of her nature, which she hadn't been that comfortable with in the first place. Maybe that's why she'd ended up with Frank. Deep down she'd known that he'd never bring out this earthy, sensual side of herself. But she'd be safe and cared for, never taking a chance or living on the edge.

Never truly living at all if she were honest.

Mewling in protest when he broke their kiss, her fingers grabbed onto his t-shirt, the material wrinkling in her tight fists as she tried to pull him back. Chuckling, he easily captured her wrists and lifted her arms so they were wrapped around his neck. Clever man. That left her torso completely open to his explorations.

She would have dubbed him Magellan – if she'd been capable of speaking at all – as his eager and talented fingers slid up and down her back before deliberately finding every spot of sensitive flesh he'd could reach. His hands had slid under her loose tank top, the rough palms grazing her already hard nipples.

No, he wasn't so much an explorer as a pirate. He was stealing moans and groans from her with every heated caress but clearly, his aim was a much more valuable treasure. His fingers glided over her hips and then to the juncture of her thighs where he found her swollen and begging for his touch. His skillful caresses quickly had her digging her nails into his shoulders and sighing his name.

So good. So very good.

He wickedly played with her, but his attention was soon pulled in a different direction. He abandoned where she needed him most and slid his hands up her ribcage to cup her breasts in his large palms, his thumbs toying with the tips until she was squirming on his lap. She was pressed directly against the hard length in his jeans and she wantonly rubbed against him until he was the one groaning her name. Payback. He wasn't the only one who could tease and torture.

White-hot need ran through her veins like wildfire and she slid her hands under his shirt, desperate to feel the muscled flesh and explore every inch of his body that she was allowed. His own impatient fingers were hooked into the waistband of her yoga pants and he tugged lightly on the elastic, letting her know in no uncertain terms what he wanted. She was happy to oblige.

She wasn't sure how he managed it but somehow her pants and tank top ended up on the wood decking at their feet. It felt wild and wicked to be completely nude while he was still dressed, the fabric of his clothes rubbing at her bare flesh and sending sparks of arousal straight to her clit as she straddled his thighs.

His hand ran down her spine and paused at her bottom, giving her generous ass cheek a squeeze before traveling to her front, his fingers delving between her thighs. She threw back her head and cried out his name as two fingers slid easily into her tight channel and his thumb strummed back and forth over the swollen button.

Her grip on his biceps tightened and the world tilted as he

found a sweet spot inside of her. He never broke his rhythm, his fingers thrusting in and out while his hot, wet mouth found a peaked nipple. Nipping at it with his teeth, he pressed his thumb against her clit more firmly, shooting her over the edge and straight into heaven. Shaking and shuddering, she chanted his name as her orgasm swept over her until eventually she was nothing but a sweaty, trembling mess in his lap, her head on his shoulder.

He gave her a few moments to catch her breath and that was all she wanted. Her need wasn't nearly sated yet. Inside of her was where she had to have him and soon. Reaching down, her fingers fumbled with his zipper and he came to her rescue, unzipping his fly and pushing down his jeans and boxers. Curses flew out of his mouth as he tried to situate them comfortably but to her surprise he gave up and lifted her as he stood, her legs wrapping around his waist automatically. Carrying her to the deck railing, he settled her bottom on it at just the perfect height. For a moment, she glanced over her shoulder and it looked a long way down to the banks of the river. She wouldn't die but she would probably be wearing a cast or two if she fell.

"I've got you, sweet. I won't let anything happen to you."

That she knew, so she wrapped her arms around his neck and pulled him down for a searing kiss that had toes curling and her lips tingling. When he lifted his head, his eyes were soft and adoring and she allowed herself the luxury of basking in that admiration, feeling sexy and desired. Now that she'd experienced this feeling, she was going to want to do it again. Often.

He nudged her opening but paused before plunging forward, his forehead dropping to hers.

"Are you on anything? I don't have a condom out here. I'm clean, by the way. Just passed my yearly physical with flying colors."

Thank goodness one of them was capable of rational thought. Her mind was filled with only one thought – being with him.

"I'm on the pill, and I'm healthy too."

"Thank God," Chase groaned, his tone pained. "I'm not sure I could have stopped long enough to search for a condom. Or if I even have any."

It was kind of cool that he wasn't the type to have birth control tucked all over his house as if he did women on his deck all the time. She'd like to think that perhaps she might be the first. If not, then at least it had been awhile.

With the less sexy business out of the way, there was nothing more to keep them apart. He pressed forward slowly but inexorably, stretching her until he was in to the hilt. Her lids fluttered closed and she moaned his name at the feeling, so full. His own breathing was ragged and labored, his jaw tight with the effort to hold back as she grew accustomed to the intimate invasion.

"It's okay," she breathed, her fingers flexing on his wide shoulders. "I want it."

Her legs tightly wrapped around his lean hips, she breathed in sharply at his first movement, slow and most definitely deliberate. With each subsequent thrust, his groin rubbed her already swollen and sensitive clit, sending her closer and closer to the pinnacle. Her body teetered there, reaching out, begging for that ultimate moment. She arched her back and let the cool, night air run over her nipples, feeling them tighten even further and sending a rod of pleasure to her abdomen. She needed him and she needed more.

"Faster. Harder."

Her voice didn't even sound like her own but he understood her plea, slamming into her with more force and speed until she finally broke into a thousand shining pieces that matched the stars above them. Chase found his own release as her body clamped down on his, their lips colliding in one last hot, sweaty, messy kiss that lasted until they were both wrung out and exhausted.

They sat for a long time, sucking air into their aching lungs and pressing butterfly kisses to cheeks, jaws, eyelids, and necks. Eventually Chase lifted her back up and carried her into the bedroom where they both collapsed into a tangle of arms and legs.

A deliriously happy tangle.

She'd made the leap and she wasn't sorry. She trusted Chase and he was worth taking a chance on.

Chapter Twenty-Nine

C HASE COULD HEAR the water running in the bathroom and had to fight the urge to barge in and join Bailey in the shower. Last night had been everything he could have hoped for and then some, but she'd been through so much. He didn't want to assume that she wasn't having any sort of regrets this morning. Maybe even a twinge of guilt. She'd been with the same man since her college days and she'd barely dated after Frank's death. An intimate relationship with Chase had to throw her off-kilter, at least a little bit. He wanted to be sensitive to her feelings but he also wanted to fuck her against the shower wall. The big question was which urge was stronger.

The inner debate was raging when he heard his name being called through the door. He opened it just enough to stick his head in while trying to avoid looking at Bailey in all her naked glory. If he saw her all wet and soapy there would be no doubt what part of him would win the battle and the war.

"Chase?" Her voice echoed off the tile walls. "Would you scrub my back?"

If she had been Eve offering him an apple she couldn't have

sounded more seductive. Or maybe all the blood had abandoned his brain and he wasn't thinking or hearing straight. All he knew was he was hard and ready just that fast, heat sweeping through his body all the way to the tips of his fingers. This woman was going to be the death of him.

Stripping out of his clothes, he opened the shower door and took in the most beautiful image he'd ever seen. Soap slid down her tempting curves, over her breasts, down her belly, and between her thighs. Her long, dark hair was slicked back, exposing her neck and the love bites he'd given her during round two in the bedroom. His woman.

Strong protective instincts welled up inside, stronger than he'd ever experienced and for a moment he knew real fear; fear that she'd be harmed or lost to him. He would do everything in his power to keep her safe.

"Chase?" she asked, her head tilted to the side in question. "Are you coming in?"

He was standing in the open shower doorway looking like the fool he was as water leaked onto his tile floor. Quickly he shed the few clothes he wore and entered the steamy cubicle, shutting the door firmly behind them, creating their own little world. At least for the next few minutes.

She handed him the washcloth and he poured some body wash into it before rubbing it into her shoulders and down her spine. She sighed and braced her hands against the tile wall, letting her head fall forward, happy to allow him to explore. He ran the washcloth over every inch of her luscious flesh, paying special attention to her nipples and between her legs. By the time she was squeaky clean, she was panting and shifting from foot to foot, her back pressed flush against his front.

Tossing the washcloth away, he wrapped one arm around her hips, his fingers delving into the juncture between her thighs while the other hand lifted her face for a kiss. Their tongues tangled and played as he pressed two digits deep inside her wet slit, enjoying the sound of her hiss as he hit a particularly sensitive spot. She mewled and wriggled her hips as he pumped in and out lazily, never giving her the exact sensation she needed to go over. This was only meant to be a taste, an appetizer, not the grand finish. That fantasy of taking her up against the wall...

"Chase," she groaned. "Please..."

"Yes, sweet. It's time."

Turning her in his arms, he lifted her until she was propped against the wall, her legs wrapped snugly around his waist. With one stroke he was inside of her, her tight walls already milking his shaft and making it hard to hold back. Luckily she was as overheated and anxious as he was. She bucked her hips, her nails digging into his back as he began a hard and fast pace, both of their needs too great. There would be other chances for slow, sweet lovemaking but this moment wasn't one of them. She was urging him on with her breathy pleas in his ear, raunchy words falling from her innocent lips and making him even hotter and more aroused than he already was. She was the perfect combination of angel and sinner and he was the lucky recipient of her debauchery.

Teeth gritted and jaw locked, he reached between them to rub circles around her clit, knowing he couldn't hold off any longer. She tightened around him, crying out his name as she tumbled over with him right behind her. His orgasm ripped through him, almost sending him to his knees with its intensity. When it was over and he could breathe normally again, he slowly lowered her legs to the shower floor, his own body trembling with aftershocks.

Bailey pressed soft kisses to his chest and abdomen, a smile on her beautiful face. She looked happy, content and he was sure his own expression mirrored hers. For the first time in longer than he could remember, he was happy. What they had together felt right. It had happened fast but now that she was here, he couldn't imagine living his life without her. Did she feel the same? When this was all over, could he convince her to give them a chance?

Of all the things they'd found out to be a lie this one thing was true...he wanted a future with Bailey Scott.

AFTER THEIR SHOWER and breakfast, Bailey and Chase had stopped at the hospital to see Peyton and been rather surprised to find she already had a visitor. Detective Ellis Hunter sat next to her bed, reading her the morning paper out loud while he sipped his coffee. Bailey hadn't thought much of the bullheaded cop but if he kept doing things like this for her friend, she might just change her mind.

"Any change?" she asked him, wondering how long he'd been sitting there. The nurses had warned Bailey and Chase about the strict rules regarding visitors in the ICU.

Ellis looked up from his paper and shook his head. "Not really. At one point I thought she sighed but it might have been my imagination. The doctor was in about fifteen minutes ago though and seemed satisfied. He said she was stable and that she simply need to rest and heal."

"They let you in here?" Chase questioned. "I'm kind of surprised about that."

Ellis smiled and folded the newspaper, laying it on the bedside table. "About that…turns out the doctor in charge of the ICU is a guy I helped when his ex-girlfriend was stalking him. When I told him that I was keeping watch over Peyton for safety purposes, he allowed me in. My relief guys have to sit outside the door though."

Standing, Ellis waved Bailey toward the chair he'd been occupying. "I think I'm going to stretch my legs and get some breakfast since you two are here, if you don't mind."

Chase shook his head. "Of course not. We'll stay here and keep an eye on things."

Lowering herself into the chair, Bailey reached out for Peyton's hand, the skin cool to the touch. She'd never known anyone in a coma but she remembered hearing that some patients were aware of what was going on around them and could remember what had been said in their rooms. It was worth a try.

"Peyton, it's Bailey. I know you might be scared but I want you to know that you're in the hospital and have the best care possible. Willow went back home to tell your family and bring them here but I stayed behind to work on the case. We're going to find out who did this to you and bring them to justice, but until then I don't want you to worry. That asshole detective? Ellis Hunter? He's going to guard you when we're not here and I think he's going to do a good job. When we got here he was reading to you so hopefully he'll keep doing that. It's supposed to help you recover faster so we'll talk to you too. I just want you to know that you're going to be okay. The doctor said you're stable and soon you'll wake up and everything will be fine. We miss you though. I really miss you, Peyton."

She was rambling back and forth but she couldn't seem to stem the tide of words and emotion. Her chest and throat had tightened painfully and tears pricked the back of her eyes as she watched Peyton's still body. So pale and fragile. None of this was fair.

She and Chase took turns talking to Peyton about everything from the weather to what their plans for the day were. By the time Ellis strolled back in they were about out of topics. His hair was damp as if he'd had a shower and his clothes were fresh. Before they could ask him if he'd gone home he pointed to his shirt and grinned.

"They let me use the showers here and a buddy brought me some fresh clothes. I'm good for the next eight hours or so, then a relief is coming to let me get some rest. Don't worry about your friend. I promise nothing will happen to her."

Bailey kissed Peyton's forehead and told her she'd be back after they spoke to the senator to give her an update. She let Chase take her hand and lead her out of the hospital and into the bright sunshine, a world that seemed far away from the beeping machines and gray walls of Peyton's hospital room.

"Ellis is in a pretty decent mood today considering he slept on a hard, plastic chair," Chase said. "I was afraid he'd be his usual dick self but he was on his best behavior this morning. He must like you."

Bailey didn't care how he felt about her as long as he protected Peyton.

ELLIS HUNTER SETTLED back into the chair next to Peyton's bed before reaching over to the bedside table where he'd stashed a half empty water bottle sometime last night. Unscrewing the top, he quickly drained the remaining liquid and tossed it in the trashcan in the corner.

"Two points," he chuckled. "Of course that was only about six feet so I guess it's not all that impressive. So Peyton, what do you want to do today? Shall we read more of the paper or maybe that paperback the nurse brought me? It looks like a halfway decent thriller. Do you like blood and guts or are you more of a romance and kisses type? I bet you like the romance, don't you? Me? I like those action, shoot-'em-up movies where you're not sure if the hero is going to live or die. I guess I like the adrenaline rush or something. You're probably more quiet, soft-spoken. A real lady."

He fussed with the sheets, smoothing them down where Bailey and Chase had wrinkled them during their visit. He didn't touch Peyton; he wouldn't do that, but he had a feeling she would want her linens to look nice. She seemed like someone who liked order.

"I don't want you to worry about anything, okay? Whoever did this to you is going to pay, I promise. I won't let them get to you again. Hell, they'd have to go through me and I'm not ready to die. Not even close, so you can just rest and get better."

He picked up the paperback on the table and opened it to the first page, clearing his throat.

Chapter Thirty

T HEY CAUGHT UP with Senator Daniel Ford while drinking a beer at the clubhouse after a round of golf. The look on his face when he saw them was priceless but he simply shook his head and capitulated when they asked if they could talk to him for a few minutes. His companions had drifted back to the locker room, leaving the three of them sitting at a table overlooking the eighteenth green.

"So I lied."

Bailey didn't much care whether he had or not. He was a politician so she expected it. "We met with Guy Eckley."

"How is he? Is he okay?"

"You could call him and ask," Chase replied. "But I guess since he's been blackballed you're not allowed to do that. Isn't that the rule?"

The senator rubbed his hand over his sweaty forehead. "It's not like that. You don't understand."

"Make us understand," Chase pressed. "When Guy found out that Frank, Alex, and Greg were all dead and on the same day, he said one word. *Evandria.* He didn't even hesitate—it was the first word on his lips. Tell me why he would say it."

Ford made a choking sound and scraped his hand over his face. "Guy is bitter, that's all."

Bailey shook her head. "Not at all. He's actually happy with his life. So try again."

Lips trembling, the senator stared out of the window. "I've made vows. There are people depending on me to keep them."

"Are they more important than your friends? Frank, Greg, and Alex were like brothers to you and this is how you treat their memories? You know more than you're telling us. Don't think about Evandria. Think about your friends."

"I think about them…more than you can imagine."

Bailey had lost patience. "Big deal. Try being married to him and thinking about him every single day. Never having real peace because I don't know what truly happened. Wondering who my husband was and why he kept so many secrets from me. Try doing that for several years, Senator, and then tell me all about your vows."

Ford's shoulders slumped in defeat and he hung his head for a minute before responding.

"I shouldn't be telling you this, any of it. They could…"

"Who? Evandria?" Chase asked. "What would they do?"

Ford shook his head, his gaze far away. "I owe what I am to them. Everything that I've become."

"And they'd take it away?" Bailey said. "Would you be blackballed too?"

The senator's gaze finally swung to them and he shrugged his shoulders. "Punishments can vary. I'm going to use the mortality rule in talking with you both today. Basically I can reveal certain things about a deceased member of the group. I will reveal only those things that are covered in the rule, understand?"

They both nodded in agreement, letting him continue. "That summer when we were invited to join there were various recruitment opportunities. Everyone has to find their place in the council and our young men and women talk to several different department captains about how they might work for the mission. The five of us were a part of that. This is no secret and is considered common knowledge so I'm not telling you anything that isn't public knowledge."

"The secret is where Frank was recruited?" Bailey guessed. "Can you tell us that?"

"I don't know exactly. We don't discuss our placement but I do know that all of us were being recruited for what were called *special assignments,* and they were to be kept under wraps. I went to work for a congressman and ended up in politics. Frank ended up in London with a man named Nigel Holmwood, some sort of investment banker. I don't know about Alex and Greg. We all lost touch with one another after that summer and I blamed it on these secret assignments."

"Uncle Nigel?" Bailey sat back in her chair, floored by the revelation. "I always thought he was Frank's real uncle."

Chase placed a steadying hand on her own. "We're going to need to talk to him."

"I have his number. He's kept in touch since Frank's death. He's a wonderful, sweet man."

"So how many other people had these special assignments?" Chase's attention turned back to the senator. "Are they still alive?"

"I don't know. The only reason I knew about us was because we were such close friends. I'd have no way of knowing that information."

Bailey tapped her chin. "Does Evandria keep records?"

Ford's face paled. "They might but you'll never see them. If they even exist, they'd keep them at the headquarters under lock and key."

Midnight Blue Beach. Willow and Josh were already there. Maybe they should make a visit to the compound.

She was done pussyfooting around the real question. "Do you think Evandria had Frank, Alex, and Greg killed? Do you think Evandria had something to do with Gwen's death?"

The man put off answering the question as long as possible, rubbing his chin, looking at the ceiling and then the floor, sighing several times. If he didn't want to answer that question, maybe he would answer this one.

"What is so special about July twenty-first?"

For the first time that day, Daniel Ford didn't seem uncomfortable. "That is the date of the First Battle of Bull Run in Manassas Junction, Virginia. The first major battle of the Civil War was fought and ended that day. The Confederates won."

Bailey and Chase exchanged a confused glance.

"I'm not sure what that has to do with my husband Frank."

"That day, Mrs. Scott, was the day the Evandria Council was born. It was created out of the chaos of a country tearing itself apart, being destroyed, not by foreign invaders, but by its own citizens. It was on that day that our founders knew that no matter who won or lost, there would need to be great healing and leadership going forward. We could never allow this to happen again."

The senator then stood, tucking his wallet and phone in his pocket. "Now I must be going. I've told you all I can."

"Wait," Bailey begged. "You haven't answered my question. Do you think the Council had my husband killed? Did they kill Gwen?"

Ford stood up tall and proud. "I can say without a sliver of doubt that whatever the Council does, it does for the good of the people. But frankly, Mrs. Scott...me, your husband, you, or Chase...we're not important enough to capture the Council's attention. What a teenage girl did one summer long ago matters little to them."

With that the man turned and strode away, leaving Bailey and Chase sitting alone at the table contemplating what they'd learned. Bailey was the first to speak.

"So was that a yes or a no?"

Chase exhaled and shook his head in disgust. "That was maybe, I think. Mostly I believe he doesn't know and even more he doesn't *want* to know. He's a foot soldier and seems to work under need to know conditions."

"Is this a war?"

Chase nodded to where Ford had been sitting moments ago. "I think *he* thinks it is."

Wars have casualties. Was that what happened to Frank and the others? Had Frank been secretly fighting a battle she'd known nothing about and had Gwen been caught in the middle?

*

BAILEY HAD TRIED to call Nigel Holmwood but there was no answer. She left a message and also typed out a quick email to him, explaining that she needed to talk to him right away but didn't give him any actual details.

Chase opened the door to the hospital ICU for Bailey as she stuffed her phone back into her purse. The nurses were sticklers about cell usage in the ward.

"I hope he's okay," she sighed before they entered Peyton's room. "I don't remember a time when he hasn't answered. He's glued to his phone."

"Don't look for boogeymen where there are none. He probably just forgot to put it on the charger. He'll contact you very soon."

"I hope so."

Placing an arm around her shoulders, he pulled her in for a brief kiss that had the nurses grinning and giggling. She slapped at his hands but she wasn't upset in the least.

"Everyone is staring, you crazy man."

"Everyone is envious."

Bailey giggled and rolled her eyes, casting a glance behind her to the nurse's station. "You bet they are. They all wish they were me. Don't think I haven't noticed how they flirt with you, Chase Jennings."

He laid his hand over his heart. "I'm a one woman man."

"You better be."

Peyton's color was a little better but the doctor still had her in a coma. Ellis had apparently gone home in the middle of the day and taken a nap and was now back, planning to spend the night. In a chair. Again. That had Bailey bustling out to the nurse's station to find him a cot or even a semi-reclining hammock or lawn chair that wouldn't force him to sit up for the next twelve hours or so.

"You've got to get some fucking rest, Ellis," Chase said when Bailey had left the room. "You can't protect Peyton if you're exhausted."

"Sam will be sitting outside the ward from nine tonight until six in the morning just in case I fall asleep. But I'm fine. I socked away three hours today. I'm as good as new."

It was true Ellis needed little sleep but there had to be a line. "Don't you trust the other guys to protect her?"

"I do but you know I like to handle things myself." Ellis reached down for his briefcase that he'd tucked next to the plastic chair and pulled out a piece of paper. "You're fucking welcome."

Chase took it – a name and address. Son of a bitch. "How did you find it?"

"It wasn't easy. She's a woman that doesn't want to be found and I find that fascinating. You never mentioned her before so I assume you didn't know her."

Chase shook his head. "I never met her. I don't think she ever attended. I'm not even sure if she knows anything."

"That friend Taylor didn't know why Gwen was acting wild that summer, but her older sister might. Girls tell each other things, secrets. I think she might be worth a visit. If you find out what was behind the behavior you just might find a motive. Good work finding that obscure reference to her. Nobody on the original case thought to interview her."

"Or wanted to," Chase replied. "Whenever I read through

that file it's like the cops back then went out of their way to not solve it."

"Careful," Ellis laughed. "Your tinfoil hat might fall off. Stop with the conspiracy theories. Secrets are too hard to keep in a group of guys. You're letting this case get to you. Now tell me about your meeting with Senator Ford."

Chapter Thirty-One

I T WAS LATE afternoon when Bailey and Chase pulled up in front of a large Victorian home that looked to have been lovingly restored. According to Ellis, Catherine Baxter – who now called herself Cathy Martin – lived in this home along with her husband of ten years. No children. They hadn't called first because frankly they were afraid that Cathy would tell them not to come.

"There's no car in the driveway so no one may even be home."

Chase pocketed the car keys. "Then we'll wait. We need to talk to Catherine Baxter."

Bailey wasn't as sure that the woman would have anything to say that would help them. She was beginning to get discouraged. Just when she thought they'd made a breakthrough and learned something important they'd have another setback and be left where they'd started. The one thing she knew for sure was that the man she'd married hadn't been the boy who had attended summer camp all those years ago. He hadn't been the young man excited about life and dedicated to making the world a better place. No, he'd been someone altogether different and she wished sorely that hadn't been the case.

Bailey swung out of the car, hitching her purse onto her shoulder. "So we're just winging it? Is that the plan?"

Chase came to stand beside her. "I don't have a plan except to tell her the truth and hope she takes pity on us. How does that sound?"

"I think that sounds like exactly what we should do. No pretending, no beating around the bush. Tell her what we know and what we don't know."

"I'm beginning to think we don't know anything for sure."

Bailey couldn't argue that fact and didn't try. Instead, she followed him up the porch steps and waited patiently as he rang the doorbell. It only took a moment for an attractive dark-haired woman in her forties to answer. She smiled guardedly, probably thinking they were there to sell magazines or religion.

"Hello, my name is Chase Jennings and this is Bailey Scott. I know you don't know us, Mrs. Martin, but we're here to ask for just a few minutes of your time. It's very important. We'd like to ask you a few questions about your sister Gwen."

The woman blinked a few times, her mouth going slack. "I–I can't imagine what you have to say being any interest to me. I think you should go."

The door started to close but before she could even think about her actions, Bailey grabbed it, holding it open. She only hoped she hadn't scared Catherine Baxter in the process.

"Please, I beg of you. We need to talk to you. I lost my husband Frank Scott five years ago, Mrs. Martin. On July twenty-first. The same day as Alex Vaughn and Greg Nelson. All three of them were friends and cabinmates at the summer camp with Gwen. All of them dated her. Frank was the last person to see her alive. I'm trying to find out if there is any connection between Frank and his friends' deaths and Gwen's. I am pleading with you to speak with us. We're not trying to bring up bad memories, I swear. We are trying to find the truth."

Bailey didn't have to exaggerate her desperation because it was real. It also seemed to do the trick. Cathy Martin's hands dropped from the door and her expression turned haunted and sad.

"The truth? My dear, I don't even know what that is anymore."

"Would you talk to us?" Chase asked kindly. "Just a few minutes."

The woman's hand fluttered to her throat, but she finally agreed. "Yes, you can come in."

They followed her into a sitting room, Cathy on one side of the coffee table and Bailey and Chase on the other. Cathy folded her hands in her lap tightly, her features now composed.

"Now how can I help you? I'm afraid I didn't catch all that you were telling me. Your husband knew Gwen?"

Slowly this time, Bailey and Chase explained how they had come to meet and what they'd done since, keeping the whole Evandria Council theory out of it unless Cathy Martin mentioned them. Gwen's sister listened closely, not interrupting often, only asking a question when she didn't quite understand something. She seemed to get that they were trying to find out who killed Gwen and how she was connected to Frank. When they were done, Cathy appeared to be holding back tears.

"I'm sorry to be so emotional. It's just that it's been so long since I've heard anyone speak of Gwen or even say her name. I don't talk with my family much any longer, to be honest, not that they would have spoken about Gwen. When she died it was like she'd never existed to them."

"Is that why...?" Bailey asked hesitantly.

Cathy nodded. "When I saw how they acted after Gwen's murder I couldn't deal with them anymore. It was as if they didn't want her murderer found. They talked to the police once and then flew to Switzerland to go skiing."

Over the top cold and unfeeling.

"You didn't speak with the police though. They didn't ask?"

Brows pulled together, Cathy shook her head. "I did speak to the police. When they questioned my parents, they talked to me too. I was living on my own at that point but I'd come home when I got the news. I was living in Philly at the time."

Chase and Bailey exchanged a look. Whatever she'd said that day had never been put in the case file.

"What did you tell them?"

"It was so long ago, but I know they only asked me a few questions. If Gwen had called me that night, which she hadn't. Also, if Gwen had argued with anyone lately and I said no. That was about it. I loved Gwen but since we didn't live in the same city I wasn't as involved in her life as her friends would have been. But I loved her like she was my real sister."

Bailey frowned at the last statement. "Your real sister? I'm not sure I follow."

"Gwen and I are step-sisters. Mine and Stephen's father married Gwen's mother and then adopted Gwen. Her own father had abandoned them when she was a baby. I'm also Stephen's half-sister as my mother was my father's first wife. Stephen was born out of his second marriage. They divorced as well and then he married Gwen's mom."

Chase steepled his fingers and leaned forward so his elbows were propped on his knees. "We didn't realize and your brother never said anything."

"You spoke with Stephen?" Cathy smiled slightly. "I'm not surprised he didn't tell you. It was always a touchy subject for him. He and Gwen had gone on a few dates and that's how my father met her mother. Of course they couldn't date after Dad started dating Gwen's mother. I think Gwen called it 'icky' or something like that. But it must have been the real thing because they're still married today. I guess third time was the charm for both of them."

Bailey's brows rose at the convoluted tale. "It's like something out of a soap opera."

Cathy shrugged and laughed. "At the time it was sort of scandalous as Dad hadn't finalized his divorce but I doubt anyone remembers all that drama anymore."

There was another question that needed to be asked and Bailey wasn't sure how to say it without it sounding awful and rude. Delicacy and tact were called for here.

"Gwen went to camp that summer," Bailey began. "From what we were able to piece together she had several admirers that year. Did she ever talk to you about them?"

"It's okay. You can say it. I heard what the other kids were saying after she died. She'd been running wild and sleeping around that summer."

"Do you know why she was doing that? We're told it was out of character."

Cathy seemed to be choosing her words carefully as well. "I loved my sister but that behavior wasn't unusual. At least not from the time I met her a year earlier. She loved the attention, maybe because her father abandoned her. Who truly knows? Maybe before I knew her she wasn't like that. Her friends would have better information. All I know is that I was worried she was going to get pregnant if she wasn't careful and I told her so before she left for camp."

"What did she say?"

"She said she had everything covered and that I worried too much."

"Did she ever mention anyone named Frank, Alex, or Greg?" Bailey asked. "Do those names sound familiar?"

Cathy shook her head and sighed. "I don't think so but it's been so many years. She knew so many boys and after awhile I didn't really listen to their names. They didn't tend to stick around once they got what they wanted."

So far this trip had been a huge disappointment. Once again they were at another dead end.

Bailey sat back and let Chase ask his questions. "We haven't been able to speak to your parents, Mrs. Martin. We've been told that they're out of the country."

"I can assure you they're in the United States but as I said they don't speak of Gwen. Ever. Honestly, I can't see how they could help you. They weren't involved parents at all. I doubt they could tell you the names of Gwen's friends or even what classes she was taking. They were hardly ever home and when they were it wasn't like we sat down to dinner together every night and talked about our day. When I was in high school, if I saw my father once a month that was a lot."

Great parenting. No wonder Gwen wanted affection and attention. She'd been starved of it.

"So there was no one Gwen was fighting with? No spurned suitor?" Chase asked. Having spent so much time with him, Bailey could hear the exasperation in his tone but she doubted Cathy Martin would notice. "Can you think of anyone that would have wanted to hurt Gwen?"

The sister shook her head, mouth turned down. "I don't know anyone. Gwen didn't have any enemies. She got along well with pretty much everyone. As for boys, as I said, she didn't have the best taste in males. They came and went, but none seemed to stick around long enough for any drama. I'm sorry I can't help you more." Her expression perked up along with a smile. "I have her memory box if you want to take a look at it. There's not much there but you're welcome to it."

Bailey nodded in excitement. "That would be wonderful. Thank you so much."

Cathy stood and headed toward the staircase. "I'm just happy that someone still cares about Gwen's life and death. I thought she'd been forgotten by everyone except me."

Chase stood as well, tension in every line of his body. "I can assure you, Mrs. Martin, we haven't forgotten Gwen."

The sister was only upstairs a few minutes before she returned with a plain cardboard box labeled "Gwen" with magic marker. Chase took the box from her and said thank you again.

"You don't know how much we appreciate this."

"I'm not sure if it will help you at all but you're welcome to it. You can return it when you're done. I just ask that you be careful with her things. It's all I have left of her. That and the memories, of course."

"I promise we'll be careful," Bailey assured the woman. "I have to echo Chase when I say we appreciate the time you've taken to talk to us and now this. Thank you so much."

Cathy's hands wrung together and her chin firmed. "If I can do anything to help find out who killed Gwen, I will do it. I've barely spoken to my family in the last twenty years because I've been so disgusted with their behavior. They ought to be ashamed of themselves. They had the money to hire the best investigators but instead they closed their eyes and coldly moved on with their lives. It's something I can't forgive or forget."

Those words echoed in Bailey's mind as she and Chase drove away, the box tucked safely in the trunk. A young girl brutally murdered and her parents blithely ignored it and went skiing. There were so many things she couldn't understand about this case but the wanton disregard of a parent was at the top of the list. Gwen had deserved better.

Chapter Thirty-Two

THE SEALED CARDBOARD box sat on the coffee table.

Bailey popped the last bite of her egg roll into her mouth. "Are we going to stare at it or are we going to open it?"

Chase pointed to an open carton. "Do you want the last dumpling?"

Shaking her head, she pushed the food closer to him. "Are you ignoring me?"

Grinning, he shook his head. "I could never ignore you, sweet. No, I was just thinking that perhaps we shouldn't open the box until we're done eating and have washed up. We promised to be careful with Gwen's things and I wouldn't want to get General Tso's chicken on any of her belongings."

That was Chase's polite way of saying she made a mess when she ate. She'd be mad but he was right. Somehow she couldn't seem to eat a meal without some of it ending up on her boobs.

"Good point. Are you almost finished then?"

He took the last bite of dumpling and began cleaning up the take out bags and boxes. There would be plenty of leftovers. They'd purchased enough food for an army. After tucking the last carton into the refrigerator, Chase retrieved a box cutter from a drawer in the kitchen.

"Are you ready?"

"What if this doesn't have anything to help us?" she asked as he slit the box open. "What will we do then? Because I've run out of ideas."

"Then we'll follow up on the Evandria angle. I'm not sure Guy really knew what he was talking about but it's worth a shot. We can't give up so we need to do something."

The insistent buzzing of Bailey's phone stopped Chase from reaching into the box. "Damn, just let me see who it is."

Willow. She had to take it. They'd been waiting to hear from her and Josh all day.

"Her fucking parents aren't anywhere to be found," Willow growled, not even bothering to say hello. "I've talked to the house staff, the family attorney, and even their neighbors. They've all called her parents – who are somewhere in the Caribbean – and left a message but they haven't called back. Their daughter is in a coma and they can't be bothered to return a phone call. What kind of parents are these?"

Just like Gwen's, apparently.

"Maybe they haven't listened to their messages yet. If they're on vacation they may have unplugged."

Willow sighed loudly into the phone. "Do you really believe that? I know Peyton mentioned that she had a strained relation-ship with her mother and father but this is ridiculous."

"You did all you could—in fact, you went above and beyond what anyone would expect. You should just come on back."

Chase held up his hand and shook his head. "Wait. Since

they're already down there. What do they think about trying to get some more information on the Evandria angle to this case?"

Not a bad idea.

"Willow, did you hear that? Do you think you and Josh could look into Evandria while you're down there? Peyton is stable and they won't bring her out of the coma for a few days."

"If that's how we can help, then we're on it. If she does wake up, please let her know I'm thinking about her all the time." Bailey could hear Josh and Willow speaking but she couldn't make out the words. "Josh wants to know what's been going on there while we've been gone."

Chase and Bailey filled them in on the visit with Cathy Martin and promised to update them if they found anything of help in the box. They signed off after setting a time to call the next day.

"I think they're getting along pretty well."

Chase laughed as they began carefully unloading the contents of the box. The last time Bailey had done this with Frank's possessions it had changed her whole life.

"Did you think they would fight and snarl at each other? Josh is a laidback guy. I doubt there's anything Willow can do that would get him angry. I've only seen him upset a couple of times in all the years I've known him. It wasn't pretty. Once his fuse is lit, get out of the damn way."

"They'll bond over dogs. I'm sure they're staying at her place and that means he's going to get sniffed from head to toe by her canine protectors."

"He'll love it," Chase assured her. "I'm betting he's scratching them behind the ears and sneaking them treats behind her back."

They laid out the contents of the box on the floor. Some concert and movie ticket stubs, carefully marked with the names of her friends that had attended with her. High school yearbooks. Spiral notebooks that looked like they were used to take notes in Gwen's classes. A few pieces of jewelry – a gold necklace, tiny diamond earrings, and a jade bracelet. A stack of paperback novels with notes in the margins and sections highlighted.

It wasn't much and Bailey's heart sank as she took it in. There was no secret diary that pointed to Gwen's killer.

"I don't know what I was hoping for but it wasn't this."

Chase gave her a lopsided grin. "You were hoping for the same thing I was. A note that said 'Here is my murderer. Go get him.' The only problem with that is Cathy would have already found it."

Bailey picked up one of the spiral notebooks and paged through the contents. "Ick. Calculus. I hated math in school. Once they added the alphabet into equations I was done for."

"I loved math. I hated history and English. At least math made sense. My English teachers were always trying to teach me symbolism but I just didn't get it. The house was a metaphor for the hopelessness in their life. Shit, how depressing. If they were hopeless why didn't he just say so?"

Bailey giggled, remembering those days well. "We read a bunch of depressing books in school. Now I only read stories with a happy ending. Look, here's one for history. Looks like they were studying the American Revolution. Here are notes on the Boston Tea Party." She ran her fingers over the handwritten page. "She must have been bored in class and sat next to her friend because instead of taking notes she and someone else were writing back and forth during the lecture."

Chase scowled. "I thought kids used text messages."

"Twenty years ago? I doubt that."

Bailey read over the short conversation.

Friday?
Yes! New skirt and shoes.
Great! Cute boys will be there.
Jerks. They all are.
You're just bitter.
I have reason to be.
They're not all bad.
Really?
I'd date him.
Go ahead. I told him I wanted to be friends.
Ugh. Two chapters tonight.

The history notes had more back and forth between Gwen and her friend. Mostly about nothing all that important – parties, boys, upcoming exams, homework, lunch, mean friends, and lame parents. Typical teenager stuff. The exchanges were all beginning to sound the same.

I'm starving.
Eat something.
Banana in my locker. Forgot it.
You forget everything.
I didn't forget Saturday.

Shit, what did Adams just say?
Papers are due Monday. You knew that.
That's next Monday.
No it's this Monday.
Fuck. No. Will you help me this weekend?

Systematically, Bailey looked through every single spiral notebook hoping for some clue but she came up empty. By the time, she closed the last one her eyes were almost crossed with fatigue.

"There's nothing here. Did you find anything?"

"Nothing earth-shattering. From all the ticket stubs she liked to see movies and eat pizza."

"Then she's in good company. I like that too. Anything else? What about those books?"

Chase held up a paperback. "All of these books were gifts. There's *To Kill A Mockingbird, The Color Purple,* and *The Outsiders* plus a few I've never heard of. She also had some non-fiction books. One on the Founding Fathers, one on the history of Greek architecture, one on the history of the United Kingdom, and one on the history of World War II."

"How do you know they were all gifts?"

"They were personally inscribed in the front."

"She saved signed books. Fantastic. Any notes in the margins that were personal?"

"Not one. All related to the story and that symbolism again. Looks like Gwen understood it a hell of a lot more than I ever did."

Bailey rubbed at her eyes and then held out her hand. "Let's get to those yearbooks. They're our last chance."

"CHASE, WAKE UP. Please wake up."

Bailey's voice. Chase normally loved to hear her speak but not in the middle of the night when he was trying to sleep. Was the house on fire? He opened one eye and sniffed but he didn't smell any smoke.

Scraping his hand over his eyes, he groaned in protest. "Is everything okay? What time is it?"

She didn't even have to answer. It was too damn early. Still dark outside.

"Five in the morning but you need to wake up."

Finally he sat up in bed and opened his eyes all the way. "Please tell me why I need to wake up. Are you sick? Did the hospital call?"

Switching on the side lamp, the immediate bright light hurt his eyes but he could still see Bailey shake her head. "No, no, and no. The house is not on fire. I am not sick, and the hospital did not call. I think I might have figured something out about Gwen's murder."

She had his attention, every bit of it.

Placing her hands on his shoulders, she turned his torso so he was looking at her. "Listen to me because it's a long shot and it may be nothing. I was lying here having trouble sleeping and I kept going over and over all the things we looked at tonight. I decided to go back through the box of mementos one more time."

"Honey, patience at five in the morning before I've had my coffee is in short supply. What hit you? What have you figured out?"

She sighed and scraped her long hair away from her face. "Stephen." She handed a book to Chase, who stared at it bleary-eyed. "It was her brother – no, stepbrother – Stephen she was talking about in her notebook. Well…maybe. Possibly."

"You were looking through the books?"

Bailey nodded excitedly. "I was looking through everything. I almost screamed when I came across this one."

She pointed to the messy handwriting in the front of *The Outsiders.*

"*To my beautiful darling Gwen, with all my love and heart, Stephen,*" Chase read out loud. "So? Her brother gave her a book. That's not all that strange."

"You don't think that sounds a little creepy? From her brother? My brother doesn't talk to me like that. When he's feeling particularly affectionate he refers to me as babyfart."

Chase needed to know the origins of that nickname. As for the book, it was a trifle over the top but that didn't mean Stephen was jealous enough to kill.

Bailey rolled her eyes and placed some items on the bed. The ticket stubs. "Look at these. Here are the tickets *From Dusk 'till Dawn* that were tucked into that book. According to Google, that movie came out in early 1996. They were dating even after their parents got married."

Chase had to be the voice of reason. "That ticket stub might not mean what you think it does. It could simply be she grabbed what was handy to mark her place in the book."

"Gwen wrote down the names of who went to the movies or a concert with her right on the stub, just like the others. She wrote one word on this ticket stub. *Stephen*. It could be that she just doodled his name but I doubt it. I think they went to this movie together and she tucked these into a book he gave her. That's a sentimental gesture you don't see between most stepsiblings. Which leads to the obvious question why didn't Stephen tell us he dated Gwen when we asked about her boyfriends? Why didn't he mention he was a stepbrother? That's weird too. We only learned about all this when we talked to Cathy who didn't live with them and wouldn't know how the relationship between them was going."

This was one farfetched theory but what else did they have?

Bailey hopped up from the bed and paced, getting more excited by the minute. "Cathy didn't mention how Stephen felt when their parents married each other. Maybe Gwen was okay with it and Stephen wasn't. Think about that. You're dating some girl and suddenly your dad wants to marry her mom. He even goes so far as to adopt her so your last names are the same. That would throw a spanner in anything you had going with her. I read through those inscriptions thinking I would see one from Frank but it was from Stephen."

Chase was trying to wrap his sleep-deprived brain around this whole situation. "So what you're telling me is that it's entirely possible we've been chasing the wrong leads, thinking that Frank, Greg, or Alex or all three of them together killed Gwen and were possibly murdered themselves because of that. What you're saying is that Gwen's death might be at the hands of her step-brother due to jealousy."

Bailey nodded. "And he could have killed Frank, Alex, and Greg for the same reasons. We never were able to check out how many of her other boyfriends have gone missing or turned up dead."

This was becoming surreal. "You think Stephen Baxter is a serial killer? He would have had to have some help. He couldn't have killed all three men himself. We've already established that there had to be multiple murderers."

Shrugging, Bailey didn't back down. "He's rich. He could have paid an accomplice. I know I'm sounding crazy but this is the closest thing we have to a clue right now."

Scratching his chin, Chase had to admit she had a good point. They'd run out of leads, everything going straight to a dead end. "We need to talk to Gwen's friend Taylor again. I don't know if those school notes were to her but if Stephen was still dating Gwen she would know."

"She didn't say anything when we were there."

Levering out of bed, he pulled on a pair of sweat pants and a t-shirt. No way was he going back to sleep now. "We didn't ask about Stephen. We asked about Frank and the other two. It's been so long she may not even think it's important. We'll go see her today but later. After the sun comes up."

Bailey blushed and slapped her hands over her face with a groan. "I'm sorry I woke you up so early but I was so excited when I read what Stephen had written and then saw the stubs. The wording struck me as odd and I just couldn't wait."

"I'm not mad. I'm cautiously optimistic. This whole theory is a longshot—you know that, right? It could be a coin—"

"Coincidence, yes, I know," Bailey finished for him. "I have to tell you I'm beginning to hate that word with a passion."

"So am I but every now and then it might happen."

"You think I'm off base about Stephen Baxter?"

"I think I need a hell of a lot of coffee before I make any decisions."

Bailey grinned and wrapped her arms around his waist, pressing her cheek to his chest.

"Bacon too?"

He'd make bacon and then they'd go back and speak to Taylor. He wasn't convinced that Bailey was right but he wasn't sure she was wrong either.

If he'd learned one thing in the last few weeks was that nothing was a shock anymore.

Chapter Thirty-Three

I T WAS FIVE hours later when Bailey and Chase pulled into
Taylor Richardson's driveway. The house looked exactly the
same as the last time they'd been there but they were certainly
different. They'd learned a hell of a lot about Gwen, Frank, Alex,
and Greg since they'd first spoken to the woman and this time
their questions would be more specific and pointed. If Taylor
knew anything about Gwen and Stephen they would find out.

Chase had called ahead of time so Gwen's friend must have
been watching for their arrival. She was standing at the door to
greet them before they even made it to the front porch.

"Come on in." She ushered into the house. "It's so hot out
there. Come in and have some iced tea."

They settled into the same positions they'd had the time before, Taylor in a chair and Bailey and Chase on the love seat.
The only difference was the outfit the woman wore today.
Instead of the cream pantsuit, she was in a soft pink A-line dress,
her hair pulled up off her neck, perhaps because of the soaring
temperatures outside.

"Now Chase, you said you needed to talk to me again.

What's going on?"

Clearing his throat, Chase didn't mince words. This time they were going to be completely honest. "I had a few questions about Gwen. Last time we were here, we honestly thought that Frank, Alex, and Greg might have had something to do with Gwen's murder but since then we've found that the men had an alibi."

Taylor's brow wrinkled. "Of course they did. The police said so."

"They might have been covering for each other but we don't think that's the case." Chase glanced at Bailey. "Taylor, how come you never mentioned that Stephen dated Gwen before their parents married?"

A flush came to her cheeks but she waved off their question. "Because it happened so long ago. They weren't serious or anything. It was a non-event."

Chase took the spiral notebook from Bailey and opened it to the page. "Was this you, by any chance? Were you the one writing notes back and forth with Gwen?"

Taylor's face lit up with a smile and she laughed, reaching for the notebook. "Oh my goodness, what a blast from the past. How did you find these? Gwen and I had several classes together and we always sat right next to each other if we could, often at tables instead of desks so it was easy to write in each other's notebook. The teacher thought we were taking notes."

Bailey pointed to the written exchange. "What boy were you talking about here? Was it Stephen? Did he have a hard time letting go of Gwen?"

Taylor ran her fingers over the page before answering. "It

wasn't like that. Stephen wasn't like that. He dated a lot of girls and Gwen was just one of them. Once their parents married they were just friends."

"Did Gwen and Stephen go see *From Dawn 'til Dusk* together?" Chase asked.

"Which one is that? We saw a lot of movies back then."

"The George Clooney movie with the vampires," Bailey answered. "Did they see that together?"

Shrugging, Taylor contemplated the ceiling for a moment. "Maybe. They could have. They were brother and sister. A bunch of us could have gone together. I don't really know. Is it important?"

Chase nodded grimly. "It might indicate that she and Stephen were still dating after their parents married. Those notes you wrote were from November. We know that because the page is dated."

Shaking her head, Taylor's lips were now a thin line. "It doesn't matter because Stephen and I started dating at the beginning of December. He even took me to the prom. So I doubt he was in love enough with Gwen to kill anyone by July and thinking anything different is just absurd."

Bailey sat back in her chair. What Guy said was true. "You and Stephen dated?"

Chin lifted, Taylor nodded. "We did and we were very happy. We broke up after my freshman year at college when I met Kyle, my husband. No hard feelings. We're still close friends."

"So that note wasn't about Stephen? Who was it about then?"

Taylor's hand tightened into a fist briefly. "So what if it was about Stephen? He could be a pain just like any guy. I guarantee you that Gwen forgot all about that note by next period." She leaned forward, her shoulders tense. "Just where are you heading with this? You don't think that Stephen had anything to do with Gwen's murder, do you? That's crazy. Stephen was incredibly protective of Gwen if you want to know the truth. He'd never have hurt her. Heck, I remember a few occasions he tagged along with us to a couple of rock concerts because he didn't want Gwen going to them alone."

While Bailey's brother would have lectured her for hours about staying safe and what boys really wanted, there is no way he would have blown his own evening to babysit her and her friends at a concert, party, or anywhere else. Maybe she just had a selfish brother. "You didn't think that was strange behavior?"

Taylor smiled. "Not at all. Personally, I think he was trying to spend more time with me."

Chase placed his hand on Bailey's knee when she would have spoken up about the book inscription. "And who could blame him? So when did they stop dating officially?"

"The beginning of 1995 maybe?" Taylor didn't look too sure. "Their parents married in March and the papers to adopt Gwen were final in May. Their dad had a connection at the courthouse and it was hurried through. He said he wanted to be her official dad since hers left her so early in life. He said that during a toast at the party they threw when it was all done."

Chase steered the conversation back to the relationship. "So when their parents announced they were getting married, Stephen was perfectly happy not to date Gwen and he never mentioned it again. Is that about right?"

Taylor shifted in her chair, her demeanor not as cool and unruffled as earlier. "That's right."

"So he wasn't dating Gwen anymore?" Chase asked gently. "And he didn't care who she dated?"

Taylor looked up at them, her eyes bright with unshed tears. "He was over her. He told me he loved me."

Bailey's heart ached for Taylor. "When did he tell you that?"

Her lips curled up into a smile. "We all spent Spring Break together in St. Lucia. He told me one night under the stars. He loved me so I know he didn't care about Gwen's other guys."

I bet he got into her pants right after he said that too.

Chase took Bailey's hand and stood. "We thank you for your time, Taylor. You've been more than helpful."

Neither of them spoke as they exited the house and climbed into the car, driving away from Taylor and everything they had learned. Bailey couldn't take the silence any longer.

"Do you believe her? Do you think Stephen transferred his affections to her?"

Inhaling sharply, Chase shrugged. "Do I think teenage boys are fickle as hell? Yes. Do I think Stephen was in love with Taylor? Maybe."

A terrible thought was beginning to grow in Bailey's mind and she had to say it out loud so Chase could tell her she was imagining things. "Could Taylor have killed Gwen? Out of jealousy? It doesn't explain Frank, Alex, and Greg but it might explain Gwen."

"At this point, I'm willing to be open to the possibility," Chase said. "After we stop and see Peyton, we need to talk to Stephen. There's only one way to know and that's to ask him some more questions about his relationship with Gwen. See how he reacts."

What could go wrong?

Chapter Thirty-Four

CHASE WAS BECOMING concerned about Ellis guarding Peyton. After they left Taylor's home, they stopped at the hospital and found the grouchy detective reading *Bridget Jones' Diary* to the comatose woman. He'd also purchased a couple of soft, colorful blankets to use on her bed instead of the scratchier hospital ones. Clearly an alien pod had taken ahold of Chase's friend.

He grabbed Ellis by the collar and dragged him into the hallway while Bailey visited with Peyton.

"What in the hell is going on here? Is there something you want to tell me because frankly I'm worried about your sanity."

Ellis scowled and shook off Chase's grip. "You're talking out of your ass, bro. Everything is fine. I'm protecting Peyton. Isn't that what you want me to do?"

"You were reading *Bridget Jones' Diary*, dude. No guy does that willingly."

A smile bloomed on his friend's face. "Insecure in your manhood? Not me. Listen, I read the few books that I had so one of the nurses let me borrow one of hers. It's not *Rambo* but who cares? Peyton just needs to hear someone's voice. Whether I'm reading the newspaper or some chick book, it doesn't matter."

That seemed like a perfectly logical explanation. But...

"What about the blankets?"

Ellis laughed and walked over to the soda machine in the corner, digging in his pocket for change. "Jesus, you're suspicious. The blankets the hospital had weren't all that warm or comfortable. I was walking through the lobby this morning and they were having a craft fair and all the proceeds went to the children's wing. I bought two handmade blankets. Figured they might cheer her when she wakes up. Is that okay? Do you think I'm trying to seduce a woman in a coma, Chase?"

Rubbing the back of his neck, Chase shook his head and sighed. "Shit, no. It's just you've been acting so strangely. You've almost been...nice."

Ellis handed Chase one of the cans of soda from the machine. "Are you kidding? This is a dream job, my friend. The client is pretty and I get lots of quiet time. Plus the nurses fuss over me and share their muffins in the morning."

"Peyton is going to wake up eventually. She'll talk and have opinions, like other people. People you don't like."

"So then it won't be a dream job anymore, but I'll still do it."

Ellis's words were running through Chase's head one more time. "Wait. Did you say Peyton was pretty?"

"Yes," Ellis shrugged. "Do you not think she's attractive?"

"She is. Very. But I'm not sure you should be thinking that way."

Ellis chugged down half of the soda in a few gulps. "She's

nice looking, Chase. It's not really a debatable thing. She's pretty and people are going to notice. You noticed."

But Chase wasn't alone with her for hours on end reading books and tucking blankets in.

"Just remember that she's been through a lot. When she wakes up she's going to find out things she never knew about her husband."

"I'll make a note of that. Now are you going to tell me how it went with Taylor Richardson this morning?"

Chase filled Ellis in on the conversation including how Taylor had dated Stephen not long before Gwen was killed.

"This is an interesting twist," Ellis observed. "It gives Taylor a motive if her boyfriend had a thing for her best friend. She was also the one that said Gwen was back in her cabin when clearly she wasn't."

Chase had thought about that on the drive over. "It does give her a motive but she still would have had to overpower Gwen to a certain degree. Although it wasn't made public, we know that Gwen suffered from blunt force trauma before being stabbed. Did Taylor have the strength to do that much damage?"

"A woman scorned? You'd be surprised. You don't like her for this? I think we're getting to the point I might want to bring a few people in for questioning. Stephen and Taylor seem like prime candidates."

"Funny you should mention that. I was thinking of going to talk to Stephen again. He never said a word about his relationship with Gwen so to my mind that makes him suspect number one. He had motive, he had opportunity, and he had the means."

Ellis grinned. "The cops' trifecta. Let me get someone here to sit with Peyton and I'll go with you. I can make this much more official."

Finally they had enough to bring in the police.

CHASE HELD THE car door open for Bailey and she climbed into the vehicle, her nerves on high alert. After the conversation with Taylor that morning, Bailey was of two minds about Gwen's killer. If what Taylor said was true, Stephen might not have a strong motive for Gwen's murder although Bailey wasn't convinced of Stephen's ardor and loyalty. In addition, if Taylor knew Stephen still harbored feelings for Gwen, it gave her a motive for killing as well.

Or perhaps neither one of them had anything at all to do with it.

Firing up the engine, Chase pulled into traffic. "I can practically hear the wheels spinning in your brain."

"I'm so confused," she confessed. "When we started out this morning, I thought I had a theory of what happened but Taylor has thrown that all into question."

"We'll find out more today when we talk to Stephen," Chase assured her. "I plan to tell him everything we know, lay it all out on the table and see what he has to say."

"I doubt he's going to confess to murder."

"He doesn't need to confess. All we have to do is punch holes in his story and let Ellis do the rest. My friend has been known to get more than a few confessions, by the way. He's quite proficient at interrogation and they bring him in to question suspects even when it's not his case."

Bailey glanced behind her. "Where is Ellis? I thought he was coming with us."

"He had to wait for his backup guy to stay with Peyton. He said he'd be five or ten minutes behind us. Tops."

Something else had been on her mind. Since she'd found the book she'd wondered if perhaps they were close to getting the answers she'd come for. There would be no more reason to be here.

"What happens when this is all finished?"

Chase glanced over, his own expression showing no surprise at her question. "To be fair, I'm not sure we're all that close to finding out who killed Gwen or Frank."

"But eventually," she pressed, her voice quivering with emotion. "What happens then? You live here and I live there. I have a business down there and you have your life and friends. How will we do this?"

He reached over and grabbed her hand. "Whoa, sweet. You're upsetting yourself about something we've never even discussed. But to hopefully make things better I'll tell you this right now. I'm in love with you and we're going to make this work. I know you have your bakery so it would be hard for you to relocate and I can work anywhere, so it only makes sense for me to move there with you. That is, if you want me to."

She only heard two words out of all of that. Love. Move.

"You love me? Enough to leave your life here?"

He flashed her that smile that had her senses humming. "Had I not mentioned that before? I meant to. I love you, sweet, and I hope you feel the same. If you don't I'm going to feel pretty stupid talking about moving down there. But if you don't I'm still going to do it and show up at your house every day with flowers and wear you down."

Happiness flooded every pore of her body and tears pricked her eyes. She had to swallow hard to push down the lump that was suddenly lodged in her throat.

"I love you too." She smacked her forehead and groaned. "Shit, I'm in love. I didn't plan on that happening."

"Just because it wasn't on one of your goal lists doesn't make it any less fucking great." He lifted her fingers to his lips. "I'm kind of on pins and needles here waiting for you to say that you want me to move down there. Do you think it's too soon?"

Probably, but she didn't care. For once in her carefully planned out life she was going to go for it. "Yes, but come anyway. Are you sure about that though? You have a home and property and friends. I don't want you to regret it a year from now when you miss playing cards with Ellis and Josh."

Chase just laughed at her concern. "Between planes, cars, and technology, I think I can keep in touch. I'm kind of looking forward to the beach and all the amusement parks. I love roller coasters."

Hell to the no. "You'll be by yourself. I don't ride coasters. I'm afraid of heights. Maybe Peyton or Willow will ride with you. I bet Willow will. She looks like a risk taker."

"You and I can ride the merry-go-round together," Chase teased. "Or maybe the bumper cars. That's pretty low to the ground."

She chuckled and playfully shoved at his arm. "It's a legitimate fear. If you fall from a high place, you can die."

The ride to Stephen's house hadn't taken long and they pulled in front of his home and parked the car. Chase caught her arm before she could climb out of the vehicle. "Let me start with the questions and feel out how open he is to talking. By then Ellis should be here and we'll let him take over. Are you okay with that?"

She was fine with it. Chase had more of a rapport with Stephen than she did so it only made sense. It was nice to be consulted though. He put his arm around her shoulders, warm and reassuring, as they walked up the driveway and rang the front doorbell. No one answered and Chase took a peek through the front windows.

"He might not be here," Bailey said. "Plus it's kind of tacky to look in someone's windows. You don't make a habit of this, do you?"

"I don't but today it paid off." Chase turned back to Bailey. "Stephen is on the back patio."

"How do you know that? Can you see all the way through the house?"

"No, but listen. You can hear voices in the backyard. Let's go ask him a few questions."

Chapter Thirty-Five

C HASE AND BAILEY strolled through the well-manicured side yard to the back of the house, the sound of loud, angry voices drowning out the chirping birds. He knew both of those voices – Stephen and Taylor. What was Gwen's best friend doing here?

"They don't sound happy," Chase whispered, slowing his steps, his hand curled around Bailey's upper arm, pulling her behind him. He wanted to keep them at an angle where the inhabitants of the backyard couldn't see them, her body shielded by his.

It was only when he peered around the corner that he realized how angry Taylor was. She was standing there in the same pink dress she'd been wearing earlier but with an additional and completely unexpected accessory. A gun. She was pointing it at Stephen who stood in front of the large gas grill, his hands raised in surrender.

"You crazy bitch, put that down. You're going to hurt someone or yourself," Stephen scoffed, clearly not all that scared he was going to be shot. He looked more annoyed than anything.

"You need to calm the hell down and we can talk. Maybe I can help you after all."

"It's too late for that. I begged you to help us and you refused. After all I did for you, you hung me out to dry. Then I find out today that you were playing me for a fool back then. You're the lowest of the low, Stephen Baxter. This is for me and Gwen."

Before Chase could even react a shot rang out, the recoil on the gun sending Taylor back a few steps as Stephen crumpled into a heap on the patio decking. Adrenaline coursed through his veins and he didn't bother to think about the wisdom of his actions, only knowing that he needed to get that gun out of Taylor's hands. She was dangerous in her current emotional state and he didn't like to think about what she might do now to get away with her crime. He and Bailey were witnesses she hadn't counted on.

Hurling his body forward the ten or so feet between himself and Taylor, he knocked her to the ground with a heavy thud, the gun skittering a few feet away, driving the air from his own lungs on impact. Taylor didn't take his intervention well and began to kick and claw, screaming at the top of her lungs as her nails dragged painfully across the side of his neck. The flesh burned and he felt the cool drip of blood as it ran over his collarbone and down his chest. A flurry of movement out of the corner of his eye had him on high alert.

Bailey. What are you doing?

His only thought to keep her safe, he took a moment to glance over his shoulder and saw her kneeling next to Stephen. A knee to his solar plexus brought his attention back to the woman he was wrestling on the grass. She twisted in his grip and turned onto her belly as he grunted with the effort to pin the violent woman to the ground. She reached out, stretching her body as much as she could, her fingertips just touching the gun but his reflexes were faster and his arm was longer. He snagged it from her, the metal cold against his palm and then he backed away, scooting on his ass until he was out of her reach.

Both of them lay there on the grass, breathing heavy, clothes ripped, scratched and bruised. Taylor's eyes had filled with tears and something seemed to give inside of her as she buried her face in her hands. Her shoulders shook with sobs, her body language one of defeat. She wasn't going to fight him anymore. She was done.

Carefully he levered to his feet, keeping one eye on the sobbing woman and the other on Bailey and Stephen. Raising the gun in warning to Taylor, he slowly backed up to where Stephen lay on the patio. His face was pale and there was a large crimson stain on his chest. If they didn't get him help soon he would bleed out.

"Is he alive? Did you call 911?"

Bailey nodded, her own cheeks wet with tears. "Yes, I called. He's alive but barely. I asked him about Frank, Alex, and Greg. He swears he didn't kill them."

His heart pounded against his ribs as he took in the scene before him. Something had gone down between these two long before he and Bailey had come into the picture. Whatever had caused Taylor to snap today had been festering for a while.

"Stay with him while I talk to Taylor."

He had to concentrate to move his legs, one foot in front of the other, as the adrenaline began to ebb away and in its place horror and pain took up residence. He thought he'd seen the worst that morning he'd watched the coroner take away Gwen's dead body but it paled in comparison to witnessing a man shot down in cold blood.

"Taylor," he said quietly. She was sitting in the grass, rocking back and forth as tears flowed down her face. Her makeup was smeared and running, giving her the appearance of a sad clown.

"Taylor," he said again, this time a little louder. He knelt down but far enough away she couldn't reach for the gun. He didn't trust her that much. "What happened here? Why did you shoot Stephen?"

Sniffling and coughing, she rubbed an arm across her nose. "He deserved it."

"Tell me why," he cajoled. "Tell me what he did. I heard you say he wouldn't help you. Why don't you start there?"

Hiccupping, the crying woman didn't answer immediately. When she did the words came out in a choked stream. "I asked him for help. I begged him. My husband's business is going bankrupt so I asked Stephen for a loan. That's all we needed to get back on our feet, but he said no. I told him that I would tell everyone the truth if he didn't help me but he said no one would believe me, that I had no evidence. He laughed at me, said they would call me crazy. I was so angry with him but my husband said to leave it alone. That the Baxters had more power than we did so I dropped it."

More sobs shook Taylor's body as the sound of sirens in the distance grew closer. "Until today. What was different today, Taylor?"

She looked up at Chase with red-rimmed eyes, her lips trembling with the effort to speak. "It was you. What you said about how he was still seeing Gwen, taking her places. He used her and he used me, made me think he really loved me. I just couldn't take it anymore. He had to pay."

Chase swallowed hard and sucked in a breath, her words hitting him dead center in the chest.

"Stephen killed Gwen, didn't he? You covered for him all those years ago. You were cabinmates with Gwen and you saw her leave with Stephen. You knew but you didn't say. Why?"

Taylor nodded. "He said he loved me."

"But he loved Gwen."

Hysterical laughter bubbled from Taylor's lips and she shook her head. "He doesn't love anyone but himself. He pretended to love her, messed with her head, just like he did with me. He didn't care if she screwed every guy at camp that summer. He only pretended to be jealous to boost Gwen's ego, flatter her so she wouldn't see what he really was. He couldn't let anyone see that. No, he used her and then he killed her. He uses everyone."

Chase rubbed his forehead, not following the logic. "But why? Why would he kill her if not jealousy?"

"Money," Taylor sniffled, more tears rolling down her cheeks. "His dad adopted Gwen so that meant the family fortune would be split three ways, not two. He didn't want to share what he thought of as his so he killed her. And he did it on July twenty-first just because he thought it was funny. After all, the cops would think it had something to do with Evandria when it was really about how greedy and cold he was. So very cold. He never loved me."

The lawn was suddenly swarmed with cops and EMTs, everyone talking at once. Ellis had a uniformed cop lift Taylor to her feet and slap cuffs on her wrists while the emergency personnel loaded Stephen onto a stretcher after hooking up an IV. Bailey stood and backed away as they worked on the injured man, a strange look on her face, something between pity and revulsion.

Ellis clapped a hand on Chase's shoulder. "Are you okay, man? You look a little worse for wear."

The claw marks on his neck were beginning to throb along with other various cuts and bruises, not to mention the headache he had from listening to Taylor's story. They'd been following the wrong path the entire time. They should have followed the money instead.

"I'll be fine. I need a shower and a beer." He wrapped an arm around Bailey and pulled her close. "How about you, sweet? Are you okay?"

She turned and pressed her face into his chest and her arms tightened around his waist until he almost couldn't breathe. "What were you thinking, charging at her like that? She had a damn gun, you idiot. You could have been killed. As in dead. You scared me, Chase. Don't ever do that again."

Realizing where her distress was coming from, he combed his fingers soothingly through her long hair and pressed a kiss to her brow. She'd already lost one man and she'd thought she might lose him. No way. He was planning on sticking around for a long time.

"Someone had to take that gun away from her and Ellis was running late, as usual." He elbowed his best friend who gave him a dirty look. "And I'm not planning to die anytime soon. You're stuck with me, baby. I'm not going anywhere."

She slapped at his chest right at the spot Taylor had kicked him with her high heel. Shit, that hurt. That woman had to have taken some self-defense classes at one time or another.

"You better not. I have plans for you."

He rubbed his nose against hers, nuzzling her ear. "I'm sorry we didn't get the answer you needed."

She shrugged, her expression stormy. "I'm not sure I believe him. He said he didn't kill them but I don't know. How can I be sure?"

There was only one way. Talk to Stephen Baxter again.

If he survived.

Chapter Thirty-Six

"STOP BEING A baby," Bailey chided Chase as she dabbed alcohol on the scratches on his neck. They were deep and raw and they probably hurt like hell but he was being extra whiny about it. He was sitting in a kitchen chair and she was cleaning the few cuts he'd accumulated during his struggle with Taylor. She was a scratcher and kicker from the looks of things.

"It fucking hurts," he hissed, his teeth gritted together. "That alcohol burns."

"Stay still and we'll be done sooner. Then we can go see Peyton." She dabbed some antibiotic cream over the marks and then stepped back to survey her handiwork. "And Stephen."

"He'll probably be in surgery for several hours, sweet, and then recovery after that. I doubt you'll get to ask him any more questions until tomorrow at the earliest."

"He said he didn't kill Frank."

Chase sighed and stood, pushing the chair back into place. "I know. I'm not sure I believe him either."

The image of Stephen being shot was going to haunt Bailey for a hell of a long time. She'd seen the look in his eyes up close.

"I've thought about it and I think he was telling the truth after all."

"Honey, Stephen Baxter was a murderer and a liar."

"He was facing death, Chase. There was no reason to lie then. Besides, jealousy fifteen years later? That's a piss poor motive, especially if what Taylor said was true and he killed Gwen for the money."

The front door swung open and Ellis breezed into the great room. "I've seen people killed over a pack of cigarettes. How are you feeling?"

Bailey smiled at Chase's friend, feeling much more friendly toward him than she had a few hours ago. "He's going to live to fight another day."

"He's a tough son of a gun," Ellis laughed with a grin. "Of course he was fighting a girl, so my money would have been on him for sure."

Chase grabbed three sodas from the refrigerator, handing them out. "She didn't give in easily and she fought dirty."

Ellis cleared his throat, scratching his chin and shifting on his feet. "Actually I came to share some news."

Chase reached for Bailey's hand. "Anything good?"

"It depends. I checked on Stephen Baxter's whereabouts fifteen years ago on July twenty-first. He was here in Williamsburg. He played in a country club golf tournament. His foursome came in third. There are photos."

"Will he—" Bailey didn't know how to ask.

Ellis' lips twisted. "It's too early to tell. He's fighting for his life, that's for sure. The doctor said it's up to him now. It could go either way. He's lost a lot of blood."

"What do we do now?" she found herself saying as the reality of everything began to hit her. "We found Gwen's killer and that's great but what about Frank, Alex, and Greg? I thought there was a link between their deaths and Gwen's but it turned out there's nothing. Not a damn thing."

"Don't discount what you've accomplished here," Ellis said. "You and Chase helped solve a twenty-year-old cold case. I ought to make you honorary deputies. What you did wasn't easy but you didn't give up. I'm proud of both of you."

Chase nodded in agreement. "Willow and Josh are still in Midnight Blue Beach checking out Evandria. At this point, all we have to go on is Guy's belief that the men were killed by the organization. Since there's no connection in their deaths, I think it makes the Evandria theory more believable."

It didn't make any sense to Bailey. "But why? Why would an organization with the power that Evandria wields kill three men? Were they some kind of threat?"

"That's what we'll find out," Ellis pronounced. "But first we have to go see Peyton."

Wrinkling her nose, Bailey elbowed Chase. "He's as bossy as you are. Wait, did you say *we*? As in we are going to find out?"

"Did you think I'd let you do this alone? I'm in now. If Evandria killed your husbands, then perhaps they're responsible for that package bomb that injured Peyton. Then there's the murder of Martina Dorrell, the swim coach. I don't like people getting blown up and shot on my watch. I've already talked to the Chief of Police and I'm taking some time off to devote to this case."

Why did she have a feeling this was more about Peyton than

anything? Something in the way his expression changed when he said her name. He was an actual human being at that moment.

"Besides, Chase and Josh need someone that actually knows what the hell he's doing when it comes to law enforcement and protecting people. I can't have civilians running around and getting themselves killed."

Well...almost human.

"Ellis, shouldn't you be getting back to the station?" Bailey asked, never taking her eyes from Chase. They needed some time alone. "I bet you have paperwork to do."

Chuckling, the detective headed for the door. "As a matter of fact, I do. I'll see you at the hospital."

The door swung shut and Bailey lifted her arms and pulled Chase down for a kiss – long, slow and sweet. "I thought he'd never leave."

"He is exhausting," Chase agreed with a laugh. "But we could both use a good night's sleep. Tomorrow we can decide if we want to investigate from here or Florida."

She'd already made her decision. "Florida, but only after Peyton recovers. They're down there and so are Frank's family. Plus we have to find Uncle Nigel. He might know something about Frank and the Council."

"Florida it is then." He lifted her hand and kissed the fingertips. "It doesn't matter where as long as we're together."

"That sounds wonderful." But there was one thing bothering her and it was time to get it out in the open. "Is it okay...you know...that I still want to find out about Frank's death? It doesn't mean I don't love you—"

His finger laid across her lips. "Don't go there. Of course

you want the truth. I would too. I don't mind. I want to help you get the closure that you need."

Tears she'd been holding back since the shooting began to leak from her eyes. Suddenly the whole day was too much for her and she doubted her entire mission to come here.

"What if it's all just a silly, stupid coincidence, Chase? A fluke of the universe and me, Willow, and Peyton are chasing our tails?"

He rubbed his chin and shook his head. "Baby, you don't believe that and I don't either. There's something there and we're going to find it. Believe it."

Her hand caressed his cheek, stubble under her palm. She loved this man so much.

"I believe in you."

"I believe in us." He lowered his head and brushed his lips against hers. "No matter what happens, I love you."

For the first time in Bailey's life, she believed those words.

Chapter Thirty-Seven

WILLOW PACED HER expansive living room, the sound of her high heels clicking on the marble floors while Josh fixed them both martinis. His calm demeanor only made her more agitated. Why wasn't he upset?

"Peyton blown up. A man shot. The swim coach dead. What's next?"

Josh held out the martini. "Willow, please relax and have your drink."

She took the glass with a huff of frustration. "How can you stay so calm?"

He smiled and lowered himself into the cushions of the over-stuffed couch, two dogs jumping on his lap immediately. He'd charmed both of her dogs within three minutes of entering the house. The traitors barely noticed she was home. "Because that's the way I was made."

Willow took a gulp of the drink, the heat traveling down into her belly. "Bailey and Chase could have been killed."

"Getting upset isn't going to help the situation. We need to keep a clear head. This Evandria lead is all we have now. They're depending on us since they can't get down here until Peyton recovers."

It wasn't that she wasn't up to the job; she was, but this was a pressure she could have done without. She hadn't known Bailey and Peyton very long but she wished they were here with her now. She could use the support of someone that understood her urgency. Josh didn't seem intense about…anything. He was the epitome of mellow, which was quite a change from the men she usually spent her time with.

She turned to the window and stared out at the backyard, remembering the last time Alex had swam in that pool. He'd been drunk – as usual – and she'd had to drag him inside, terrified he'd pass out and drown.

"How are we going to help? We can't get the head of the Council to even meet with us."

Josh ruffled the fur behind her German Shepherd's ears. "I've been thinking about that. I think you should take me out on a date."

She whirled around, scowling at him. "A date? You want to go have fun at a time like this?"

"Willow, where there are rich and powerful people there are social events. I think we should attend one of them. Don't you agree?"

He was smarter and more devious than he looked and her respect for him inched up several notches higher.

"I've never met this guy and I go to a lot of parties. It might take some doing to get an invite to that social circle," she warned. "I run with a rich and powerful crowd but this guy is in a whole other league."

"I think you can do anything you set your mind to."

That was true. She certainly had so far.

The answers had to be out there and she would find them.

For Peyton, for Bailey. For herself.

Thank you for reading Midnight Blue Beach –
Wicked After Midnight

Sign up to be notified of Olivia's new releases:

oliviajaymesoptin.instapage.com

About the Author

Olivia Jaymes is a wife, mother, lover of sexy romance, and caffeine addict. She lives with her husband and son in central Florida and spends her days with handsome alpha males and spunky heroines.

She is currently working on a series of full-length novels called The Cowboy Justice Association. It's a contemporary romance series about lawmen in southern Montana who work to keep the peace but can't seem to find it in their own lives in addition to the erotic romance novella series – Military Moguls and the romantic suspense series – Danger Incorporated.

Look for Olivia's new romantic suspense trilogy Midnight Blue Beach in Fall of 2016!

Visit Olivia Jaymes at
www.OliviaJaymes.com

Danger Incorporated

Damsel In Danger
Hiding From Danger
Discarded Heart Novella
Indecent Danger
Embracing Danger
Embracing Danger
Danger In The Night

Cowboy Justice Association

Cowboy Command
Justice Healed
Cowboy Truth
Cowboy Famous
Cowboy Cool
Imperfect Justice
The Deputies
Justice Inked
Justice Reborn

Military Moguls

Champagne and Bullets
Diamonds and Revolvers
Caviar and Covert Ops
Emeralds, Rubies, and Camouflage

CPSIA information can be obtained
at www.ICGtesting.com
Printed in the USA
LVHW04s1924130718
583665LV00001B/27/P